D1323539

Liberty Hall

'We'll start with humiliation, and just a soupçon of pain to let you know what's to come. After all, we wouldn't want you disgracing yourself in front of the cameras, would we?'

I didn't bother to answer, and I kept my eyes closed when Lance knelt in front of me again. Pathetic, I know, but I couldn't face seeing his intent expression, knowing he could do whatever he wanted with me. He clipped a longer length of chain between the wrist cuffs, then a matching one between my ankles. Only when I was trussed to his satisfaction did he unfasten the spreader bar and the chains that held my arms to the chair arms, and yank my wrist chains until I opened my eyes and stood up.

'This way.' His smile was as twisted as his nature. 'I'll enjoy this.'

Liberty Hall
Kate Stewart

BLACK LACE

Black Lace books contain sexual fantasies.
In real life, always practise safe sex.

First published in 2003 by
Black Lace
Thames Wharf Studios
Rainville Road
London W6 9HA

Copyright © Kate Stewart 2003

The right of Kate Stewart to be identified as the Author of
the Work has been asserted in accordance with the Copyright,
Designs and Patents Act 1988.

Design by Smith & Gilmour, London
Printed and bound by Mackays of Chatham PLC

ISBN 0 352 33776 1

All characters in this publication are fictitious and any resemblance
to real persons, living or dead, is purely coincidental.

This book is sold subject to the condition that it shall not, by way
of trade or otherwise, be lent, resold, hired out or otherwise
circulated without the publisher's prior written consent in any form
of binding or cover other than that in which it is published and
without a similar condition including this condition being imposed
on the subsequent purchaser.

1

My father had always claimed that I'd come to a bad end, but I'd never considered that he might be right until the night I found myself lying with my wrists cuffed to the framework of an ornate iron bed. I'd always been sure that I was really a good girl underneath my bolshie persona, no matter what I had to do to get along in this less than ideal world. Only a no good girl would have had her feet cuffed to a spreader bar that held her legs so wide apart that her thigh muscles hurt, so I'd probably been wrong about that too.

But that was the least of my problems just then. I winced as they lifted the bar and hooked it onto chains that dangled from the ceiling. Now my buttocks were displayed to the world, giving the watching men a great view of my oiled and temporarily virgin arse. The man who reached for my breasts had the best view of all, and his expression made it clear he was looking forward to humiliating me. The cameras they were adjusting to record every moment of my shame made it blatantly clear that I was in one hell of a mess, and knowing exactly how I'd got there didn't help one little bit.

None of it would have happened if Imo hadn't wanted to borrow a couple of aspirins that Saturday morning at the end of the third term of my second year at university. She'd had that radiant look a girl gets when she's had a vigorous shagging. All I'd had was a thick handful of overdue bills, a student loan that had run out weeks ago and a letter from a very annoyed bank manager who wanted my credit card back.

'What's up?' she asked as she sauntered in and sprawled herself across my bed as if she owned the place.

I've never understood Imogen Hall, and I don't think I ever shall. To start with, she's one of those tiny, delicate blondes who looks more like a porcelain doll than a real girl. But she's anything but delicate, as I found out when she made a pass at me two days after we became roommates in our first year. Don't get me wrong, I've got nothing against lesbians, or sexual fun and games. I just happen to like my sex simple, and with a bloke. I'm not a prude, and I've done my fair share of experimenting, but I'm not into the kinky stuff. Not like Imo. You name it, she's done it and she doesn't care who knows about it. Mind you, what else could you expect with a mother like hers, as my mother would say with a disapproving sniff.

Even a country vicar's wife knew about Imo's mother. Anyone who'd picked up a newspaper in the 80s or 90s would have heard of Liberty Hall. GIRL FROM THE BACK STREETS EARNS FORTUNE was one way of putting it, and the one that the tabloids preferred to use rather than find themselves in court on libel charges. The simple truth was that Liberty Hall had been a porn star back in the late 70s, the owner of a face and body that launched a thousand wanks. Some people I knew even viewed her as a cult figure, maybe even a feminist heroine, but people talk all sorts of rubbish at university so I took that with a pinch of salt. They might claim to admire her, but I'd bet you anything you like that they wouldn't tell their posh mummies and daddies that they were friends with Imogen – even assuming that Imo wanted friends like that, which she didn't. She didn't seem to need anyone, including me, which suited me fine.

Still, whatever Liberty Hall had or hadn't done in her youth was all firmly in the past and none of my business, although I'd read just as avidly as anyone else the rumours in the Sunday tabloids about what went on at the luxury hotel she now owned and had named after herself. Maybe I'd even been curious about it too, but not because the idea of a country house hotel that pandered to the wildest fantasies of the rich and famous tied in with any of my own.

No, I'm going to be a journalist, so I knew better than to believe that sort of rubbish, but mud always sticks, so poor Imo had a bad reputation before she'd set foot in the college. And she'd spent the last two years gleefully living up to it. Or do I mean down to it? Not that Imo ever seemed to care what anyone thought of her. She never took anything seriously, gliding over the surface of life like a swan on a river, but then she could afford to. She had a rich mummy to bail her out and a nice fat allowance. I'd only got myself to rely on, and I was clean out of options. If I wanted to finish my course, I had to earn some money fast.

'You've got your vicar's daughter's face on again,' she giggled, and I scowled.

It wasn't my fault that I'd been born into a family with no spare cash, and the sort of morals that the most repressed Victorian would have called out-of-date. Dad and I don't get on at the best of times, and after the last time ... well, he didn't quite tell me never to darken his door again, but it was pretty damn close. That meant asking him for cash was out, and going home when term ended was about as far out as it's possible to be.

Not that I'd wanted to spend the summer in the back of beyond, but it did leave me effectively jobless, penniless and homeless. Not good.

'I'll get those aspirins,' was all I said, but Imo's a bright girl. We both are, or we wouldn't be at this posh university.

'What's up?' she asked again, and followed me into the bathroom, her high heels clicking on the vinyl floor.

Typical Imo. It might only be eight o'clock on a Saturday morning, but she was beautifully dressed in Earl jeans that rode low on her skinny hips and a white T-shirt that was so simple and elegant that there was no way it could ever have come from a chain store, and as perfectly made up as if she was off to some posh do. I was wearing a pair of black leggings from the market and a gypsy style top that I'd bought in Top Shop's sale, and neither of them were fresh on that day. It's not that I don't care how I look, but I'd pulled on the first things I could grab when she'd knocked at the door. Now I wished I hadn't, because the more I looked at her the scruffier and tackier I felt.

My long dark hair was uncombed, and curling everywhere that it shouldn't, and my face was as innocent of make-up as the day God made it, which isn't very innocent. I've got a good body, and I look pretty good too. Most men think I'm sexy, and I plan to make the most of that because I might have started poor, but I don't intend to stay that way. Dad says that's yet another sign of my lack of morals. I reckon morals are a luxury that I can't afford yet. Someday, I will, once I've got all the stuff other women take for granted. Till then, it's a hard world and I'll do whatever it takes to get by.

I know that makes me sound like a materialistic bitch, but can it be so wrong to want to live a life where a Marks and Spencer ready meal isn't a massive extravagance? To be able to buy clothes without waiting for sales, to drink the best champagne rather than a half of lager in the student union bar? To live somewhere that wasn't a grotty bedsit in a student hall of residence where the walls were so thin that everyone knew exactly what everyone else was doing – and with whom? All I wanted was what people like Imo took for granted. I deserved it too, so I didn't much care what I had to do to get it.

'Is it money again?' Imo asked.

'Show me a student who isn't skint.' I tried to make a joke out of it, because the last thing I wanted was pity. 'Except you, of course.'

We all knew that Imo's allowance must run into six figures. She never flaunted it, but we all knew, the same way that we all knew about her mum.

'Believe me,' she said, unusually seriously, 'I earn every penny of it.' She looked me over in the same appraising way that she had before she'd made that pass, then stunned me by saying, 'And so could you.'

'You what?' I almost dropped the packet of aspirin I was getting out of the cupboard above the sink, but she wasn't thrown. She never is. Alfred Hitchcock would have loved her cool blondeness.

'You could earn plenty of money if you wanted to.'

'Like how?' I handed her the aspirin, trying to sound as if I didn't already have a fair idea what she meant. I was more of a vicar's daughter than I'd realised, because I was shocked, but that didn't stop me seriously considering it.

'Look.' Imo used that tolerant tone that some people use to talk to kids or idiots, which didn't improve my mood. 'You sleep with enough blokes, don't you?'

'I've had my share.' I wasn't the college bike, but neither was I into sleeping all night alone in my own bed and spending my evenings with a book. If I had been maybe I wouldn't have been so skint, but I reckon life's for living, not watching from the sidelines.

Watching Imo breaking the habits of a lifetime and trying to be tactful made me feel better. 'And sometimes you don't know them that well,' she pointed out.

'And sometimes I'm so plastered that I don't know them at all, and sometimes . . .' I shut up as I remembered how I'd rescued my grades last Christmas. I didn't think that anyone else knew about that, and that's how I wanted it to stay. I'd done it because I had to, but I'd hated every second of it. It wasn't that the lecturer in question wasn't fanciable; he was actually quite good-looking, but he was shockingly depraved in his tastes. Now I was doing my best to forget that it had happened, and making sure that no one could manipulate me ever again, so I wanted the subject changed – fast.

'What are you suggesting?' I asked before Imo could suss that I'd got anything to hide. 'That I turn whore for the holidays? The college would love that!'

Our dear alma mater is one of the ones with a long pedigree and tons of history and traditions. They're also real hypocrites who haven't made it into the twentieth century yet, let alone the twenty-first. Blokes who slept around were called real lads and jokily admired. If a girl tried it, she was a slut. Still, the college name would open doors, and I could ignore the old fools easily enough, so I just put up with it. I've had plenty of practice. I've ignored my father all my life.

'I wouldn't have put it quite so bluntly,' Imo murmured, still watching me in that weird assessing way, 'but if there were a way for you to earn say –' Imo was doing business studies and had a calculator for a heart, so I knew she was doing sums when her blue eyes narrowed '– No guarantees, but would you be interested in earning ten grand in the long vac, doing something confidential but legal?'

'Does shit hit the fan? You know damn well I would be, but doing what? I'll do most things, but I've got limits, and that's a word that the Hall family didn't seem to understand. As long as I kept to my rules, I was still the 'good girl' I secretly wanted to be seen as, no matter how much I pretended not to care what anyone else thought of me.

'I can't make any promises.' Imo seemed to be having doubts. 'But I could talk to my mother, if you like. I know she's looking for temporary staff.'

'And she'd pay me ten grand for being a waitress for eight weeks? Come on, Imo, I wasn't born yesterday.' I wasn't sure if I wanted to do it either, but I was definitely intrigued.

'She'd pay you ten grand for doing what you already do for free,' Imo said bluntly.

That was when I should have laughed it off, given her the aspirin and got rid of her. But I needed the cash, and she'd got a point. Besides, I'd just worked out how I could earn a damn sight more than ten grand, and start my career with a real scoop. A few months ago a journalist from one of the red-topped papers had come down to give us a talk about life in the big wide world of journalism. You know the sort of paper; the type where who's sleeping with whom, or preferably what, is far more important than world news. He'd been an oily little toerag, and afterwards he'd oozed that oil over me, buying me a very expensive dinner while he pumped me for information about Imo.

I hadn't given him any, partly because I'm not into selling out my friends, mainly because I didn't know anything worth selling, but he'd left me his card just in case I changed my mind. Now, if I played my cards right,

I could get an exclusive that'd get me started on the career ladder and pay off my debts twice over. I wouldn't mention Imo in whatever I wrote, because there are limits to what I'll do. But if I lost a friend because of what I'd written, tough. I was a big girl on her own in a big hard world, and friends are luxuries that the sort of rich, powerful woman that I intend to be sometimes can't afford.

'What would I have to do?' I asked.

Imo smiled as she gulped down the aspirin. 'Like I said, no promises. You'd have to get my mother interested first.'

'I don't do lesbian,' I reminded her, and she smiled more tolerantly still.

'So you keep saying, especially when you're drunk.' I watched her carefully, wondering if I'd admitted anything else incriminating while I'd been drunk, but she just went on reciting my personal sex mantra. 'You don't do lesbian, you don't do anal, and you're not into pain or humiliation.'

I'd made that list after that lecturer had put me through enough humiliation to last me a lifetime, but playing his sick games had got me the grade I'd needed to be allowed to stay at the university. He'd got just as much to lose as I had if the truth came out, so I was pretty sure that he wouldn't talk about it either. Therefore, nobody knew about it, so it didn't count. Sometimes I could convince myself that it hadn't even happened, but I was still on the defensive when I answered her.

'Got a problem with that?'

'None whatsoever, although it's such a waste,' Imo pouted.

I know I should have told her where to get off, but I just laughed. You couldn't help it with Imo. She might have been a shameless tart, but she was also such a nice person that I almost felt guilty about what I was planning to do to her mum. Only almost though.

'If you wrote a job application right now, I could give it to her when I meet her for lunch today,' she went on. 'Then she could see you this afternoon if she's interested, and there you are.'

'Job application?' I knew I sounded as if I was turning into a parrot, but it's not the sort of offer you get every day. 'Like what?'

'You're the one who wants to be the big journalist. Get her interested. Convince her that you could do it.'

'Do what?'

'Guess!' With that cryptic and unhelpful comment Imo left, leaving me with a lot to think about.

I considered my options for a good ten minutes, then found that business card and gave Dickie Lawrence a ring. Dad's God must have been on my side for once, because Dickie was in the office and picked up his phone. He didn't remember me, but he was interested in what I had to say.

'You get me the dirt, and I'll see you right,' he promised, but I'm not that naïve. I wasn't telling him anything until I'd got a proper contract. If I was about to get fucked for the sake of a story, I intended to be well paid for it.

'How much, and what sort of dirt?'

'What sort of dirt? Come on, Tess, half the top politicians and showbiz stars go down there for 'rest and recuperation'. If you can't work out what I want, then I'm not interested. As for how much, that depends on what you get, doesn't it? Since you're just starting out . . .'

'I don't come cheap,' I warned, but I knew I'd been

right. If I got this story, I'd have the less reputable half of what used to be Fleet Street panting round me like dogs on heat. 'I'll let you know,' I said when he'd finished explaining how good he could be for my career. I put the phone down, then turned on my word processor.

I had to write a job application that'd get Liberty Hall interested. Well, words were supposed to be my trade, so it couldn't be that hard. 'My name,' I typed with growing confidence, 'is Tess Morgan.' Actually it's Teresa, but most of my worst memories are associated with my father using my full name in a disapproving tone that meant I'd broken yet another of his precious rules. I went on to say that I was twenty years old, and a vicar's daughter, hoping that unusual detail would add to my appeal. I made my limits clear, but I also stressed that I was willing to try anything else.

I was about to add that I'd worked as a waitress before and list the hotels when I realised that this wasn't that sort of CV. I had to catch Liberty's eye, and convince her that I'd be an asset. I was pretty sure that I would be, because I was young and good-looking and, with a good career ahead of me, unlikely to want scandal any more than she did. Those would all be points in my favour, because what she was really selling was sex. Not the vanilla sort that you can get anywhere, but the extreme stuff. The type that's not actually illegal, but definitely isn't the sort of thing you'd want your friends and family to know about, let alone the Great British Public, and suddenly I knew just what to write. It felt funny typing up one of my deepest darkest secrets, but it was also a real turn-on. I've read erotica, of course, but this was different. More real, more immediate, and much, much more of a turn-on.

'I can't go home because I disgraced the family name

last summer,' I typed, then added words with growing confidence.

I went home for the recess, and noticed right away that Dad had a new curate. He was tall, slim and blond, with innocent blue eyes that gave a part-time bad girl like me all sorts of wonderful ideas about corrupting him. It wasn't hard to let him know that I was interested, and the more he watched me whenever he thought I wouldn't notice, the harder he got!

It was a hot summer, so I'd got every excuse for wearing short shorts and skimpy T-shirts, and the more I saw Nigel watching me, the shorter and skimpier they got. Dad hated it, but he couldn't say anything without admitting that he'd noticed that I'd grown up. He doesn't like doing that, so watching him fume just added to the fun. As far as he's concerned, I'm pure and innocent. I'm pretty sure he knows that I'm not, but admitting it would mean admitting that his careful illusion of happy families was a lie. So he pretends that he doesn't know what I'm really like, I pretend that I love him and, if we don't get on brilliantly, we at least manage to tolerate each other.

After a few days, Nigel had begun to watch every move I made until I began to realise what being stalked must be like, but he didn't make any moves of his own. That didn't surprise me. He was a real boy scout, which just added to the challenge. When he decided to clear the brambles from the overgrown churchyard, I saw my opportunity.

'I'll help,' I said, and Dad snorted.

'Wearing that? You'll be ripped apart. Besides, it's not exactly your thing is it?'

'You're the one who keeps complaining that I

never do anything useful,' I said sweetly. He bristled and, just as I'd expected, Nigel, being a good Christian lad, intervened before we could really get started.

'I could use the help,' he admitted, and smiled at me.

I smiled back, thinking about all the wonderful things I could do with him. Chances were that he was a real innocent, maybe even a virgin. I knew he wasn't gay. I'd seen the look on his face when he didn't know that I was watching him watching me too often to doubt that he wanted me, but he wasn't the sort that you could imagine with a different girl every night. I reckoned his girlfriends had always been the sort of daughter that Dad had always wanted: a good girl who went to Christian Union every week and saved herself for marriage. Definitely not the sort whose idea of a good night out involved getting thoroughly wasted and who was into one-night stands in a big way. But I'd bet that Nigel would secretly prefer a bad girl like me, and I had a feeling I'd find out that afternoon.

'Right.' I stood up and stretched, making sure he got a good long look at my breasts and, ignoring Dad's purple-faced glare, I said, 'I'm ready when you are.'

At first, Nigel acted as if he'd never had a sexy thought in his life. I'd begun to think that I was wasting my time and all I'd get out of it was blisters, when I spotted him watching me and put down my shears. 'God, I'm hot!' I said, wondering how blatant I was going to have to be.

'It is a hot day,' he agreed, smiling shyly.

'So you could take your T-shirt off?' I suggested,

touching it playfully. 'It's all right. I promise I won't ravish you.'

He stared at me, then swallowed and moved closer, and I knew he was tempted.

'Unless you wanted me to,' I murmured, leaning closer still. He smelt of sweat and beneath it, there was the tang of that musky smell that men get when they're turned on, but he still had a conscience. That didn't matter, because working out how I'd overcome his scruples made me feel even hornier.

'You haven't done it before, have you?' I whispered, so excited that my nipples felt as hard as pebbles as they pushed against my tight T-shirt.

'Haven't what?' he muttered, but I knew that he knew what I meant.

'Fucked a girl.'

For a second I wondered if I'd been too blunt and put him off. Then he pulled his T-shirt over his head, and I could only think what a waste it was if he hadn't. He'd got a broad chest, with a nice-looking six pack that was just hidden by a light coating of fair curly hair, and narrow thighs that were currently encased in old jeans that bulged at the crotch.

'Do you want to?' I asked, keeping a careful distance from him rather than risk scaring him off.

'You don't mean . . . ?' He looked so stunned that I couldn't help smiling.

'That's right. Here. Now. It's quiet enough.'

And I couldn't think of a better place. The jungle we were meant to be clearing would provide both a screen and a comfortable bed and the sheer wickedness of seducing Dad's curate in Dad's own churchyard, with his church tower looming overhead and his study overlooking the long grass made it perfect.

'But . . .' Nigel didn't seem able to believe his luck. 'You're sure?'

'Very.'

One of us would have to make the first move, and I knew it wasn't going to be him, so I moved closer and ran my hand over that tempting bulge in his jeans. He gasped, and I thought he'd come there and then, but he didn't. Instead, he grabbed me. No finesse or skill, just a hungry kiss as his tongue thrust down my throat and his hands shoved the thin straps of my T-shirt down.

'You're beautiful,' he muttered, staring at my breasts like a starving man at a feast, and I'd never felt sexier. He'd never done it before, so I could teach him just how I liked it, and I'd got all summer to do it in. Dad would have a fit if he found out, but I wasn't planning to tell him, any more than I reckoned Nigel was. And knowing how much he'd hate what I was planning made it even more fun. Sort of my way of getting back at him for all the times he'd made me feel six inches tall and as if I'd never amount to anything.

'You're not bad either,' I murmured and made a closer check of those muscles I'd been admiring ever since I came home. They were every bit as hard as they looked and, when I unzipped his jeans, his cock more than lived up to my expectations. It jutted upwards, hard and red and swollen, just asking to be kissed and squeezed. It was also so sticky that I knew I'd have to change my plans. Otherwise it'd be over before it had begun and Nigel would have a chance to remember his precious principles and chicken out.

I knelt in front of him, shoving his jeans down just enough so that I could reach him, but not enough that he could run away easily if he had a sudden attack of conscience. Not that it looked as if he was suffering from that. He was staring at me, dumbstruck, but he grabbed my breasts when I reached for his cock. I yelped, but not loudly enough to put him off. I like it rough, when I'm in the right mood, and besides, he didn't know any better. Yet.

I licked him slowly, tasting his lust, enjoying the way his body quivered with each stroke, until he was shaking as if he was high on something. My tongue flicked round his balls, then he groaned as I took him into my mouth. I wanted to suck him long and slow, but his body had other ideas. I'd barely run my tongue beneath the tip when he gave a convulsive jerk and shot his load down my throat. I swallowed.

'I'm sorry,' he muttered, looking anywhere but at me. 'You're just so sexy.'

'It's all right. It doesn't matter.'

For once I wasn't lying. I'd always known that he'd come as soon as my mouth touched his cock. I also knew that he was young and fit enough to get it up again in a few minutes. Until then, I had plenty of other ideas, so I wiped the come from my lips and lay back on the soft grass, letting my thighs fall apart and wondering if he'd take the initiative.

'Aren't you going to laugh at me?' He was so unsure of himself as he lay down beside me, and so needy that I knew he'd do anything I wanted him to. The combination was intoxicating, and as much of a turn-on as his gorgeous body.

'Why should I?' I kissed him, feeling him recoil as he tasted himself on my mouth, but his revulsion didn't last long.

'Because I've never . . .'

'You were waiting for the right girl,' I teased,

knowing that I was about as much the opposite of that girl as it was possible to get. He was the sort who'd be thinking marriage and loads of babies. All I wanted was good hard sex, and plenty of it, and I wanted some right then.

'Shall I tell you what to do?' I suggested softly, and he smiled.

'Take charge? I'd like that.' His hand strayed to my breast again, this time more gently.

'I like it when you kiss my nipples.'

He bent that fair, close-cut head over my body, his tongue working with growing enthusiasm. It was good, but it wasn't enough.

'Undress me,' I ordered.

He paused for so long that I almost lost it and screamed at him to get on with it, but then he reached for the button of my cut-off jeans. He undid it, pulled the zip down, eased the jeans down my thighs, then stopped with them just below my sex.

'You're wet,' he whispered, and I smiled and sat up.

'I want you. Aren't you going to finish?'

'No!' I'd been sure he was a bit of a wimp, but I'd been wrong. 'You want it!' he panted, twisting my knickers until the thin sidestring gave up the fight and tore. 'You can damn well have it.'

He shoved me back against the ground, and I revised my estimate of how long it'd take him to get another stiffy.

'Nigel, please . . .' I made the token protest that he'd expect me to, more turned on than ever by the sudden role reversal.

His face contorted in a grimace as he pinned me down, and I knew he wouldn't have been interested if my protest had been genuine. Right then, he only wanted one thing; which was fine by me. I wanted it too, and the guiltier he felt afterwards, the more certain I could be that he wouldn't confess what he'd done to my dad. Then we could keep up the illusion that I was his sort of good girl and make the rest of my summer vacation bearable.

'If you fight me,' Nigel muttered, and I began to wonder what I'd unleashed. Not that he'd have to force me, because I fancied him more than ever, but my innocent curate had turned into a tiger.

'What?' I challenged, and he tugged at my knickers again. The other string broke, and he jerked the cotton through my legs. It brushed tantalisingly over my clitoris as he pulled the sticky, moist fabric free. He stared at it for a second, then threw it into the long grass, and smiled cruelly.

'Only you won't fight me, will you? You want it as much as I do.'

I wanted it a damn sight more than he did, but this was no time for technicalities. Instead, I settled for another moan when his thick, grass-stained fingers parted my lower lips. I keep my bush trimmed because it makes it easier for swimming and bedroom sports. It was wet then, and it got wetter still when he shoved two thick fingers inside me. His mouth fastened on my breast, his teeth savaged my nipple and I grunted with pleasure as he began to thrust.

'You want me.' His free hand replaced his mouth, and he raised his head to study me, his face so darkened with lust that I hardly recognised him.

'I want you,' I admitted, wishing I dared risk yelling at him to go on. My hips were bucking as I rode his hand, but it wasn't enough, and the bastard knew it. He might be a virgin, but he'd obviously done some research, and a hell of a lot of fantasising. Now I was getting the benefit of all that pent-up lust, which beat clearing graveyards as a form of exercise any day.

'Touch me.' I'd meant to stay cool and in control while I initiated him, but I wanted him too much for the words to be anything but a plea.

'Where?'

I blinked, wondering how anyone could go through all that sex education we'd had drummed into us at school and still know so little, but it was incredibly erotic to know I was the first girl he'd done this to.

'My clit.' I guided his hand from my breast to where I wanted it most, parting my lower lips for him, then had a better idea. 'Kiss it, the way I kissed you.'

'I'm in control here,' he reminded me, and I gasped as he jerked his fingers free.

'Please, I'll do anything you want if you just suck me.' Part of that plea was pandering to his unexpected control-freak streak, the rest was genuine lust.

'Anything?' His eyes widened, and I started wondering what sort of dreams my allegedly innocent little friend had been indulging in. Not that I really cared. He shoved my jeans down another inch, and I spread my thighs as wide as I could to help him. There was still barely enough room for him to get his head between my legs, but he managed it somehow.

His tongue brushed across my bush, and I shoved my hand into my mouth, knowing I daren't make too much noise in case someone came to find out what we were up to. Then that virgin mouth fastened on my clit, tugging it the way he'd savaged my breast. His fingers were back inside me, and there were three of them now. No gentleness, no finesse, but I didn't care. I'd got what I wanted; a good hard fucking. I could hear him slurping at me, feel my clit hardening and my stomach tightening, but seconds before I'd have come he sat up, leaving me whimpering as the incredible feelings faded.

'Not like this,' he muttered and yanked at me again, rolling me onto my belly.

'Wait!' I gasped because, although I might have been acting like a slut, there was no way he was having me without a condom. It was a safe bet he wouldn't have one, but I'd been a Girl Guide until they'd thrown me out when they caught me smoking, so I was prepared. I reached into the rear pocket of my cut-offs and pulled out a condom.

'You knew this was going to happen, didn't you?' he snarled as he grabbed it. I just smiled. Of course I'd damn well known, but nice girls of the sort he was deluded enough to think I was wouldn't have even thought of such a wicked idea.

'I hoped it would.' I tried to sound coy rather than smug as I listened to him ripping the foil covering away. Imagination let me fill in the rest. That massive erection I'd felt in my mouth would be inside me in a minute and I couldn't wait.

He put his hand under my stomach, urging me onto my hands and knees, and I began to get a bit scared. Had I been wrong about him? Had he not had a girl because he went the other way? I was opening my mouth to make it clear that that entrance was out of bounds when he shoved his cock into my fanny. That was one problem solved, and I soon wondered why I'd ever thought I'd have to teach him anything. He was thick, he was hard, and he was ramming himself right where I wanted him, but that wasn't enough for him. He leaned his weight on me until my elbows collapsed, leaving me with my arse shoved in the air to meet his thrusts, and my head pressed against the grass.

It was hellishly uncomfortable, but I didn't care. One of his big, firm hands stretched my buttocks wide, making me feel deliciously dirty and depraved, and the other was working my clit. In and out he thrust, each movement harder than the last. His grunts were as loud as my moans, and I was feeling the first glorious cramps of orgasm in my belly when a cold voice said, 'What, precisely, is going on, Teresa?'

It was Dad, of course. We should have been quieter, or more careful, or maybe he'd had his suspicions about what I was up to all along. Either way, we were about as caught as it's possible to be, and poor Nigel had reached the point of no return. It couldn't have been worse for him, really: under the accusing eyes of the vicar of his parish, only a few yards away from the church he preached in on Sundays – with his cock buried in the vicar's daughter – the promising new curate let out a last wrenching groan and came. I buried my head in the grass, torn between laughter and tears. I was so near, and yet so far, and one thing was certain: I wasn't going to get my orgasm, or a second chance with Nigel.

Dad, as you'd expect, was livid. At any other time I think he'd have blamed me, but it was clear who'd been in control so he just watched while Nigel withdrew and grabbed his jeans. I picked up my shorts and T-shirt and got dressed, knowing Dad could see the torn knickers that still lay on the grass.

'It's not how you think,' I said before Nigel could do the hero bit and claim that he'd forced me.

'I don't need to "think" anything, Teresa. I know exactly what happened, and who started it.' Dad's voice was so cold that I knew he was seriously angry. 'In the churchyard, above the graves, where anyone could have seen you. Nigel, how could you?'

I was obviously a lost cause, which didn't surprise me, but Nigel had been his big hope. Nigel looked at me, and I waited for the truth to come out, but he had to play hero, didn't he?

'I took advantage of her,' he said, and at any other time I'd have laughed at his pathetic explanation. 'She sat down for a rest and . . .'

'She didn't struggle, did she?' Dad turned on me. 'You never do, do you, Teresa?'

Then all the secrets that I'd hoped I'd kept came out. Well, not all of them, thank God, but more than enough to make it abundantly clear that I was not a suitable vicar's daughter, and neither was I welcome in his house. According to him I was an ungrateful, callous disappointment who deserved the bad end she was undoubtedly going to come to. It wasn't anything I hadn't heard before, and I felt much the same way about him, so I didn't bother to bite my tongue, let alone apologise. I was tired of living my life to comply with his rules, tired of never having any cash, and lying about what I was really like. I left home that day, and I haven't been home since which is why I need a summer job.'

I had to stop because my fingers were aching; not surprising, as I'd been typing for a good half hour. I was almost as wet between my legs now as I'd been then, but at least I could do something about it this time. I hit the save key and headed for the bed, pausing only to get my vibrator out of the drawer where I'd hidden it beneath the pile of textbooks I did my best to avoid reading. I stripped off the leggings and top that I'd pulled on when I'd opened the door to Imo, and lay down on the bed, spreading my legs as wide as I'd longed to be able to spread them that day in the churchyard.

Briefly, I wondered if I was doing the right thing. No matter how you dressed it up, if I took this job I'd be a hooker. That didn't fit my vision of what a good girl did, let alone tie up with Dad's antiquated ideas. It'd hurt him as well as my future if anyone found out what I'd done. Then I thought to hell with it. Why shouldn't I make the cash I needed by doing what I already did for fun? Being paid added a frisson to it, and I won't deny that the idea of revenge was there too, adding a spice to my feelings as I turned the vibrator on.

At first, the steady pulsing against my clit was enough, but I soon needed more, so I conjured up an image of Nigel with his contorted face and massive erection. I slid first two fingers, then a third, inside myself and tried to conjure up every detail of how I'd felt: the smell of the crushed grass beneath my back, the sound of grasshoppers and his increasingly frenzied grunts. It wasn't enough, so I let the images darken. If I worked for Liberty Hall, not only could I be asked to do anything, but I'd be well paid for it, and the combination of those two wonderful ideas sent me tumbling over the edge into orgasm.

2

Once it was over I closed my aching thighs and considered my options. I wasn't sure if I really wanted to work at Liberty Hall, although part of me was really turned on by the idea; and not just because of the cash either, but I was pretty sure that I didn't have much choice. I needed the money, and I wasn't so inundated with job offers that I could afford to be choosy about how I got it. Besides, I could always walk out if it got too kinky so I wasn't even really taking much of a risk. I won't deny that I considered the possibility that I mightn't be able to leave, or that it gave me a weird sort of thrill, but I didn't think about it for long. This is the 21st century, where no girl worth her Guccis goes anywhere without her mobile phone. As long as I'd got that, I'd be perfectly safe, so I dismissed the idea of being held prisoner as the cheap fantasy that it was and got up, not bothering to dress before I read back what I'd written.

I didn't have time to waste, because it was almost eleven o'clock. Imo would soon be here to collect that letter and the last thing I wanted was for her to find me naked and dishevelled, obviously turned on by what I'd done. That'd make me too much like her, and might have given her ideas. I couldn't help thinking that I'd be more likely to get the job if we were lovers, but I dismissed that idea right away, because there were some things I wouldn't do, no matter how much I needed the money; and one of them was fuck up a good friendship when I didn't have to. Instead, I ran the spell check, then started my 'CV' printing and headed for the shower in the cupboard that claimed to be my bathroom, cursing the dribble of lukewarm water that emerged. Someday I'd have a power shower, and a jacuzzi and all the expensive clothes I wanted. I'd go to all the designer shows and dress in Versace and Armani from head to toe, and people would turn their heads when I walked by and wonder who I was and how they could be like me. If that meant treading on a few people on the way then it was nothing more than Liberty Hall had done so I didn't waste any time feeling guilty about what I was planning.

I rubbed shampoo into my scalp, kneading the long curly hair that was the bane of my life. It never stayed tidy for more than five minutes, but I liked it too much to have it cut, even if I could have afforded the sort of hairdresser who'd make a decent job of it. As I worked, I made an audit of my body, trying to see it as an asset, the way that Imo no doubt would have done.

Good breasts – 34C with prominent dark nipples. A narrow waist, wide hips with a bit too much flesh on my bum for me to be a fashion model, but men liked it like that so I didn't care. I'm tall, wear a size ten, and I knew I was presentable enough to make a high-class call girl. But had I done enough to intrigue Liberty Hall? There was only one way to find out, so I got out of the shower, wrapped my hair in a towel and, in case she decided to see me straight away, dressed in my one respectable short black skirt and the white shirt Mum bought me for interviews and stuff. Then I read through the sheets I'd printed off one last time, and shoved them into an envelope just as Imo knocked on the door.

'Well?' she asked as she came in without waiting for me to call out.

I tried to act tough, and not as if my belly was suddenly tight with nerves. I had to do this, even if it meant betraying Imo. I tried to convince myself that I was being melodramatic, but I still couldn't shake the feeling that I was being seriously stupid. 'Have a look,' I said and gave her the envelope before I could chicken out. She read it through, then whistled softly.

'Oh, Tess, what a naughty girl you are.' Her expression reminded me of Nigel, as if it wouldn't take much for her to ravish me.

I smiled, tantalisingly I hoped. I wasn't going to let her do anything, but she'd be more likely to talk me up to her mum if she thought I might. By the time she discovered the truth, I'd be well in at the hotel and there'd be nothing she could do about it. I felt a bit guilty about that too, but the feeling didn't last long, especially when I remembered my overdraft.

'Am I naughty enough for your mother?' I asked, but she just shrugged.

'You can never tell with Mum. I'd better go. I wouldn't want to be late.'

'What happens next? How many people work at the hotel? What would she expect me to do?' I asked, because I'd got a mammoth attack of cold feet as soon as she'd tucked that envelope in her Prada handbag, but she just smiled enigmatically and left.

What happened next turned out to be sod all. By six o'clock, my limited reserves of patience were exhausted. I went across to Imo's bedsit to see what she was playing at, but the door was locked. The girl opposite said that Imo and her mum had come back a few hours ago, packed up all her stuff and gone home in Liberty's Mercedes. That was just dandy for Imo, but where did it leave me? Still skint, still going to be homeless at the end of the week, and still with a roomful of stuff that I'd got to pack up with no idea where I'd put it.

Sorting my possessions out occupied my Saturday night and Sunday, because for once I didn't fancy going out on the pull. Most of our crowd had already gone home and, while there were plenty of tourists around, I kept remembering what Imo had said about being paid for something that I currently gave away.

I'd never thought of myself as the prostitute type before, and I can't say that I liked it. I'd always considered myself liberated because I slept with anyone I liked the look of, but Imo had been raking in the money I so desperately needed for shagging the same number of men without the fancy gift wrapping. Now I kept wondering which of us was wrong, assuming that either of us were. Dad would have said that we were both heading for hellfire and damnation, but I'd given up listening to him years ago.

First thing Monday morning I went down to check my cubbyhole, hoping that the postman would have brought something that wasn't a bill. For once I got lucky. There was an envelope, addressed in a beautiful copperplate hand. It was thick parchment, obviously expensive, and the postmark started my heart thudding. St Paul's Head was where Liberty Hall lived, in the expensive and secluded hotel that bore her name.

I took the envelope back up to my rooms and locked the door, not sure if I actually wanted to open it. If I did, I'd be facing something about myself that I wasn't sure I could handle knowing. But I needed the cash, and part of me was intrigued by the chance to live out some of my teenage fantasies. There'd been a time when I'd existed mainly in my imagination, retreating from the boring reality of my boarding school into a series of increasingly lurid sexual scenarios. Even now, when I masturbated, I summoned up some pretty dark images, and I couldn't deny that I'd occasionally wondered what it'd be like if I ever found the courage to turn them into reality.

So it wasn't as if bringing it out in the open would change anything. I already knew that I liked sex, and I wasn't too fussy about who I had it with, and I couldn't see why I should be ashamed of that when it didn't make me any different from hundreds of other girls. Fuelled by bravado, I ripped the envelope open, and took out a sheet of paper, and a train ticket. One way. First class. That had to be a good sign, so I unfolded the page and read.

> 'Dear Tess, I read your letter with great interest, and should be happy to offer you an interview for the position of temporary guest greeter at Liberty Hall. Should you wish to attend, please be on the twelve o'clock train from Waterloo today. Should you be offered and accept the vacancy, you will commence your duties immediately. All necessary clothes and uniforms will be provided so please do not bring any of your own clothes. You will be paid two hundred and fifty pounds for attending the interview no matter what the outcome.'

All necessary clothes and uniforms provided? That sounded a bit ominous, so I did something that I hadn't planned to do and rang Dickie Lawrence to make sure that someone knew where I was going. It took a bit longer to get hold of him this time, but judging by the speed at which he rang me back, I'd definitely got something he wanted.

'I've got an interview for a job at Liberty Hall. I'm going today.' Adding 'come and rescue me if I don't get in touch' sounded melodramatic, but it was what I meant. I don't believe in rubbish like white slavery, but neither was I stupid. Playing at being a sex slave was one thing; being turned into a real one was something else entirely; and I didn't intend for it to happen to me.

'I'll keep in touch,' I settled for saying, and Dickie laughed.

'You do that, love, and I'll make it worth your while.'

'How much?'

He thought that I was as naïve as a little kid. The more he haggled, the more I realised that he might be right, but by the time I caught the train I'd signed the contract that he'd faxed to me, and I reckoned I'd got the best part of the deal. He now had first refusal of my story, and I had the promise of ten thousand pounds, or five thousand if he got cold feet and decided not to use whatever I uncovered. That'd solve my problems even if I decided not to work for Liberty Hall, but I knew I'd have to be careful and, to be honest, I was really nervous. I'd known that Liberty guarded her privacy, but Dickie reckoned that she was paranoid, and dangerous. Other people had tried to investigate her hotel, but no one had ever filed a story or been prepared to talk about why they hadn't. She was less likely to suspect me because of my friendship with Imo, but my notes were still going to have to be very well hidden. That wouldn't be hard. Imo knew that I kept a diary and that I always kept it locked. Besides, I hadn't got the job yet, so I decided to save worrying about how I'd handle it until I knew that I'd have to.

I could get to like travelling first class. I had a compartment to myself, the seats were wide, clean and comfortable and, miracle of miracles, the train was on time as it pulled in at the pretty station with its twee hanging baskets. I told myself that it was now or never, then realised that it wasn't. The ticket was only a single, so I was already committed.

Even if I hadn't been, I still wanted to do it so I grabbed my bulky handbag and got out, then stood alone on the platform, wondering who Liberty would send to meet me. Probably Imo, or maybe some member of staff. But then, realising I'd just got lucky, I saw a really gorgeous bloke. Imagine a blond Hugh Grant, complete with floppy hair and self-deprecating smile. He was wearing tan chinos and a blue shirt, open at the neck, and handed me an envelope as soon as he'd said 'hi'.

'This tells you what you've got to do.' His voice was soft, tenor and as fanciable as the rest of him, and I tried not to lust too obviously while I opened the envelope. Inside was another sheet of that heavy, expensive paper, giving me terse instructions to go with Rupert and do as he told me.

'So you're Rupert?'

It wasn't exactly sparkling dialogue, but it was all I could do not to run. Sleeping with a stranger wouldn't be a new experience for me, but I didn't like not knowing what this interview would consist of, or what would be expected of me if I got the job. People don't pay for sex unless they can't get it any other way. That meant that any 'client' as Imo would no doubt call them would either want something really odd, or wouldn't be any self-respecting girl's type.

'And you're Imo's friend, Tess. She's told me all about you.'

'Oh, God!' I said involuntarily, but he just laughed and opened the car door for me with old-fashioned courtesy.

'Nothing bad, and there's nothing to be nervous about. We're only going to go back to the hotel and have something to eat. I bet you're hungry.'

Until I'd seen him, I'd been starving, because I'd been too nervous to eat on the train, but my appetite had vanished. 'That's fine by me,' I said, because there was no way I intended to let him guess how scared I was. 'It's a pretty place,' I went on as he started the engine.

'Nothing but the best for our visitors,' he agreed, brushing his hand through his hair in just the way Hugh Grant does; only it looked much sexier when Rupert did it.

'Have you worked here long?' It'd be good if he had, because I could pump him for information that I could use during the interview.

'This is my third summer. I'm at film school. First London, now UCLA.'

He must be good to get a place in the top film school in the States – the college that had turned out Spielberg and Lucas – but I was good too, so I didn't need to waste time feeling intimidated or second best. Maybe my grades hadn't been that brilliant, but that slimeball lecturer had as good as admitted that he'd marked me down in order to get me to put out. I got my 'A' in the end though, and I more than deserved it for effort. I shivered as I remembered a night I'd thought would never end. One firm, tanned hand left the steering wheel to rest on my bare knee.

'Are you all right?'

He really seemed to care, and I found myself admitting, 'A bit nervous.'

'Don't be. Liberty loved your letter.' He grinned. 'So did I.' I'd expected that letter to stay private, but the frank admiration was very soothing. 'Here we are,' he said before I could think of a decent answer to that, and I gasped.

I'm not easily impressed, but it was a pretty incredible place. A tall, white building, with two castle-like towers, set at the very edge of the headland. Not the biggest hotel in the world, but then if the rumours were right, it wouldn't need to be. It'd only need to handle a few guests at a time; the sort of people who'd pay well for absolute privacy. Beyond it I could see the cliffs, and beyond that, I guessed, would be the shore. Sandy, Imo had said, and since it was the Hall's private beach, a great place for swimming without the hassle of a swimsuit. The grounds jarred with the polished image. Behind the high iron gates we'd stopped outside was an appealing wilderness that reminded me of the graveyard. It wasn't the sort of place you'd expect to find in a normal resort, and those gates were a bit ominous too. I got more nervous still when a uniformed porter came up to the car, and Rupert gave him the keys and got out.

'We walk from here. Miss Hall doesn't like cars on the premises. She says they spoil the ambience.'

Not having cars makes it harder for people to leave too, I thought, but I didn't say anything. I was too busy trying to convince myself that I'd got a bad attack of cold feet. I knew it couldn't be anything more, because I didn't believe in intuition, so I smiled at the uniformed guard. He didn't smile back.

'This is Tess Morgan,' Rupert explained. 'She's here for an interview.'

'Right.' The guard hit some sort of electronic gadget and the gates swung silently open.

'Real Hammer house of horror stuff,' I said, struggling to grin.

'With you as the innocent virgin?' Rupert's admiring

expression was an open invitation to prove that I was neither, but I wasn't there for that, which struck me as being a real pity.

'Hardly, but it's incredible,' I settled for saying, and that was no lie.

We were walking up a long, winding gravel driveway, and it took about five minutes to reach the house. The front doors were flung open, but I guess they didn't have to worry about thieves with all that security lurking in the background. We didn't go in that way – we were just the hired help or, in my case, the hoping to be hired help.

'My humble home,' Rupert declared as he escorted me into a room that was anything but humble.

It was large and airy, with one of those wicker and brass ceiling fans you see in old films set in India rotating overhead. Through an open doorway I could see a starkly simple bedroom, but the room we were in was furnished as a living area, with a table set in the window, looking out over the cliffs.

'Nice,' I murmured and stroked the chintz upholstery on a wicker chair, very aware of how close he was to me. Then he touched my shoulders, and eased me round to face him.

'Do you want to eat first, or shall we get on with it?' he asked.

I did a good impersonation of a goldfish that's just fallen out of its bowl and discovered that it can't breathe air. 'That's up to the interviewer, isn't it?' I pointed out, trying to concentrate on the job rather than the man.

'In a manner of speaking.' His grin seemed sexier than ever. 'Because you're going to fuck me, as your interview.'

'Right,' I said, after a moment when I hadn't known what to say, which as anyone who knows me will tell you, is pretty unusual. It wasn't as if fucking him would be hard, but I couldn't be as liberated as I'd always reckoned, because I was shocked. I'd met more than my fair share of men whose idea of brilliant repartee was 'Get your coat, you've pulled,' and I'd been contemplating a foray into prostitution for days, but that blunt statement really got to me. Then I realised that it was meant to, and decided to take him at his word.

'Let's order anyway,' I smiled, I hoped wickedly. 'Think of the fun we could have with a chocolate eclair!'

I looked round, wondering whether to go into the bedroom, then realised that wouldn't show him what I was capable of. He'd tried to throw me with that sudden blunt statement, but I wasn't easily thrown, as I intended to show him. I wouldn't ask questions or wash beforehand, or even lead him to that bedroom and fling him down on the bed and rip his clothes off, even though that was what I really fancied doing. He'd ordered me to seduce him, and I would. I'd also make his balls turn blue before I let him come, and show him who was in charge.

Tossing my hair back over my shoulders, I began to unbutton my shirt, glad I'd added to my debts by buying new undies. The chain-store white cotton that I usually wore wouldn't have cut it for what I was planning, but the black satin bra and matching high-cut knickers were ideal and no one looking at them should guess that they were Marks and Sparks rather than the Agent Provocateur I'd be able to afford by the time I went back to university.

'Do you like what you see?' I asked once my shirt hung open. I didn't bother to take it off as I crouched in front of him and slid my hands beneath his shirt to feel his nipples. The bulge in the front of his trousers made it clear how much he liked what he was seeing, but he didn't answer, and I knew it wasn't going to be as simple as I'd first thought. Imo had said I'd be being paid two hundred and fifty pounds a fuck. The punters would be entitled to something really special for that so I kissed him, long and hard, then sat on his knee and rubbed myself against his bulging crotch. Then, just as his hands moved towards the fastening of my bra, I stood up and stepped back.

'Not yet,' I whispered, and reached for the zip at the back of my skirt, wishing I was wearing stockings that I could have slowly peeled off.

I couldn't believe how turned on I was getting, both by what I was doing and by the look in Rupert's eyes. He might be playing it casual, leaning back on that plush leather sofa with one leg crossed over the other ankle, but I knew that he wanted me. I also knew he'd want me far more by the time I finally let his cock slide up my wet and sticky sex.

I stepped out of my short, tight black skirt, then did a slow pirouette only wearing that bra, those knickers, now distinctly damp around the crotch, and my high heeled black shoes. As I turned, I spotted the fruit bowl, and inspiration struck. Wriggling my bum as I walked, I went over to it and chose a thick banana. Nothing too soft, or too short, but unmistakably phallic. I held it up, as if measuring it against the erection I'd felt, but not yet seen, then dragged one of the cane-backed dining chairs across the room and straddled it.

'You want to see whether I'm worth it, don't you?' I'd got so many doubts that it was all I could do not to run, but that didn't stop me giving him my most sensuous pout. 'You want to see what I can do, and I want to show you.' I licked the fruit, imagining it was him. He didn't move a muscle or speak, but I wasn't fooled. He wanted me as much as I wanted him, and I began to feel better.

'Well.' I drew the word out, leaning on the back of the chair with my tits propped on the top of it, making sure he got a good long look. 'I like to be fucked. The longer and harder the better.'

He didn't bother to nod, let alone react, so I pushed the underwired cup of my bra down, and freed one breast. It peaked, hard and heavy, the nipple red and erect, and I felt a hot pulse of lust in my stomach. I longed to unzip those elegant chinos and use him the way I'd be used by the men who paid for the pleasure of fucking me if I got the job, but I wasn't giving in that easily. This was my audition, and I knew that you always have to give the punter what they want. My dad's never understood that, which is why I've always been the poor scholarship kid in a classroom full of rich girls. But that was going to change and I didn't much care what I had to do to change it.

'I like a good, hard, cock.' A combination of nerves and raw desire made my voice huskier than usual, but that just added to the effect.

My thighs felt sticky against the chair when I spread them wider still, gripping the fruit one-handed while I slid the knickers away from my crotch with the other. Then I hit a snag. There was no way that I could look graceful masturbating like that, so I fingered my clit instead. It was as hard and ready for action as Rupert, so it was easy to moan enticingly. He still hadn't moved, but his breathing was coming faster, and knowing that I was winning spurred me on. I made a real production number out of wanking until my breasts ached with the need to come, then walked across until I was right in front of him, but just out of reach.

'Do you like what you see?' I repeated, and this time he nodded.

I smiled again, knowing I'd got him, then pulled the knickers to one side and slid the banana up my soaking pussy. My muscles clamped down on it right away, and I felt the first ripples of orgasm cramp my stomach. It would have been easy to ram it in and out of me and rub my clit until I came, but I was meant to be seducing him, and that wouldn't do enough for him.

'It feels good,' I murmured, 'but I know what'd feel better.'

'Yes?' he breathed, and I knew I'd won. He lowered that insouciantly crossed leg, revealing trousers tented upwards by a massive erection. He was creaming himself at the sight of me fucking myself with a banana, and that put me in the driving seat.

My smile widened as I worked that fruit inside me, almost removing it, then ramming it home again, knowing that he was imagining his cock replacing it. When he began to pant, I crouched on my knees in front of him, tightening my muscles round the banana.

'I like feeling really full. You know, my mouth and my cunt.'

I'd never had two men at once, but I'd fantasised about it, and Rupert obviously liked the idea too. He didn't wait for me to unzip him, just yanked his trousers down. Beneath them, he was naked and I smiled as I looked at his cock, exhilarated by what I was doing. He was big, he was hard, he was wet, and I was about to be paid serious money for the privilege of doing something I was aching to! I leaned forward, reminding myself that there was no need to hurry and licked my way up and down that tempting penis, tasting him as if he'd been an ice cream.

He still didn't make a sound, and I swore I'd make

him beg before I took him inside me. I reached for his balls, pushing my head between his thighs, smelling him as well as tasting him. His chinos were round his thighs so he couldn't spread his legs to help me, and he didn't show any sign of wanting to anyway. He just sat there and let me service him like the whore I was auditioning to be. Not only did I not care, I was enjoying myself. I like giving head. Blokes tell me I'm good at it too, and I swore that this time would be the best ever. I started by taking his balls in my mouth, squeezing them gently, and wriggling my bum so that he couldn't forget that I was stuffed full of banana right where he wanted to put his cock. I licked and sucked until his balls bulged and his breathing came in fast bursts. I watched his eyes the whole time.

They were very blue, with the sort of lashes that mascara companies would kill to have in their adverts, and the expression in them was changing as his body became mine. I was in control now; I could make him come or I could leave him hanging. To demonstrate that, I switched targets, letting my tongue dance in enticing circles over the delicate skin that had been revealed when his foreskin retracted while my hand moved up and down his cock, giving him a good firm sheath to thrust into. He began to jerk his hips, so I bit him. Not hard, at most a graze, but it was enough to stop him in his tracks.

'Not yet,' I breathed, more turned on than ever by the sense of power. 'You don't want me enough yet.'

'Bitch,' he breathed, in the way most men would have paid a compliment. 'Hot, horny bitch.'

'That's right. Are you man enough for me?'

Seconds later, I realised that that wasn't the most intelligent thing I could have said. I'd known he was young and hard and fit, but I'd been sure that he was also a gentleman. If he was, he wasn't showing it now. He came off that sofa in a single pounce, kicking his chinos away as he flung himself on top of me. I overbalanced, landing crouched on hands and knees. He grunted with pleasure, then reached for that banana.

'You claim to want it!' he gasped. 'Now let's see if you can handle it.'

He shoved me down until my face was pressed against the carpet and his bare, hairy leg forced my legs apart. I knew I should have been scared, or at least made a token protest, but I was past caring about anything except my throbbing need. I rode each thrust as he shoved the banana up inside me, ramming it home until it split its skin and went mushy. Then he gave another grunt and rolled me onto my back, yanking the knickers away and shoving them under my nose so that I could smell what I already knew. I was as turned on as hell, and he was in charge now.

'Filthy bitch,' he whispered as he tossed them away. Then he gripped my breasts and worked his cock between them, sliding it first between soft black satin, then along my hot, hard flesh. I tried to close my legs, but he wasn't having it. His hand came down hard on my thigh, sliding in the remains of the squashed banana. Then he smiled. Not cruelly, but with such pent-up lust that I got hotter than ever.

'Filthy,' he repeated, and slid his fingers downwards. This time I didn't want to close my legs. I knew exactly what he wanted, because I wanted it too. I moaned, and shoved my hips against his face as he began to lick me clean. I wasn't the only one who was good at tongue gymnastics. The bastard kept me right on the edge, but he wasn't letting me anywhere near orgasm. I moaned and pleaded, but he didn't give a damn. He just kept licking me, slapping my hands away when I tried to reach for him, his tanned skin dark against my pale, widespread thighs. Then, when I was pleading with him to let me come, he rolled me over, shoving my head against the smooth leather sofa.

'Please,' I whispered, lust replaced by fear when he moved away from me. I tried to move, but he slapped my arse.

'You'll do exactly as you're told. You're mine, remember? Bought and paid for.'

At any other time I'd have told him where to get off, but he was right, so I kept my mouth shut, and just crouched there, trying not to think about what he was up to. He padded away, I heard a cupboard open, then he was back and parting my buttocks.

'No.' I didn't have to be able to see his face to know that he was smiling, but I didn't know if it was from genuine amusement or some sort of nasty anticipation. 'You're not into that, are you?'

I tightened my muscles when his finger pushed against my anus, wondering how quickly I could grab my clothes and run, or if I should just run and to hell with what little modesty I had. For a moment there was a feather light pressure, then, seconds before I'd have begun screaming and fighting, his cock plunged inside my pussy. The hand that had been tormenting me slid round to my belly, lifting me to meet his thrusts while his other hand squeezed my breasts until I was yelping.

He didn't give a damn about what I felt. Why should he? Like he'd said, I was a whore, bought and paid for. Realising that added to the dirty thrill of what I was doing, and I was smiling as I shoved my arse up at him, more than matching his lust, our grunts mingling. No words of tenderness; no lies about it meaning anything except pure physical gratification, and it was all the better for it. His body slammed into mine until my face was rammed so hard against the sofa that I could hardly breathe, and I went very still as my orgasm became inevitable.

There are girls, ladylike ones of the sort I'd gone to school and university with, who can come without making a sound. I'm not one of them, and I'd really lost it. I was keening my pleasure, yelling at him to give me more, harder, and he was giving it to me. He abandoned my belly, and grabbed my other breast, clamping down until I wondered if he was planning to twist it off, but I was so high that I didn't care that he was hurting me.

Then he drew back until his cock was barely at my entrance and laughed as he thrust himself into me until I could feel his balls pressing against my buttocks. He tightened his grip on my nipples, and everything came together in one titanic surge. I came like an express train, feeling him pumping inside me. He slumped forward when he'd finished, pinning me down, but I was too busy jerking like a stranded fish as I came again and again to care. My bra was shoved down, my thighs were smeared with an unappetising mixture of my juices, lubricant from the condom and mashed banana, but I didn't care about that either. I'd forgotten why I was there, and what I was doing, forgotten everything except the urgent messages that my body was sending me to get fucked.

Then I heard a quiet voice behind me – a woman's voice that I didn't need an introduction to identify – leaving me wondering how long she'd been watching and if I was good enough. 'An interesting technique,' she said coolly.

'Damn effective,' Rupert retorted, and the gulf between me and the staff of Liberty Hall widened until it made the Grand Canyon look narrow. I was still shaking, my hair was all over my face and a mass of tangles, and my make-up was smudged and smeared. I was also naked except for that bra that revealed more than it covered and even that was smeared with stuff I suddenly didn't want to think about. Forget the practised, powerful seductress I'd felt like a few minutes before; now I was the cheapest of cheap tarts and there was nothing I could do to make myself look any better.

Rupert just pulled free, slid off the condom I hadn't realised he'd put on and tied a knot in it, then put his trousers back on and looked as if nothing had happened. I knew exactly what had happened. I knew that I'd enjoyed it too. Worst of all, I knew that for all my so-called morals, I wanted to do it again. Until then, I'd kidded myself that I could always refuse Liberty's offer and walk away as if nothing had happened. Then, I knew that I couldn't, and not just because I needed the cash.

'They won't have seen anything like her.' Rupert was as cool and aristocratic as ever, and I knew there was nothing else for it.

I pulled my bra back up, then considered using my hands to cover my crotch, before abandoning the idea. She'd already had a good look at me, and I was no different from any other woman so I'd got nothing to be ashamed of, no matter how I currently felt. Besides, there was no way that I was letting this woman know that she'd got me off balance. This had to be Liberty Hall, the star of a thousand teenage fantasies. She'd been younger then, of course, but she was still impressive now. She was tall and slim, with long blonde hair that was as immaculate as mine was dishevelled. Her eyes were green rather than blue like Imo's, but they had the same catlike intensity, and they watched me without a trace of emotion.

'Well?' I challenged. 'Will I do?'

'Funny.' Her mouth smiled, her eyes didn't. 'You didn't mention that you weren't the submissive type in that list of things you won't do. They'll reduce your value, you know.'

'But you still wanted me.' I stared stubbornly up at her, knowing that she'd value me just as much as I valued myself, and determined to make her realise that the one thing I never intended to be was cheap.

'It might be interesting to try you,' she conceded, and I wished I'd used any words but those.

Perhaps I was being stupid, or at best naïve, but those rules that I'd set myself really mattered to me. As long as I kept them I didn't give a damn what the rest of the world thought about me. Right then, I knew exactly how vulnerable I was, and I wasn't sure that I'd be able to keep them.

The more Liberty watched me the more scary possibilities my imagination produced. By the time she smiled I was half expecting her to order Rupert to hold me down while she raped me.

'You'll do, but not looking like that,' was all she said, and suddenly I could breathe again.

I almost asked if she could manage to fuck like that and still keep her make-up intact, but I did have some sense left. Besides, I'd seen Imo come home stinking of sex but still looking as virginal as I knew she wasn't, so Liberty probably could too.

'Stand up,' she ordered. I stood. 'Take the bra off.'

I did, without the histrionics that had accompanied my earlier undressing.

'Now turn round.'

I made a slow pirouette, standing straight so that my breasts were shown off to their best advantage, and she smiled.

'I rather think you'll do. Rupert, fetch the contract.'

I knew she was expecting me to ask her permission to put my clothes on, maybe using the contrast between my nakedness and her classy Chanel suit to emphasise the gap between us, but I wasn't giving her that satisfaction. Instead, I sat on the chair I'd straddled while I masturbated, and read the contract through twice, acting as if being naked meant less than nothing to me. I noticed no less than a dozen clauses about confidentiality. She saw me noticing them too and smiled.

'Some of our clients have a lot to lose,' she said serenely.

I had a lot to lose too, like ten grand from her, another ten grand from Dickie, and my big break and I wasn't planning to lose any of it. Liberty might think she had all the cards, but I could walk out whenever I chose, and by the time she realised how wrong she'd been about me it would be far too late for her to do anything about it. With that comforting thought in mind I signed my name with a flourish, then asked confidently, 'What do I do first?'

3

Liberty favoured me with another unreadable smile. 'You'll do exactly what you are told, within limits, of course,' she amended before I could protest. 'As long as you keep my rules, I'll indulge your limits.'

She put the papers I'd just signed in a cardboard file. I spotted my letter in there too, along with a copy of the medical I'd had at college a few weeks before and realised that Dickie had been right about one thing. Liberty knew all the great and good; and probably had something incriminating on most of them. As a result, she'd got the sort of power that most government ministers can only dream about. For a second I wondered if I should get out while I still could. Then she smiled again, and the feeling of being outclassed grew until I reminded myself that she was no better than I was. She was just older and richer, and one of those is no advantage for a woman.

'Should the situation change, that too will change,' she murmured.

I nodded, knowing that wasn't an idle threat, and swearing that I wouldn't get caught.

'Get dressed,' she ordered, and watched while I obeyed, leaving me feeling humiliatingly conscious of my sticky thighs and the way I stank of sex. 'Now go to your room, and have a shower. As you'll remember, part of your duties are to look good at all times. The rest will be flexible. Leave your clothes outside the bedroom door. They'll be washed and stored for you until you leave.'

'I see.' I did, all too clearly. Without my own clothes or any sort of transport I had no chance of doing a runner. Those guards I'd seen on the gate would be able to catch me long before I caught one of the two trains a day the station boasted. Even if they didn't, I didn't fancy all the attention running away dressed like something out of a cheap male fantasy would bring. Still, there was no point alerting her that I could be up to something by arguing when I'd got a way round it. As far as she knew, I'd obeyed her orders and didn't have jeans and a sweater stuffed into the bottom of my oversized handbag.

'Sure,' I said again.

She favoured me with a long, level stare. 'No doubts? No questions?'

'I know what I'm here for.'

'I'm sure you think that you do.'

Her smile was warm and amused and somehow invited me to join her in either a private conspiracy or a glorious game, and I began to see how she'd enslaved so many men. It was as if she knew it all and was offering to share it. I longed to please her, and almost felt guilty about what I was planning to do to her little empire.

'Rupert, show her to her quarters. You'll be sent details of your first job shortly, Tess.' She turned and walked away without bothering with any of the usual platitudes. I watched her go, then, once the door was safely closed, let out my breath in a long hiss.

'She's really something else,' I said, sounding as respectful as I'm ever likely to.

She was, and that something else was what I wanted to be. She knew what she wanted, and she'd do whatever it took to get it. I was also pretty sure that she suspected me, so I knew I'd have to be a perfect whore, at least for the first few days. Only she didn't call them that, did she? I was a personal services provider. So, I guessed was Rupert.

'You're not bad yourself,' he said with a faint smile.

He was acting as if the last hour hadn't happened, but I had an ache and a stickiness between my thighs that reminded me of what I'd not just done, but enjoyed. I could smell myself too, so it was a relief when he escorted me to my quarters. My room was nothing like as glamorous as his, but it was on the ground floor, so getting out would be easier. Their security might be impressive, but I'd been at a boarding school that had rivalled Colditz when it came to keeping people in although I reckoned that the conditions had probably been better in that German prison camp. I knew how to beat security, and I was damn well going to. That decided, I looked round the pretty, white painted room that was dominated by an iron bedstead that came straight out of a B & D fantasy. A pure white quilt covered the bed, masses of pillows that could be thrust under my hips to make me more helpless still were piled at the top, and there were odd marks at the posts, as if someone had struggled as they'd been handcuffed to it, spoiling the shiny finish.

'Are you into being tied up?' Rupert asked before I'd finished taking everything in, the way a normal bloke might ask if you wanted wine or lager in the pub.

'I've never tried it.' I tried to sound just as casual, which wasn't easy when I was still fighting another rush of lust. Until then, I'd have sworn I wasn't into that sort of stuff. Now ... well, let's just say I was open to new possibilities.

'Would you like to? Sometime when we're both off duty?' His eyes gleamed, and those full, eminently kissable lips parted sexily as he waited for me to answer.

'Can't I tie you up instead?' That'd turn me on far more than playing helpless ever could.

'Maybe, after I've had you again.'

'Is that part of the job?'

It hadn't been in the contract, but I wouldn't really care if it was. I just wanted the rules clear from the start. I wasn't planning to keep them, but I always like to know when I'm breaking them. A bit of deliberate disobedience makes life more fun, too, so I wasn't sure whether to be disappointed when Rupert shook his head.

'What we get up to in our own time is up to us, as long as we've got enough energy for the job.'

'We?' I asked, warily curious. 'How many of us are there?' I'd have to be careful how many questions I asked, but surely I could be expected to be a bit curious about my new colleagues?

'There's you and me, Imo, of course.' When he smiled I had a real attack of the green-eyed goddess. Had he fucked Imo too? If so, which of us was best? But there was no way I was making myself seem vulnerable by asking that. Even if I had been that stupid, he'd already gone on. 'You'll be working mainly with us to start with, so I'll introduce you to the others as and when necessary.' He didn't give any sign that he'd been ordered to keep any information I was given on a 'need to know' basis, but I wasn't stupid. I was a little worried when he frowned, then added slowly, 'And Lance. You want to watch him.'

'Why?' That could have been said to get me off balance, but I wasn't taking any chances.

'All the stuff you're not into, he is.' Rupert frowned. 'And the less you want to do it the more he wants to do it to you. He runs the health club here, and he likes a challenge.'

'He can like it all he likes, but he's not trying anything with me,' I retorted, then looked pointedly at the bathroom door. 'If you'll excuse me?' We might just have fucked, but that didn't give him any rights over me, and I wanted to be on my own.

He smiled again, then ambled towards the door. I locked it behind him then explored my temporary home. There wasn't much in the way of furniture, but I didn't have much in the way of possessions, so that didn't matter and what they'd provided didn't take up a quarter of the space. There were half a dozen of the white shift dresses that my contract had said I was to wear unless otherwise instructed, and a selection of underwear that any sex shop would have envied, but no Gideon bible. That didn't surprise me, because it wasn't that sort of hotel.

I stripped off again and wrapped myself in the soft cotton robe that someone had thoughtfully left on the bed, opened the door to check that there was no one lurking in the corridor, then, once I was sure I was alone, got my mobile phone out of my bag. Seconds later, I put it back in again, and swore under my breath. So much for the phone company's boasts of 90 per cent coverage. I couldn't even get a fucking signal, so there'd be no way that I could call for help if I needed it.

I wondered if I ought to pull out – for all of thirty seconds. Then I dumped my clothes outside the door just as I'd been ordered to, and had a long, hot shower. Rupert hadn't left any bruises, which was a surprise, but I suppose they didn't want me marked because the clients wouldn't like it. I wondered about what those clients would like while I luxuriated under the powerful jets, surprised how calm I felt. I'd just had sex for cash with someone whose surname I didn't know. Was I ashamed, the way the nice girl I'd always thought I was should have been? Was I worried about what lay ahead? Wondering whether I could go through with it? No way. To be honest, I was looking forward to it. There'd be no expectations or emotional baggage to worry about, just a chance to fuck and forget the way that men have done for centuries, but with the added bonus of lots of lovely cash to sweeten the deal.

Only I wasn't planning to forget about it, and I didn't feel guilty about that either. So what if what I wrote ended a few careers? It was nothing more than they deserved for paying me to pander to their sick little fantasies. That reminded me that I'd better make some notes while things were fresh in my mind, but how? Imo knew that I kept a diary, so hiding it would arouse suspicion. But I had a way round that too. I'd write in that book like a good little girl, then tear the pages out and hide them underneath the insulation on the hot water tank, leaving only something innocuous for anyone who searched my room to see. And I wouldn't write about what had just happened, because Rupert wasn't rich or famous yet. He might be someday, so I'd put it in my own diary, which tricky Dickie wasn't going to get a look at.

'Always keep a diary, and some day it'll keep you,' I quoted as I got out of the shower, taking my time over drying myself, and rubbing in some of the unscented body lotion that had been left on the side. I combed out my wet hair and was considering blow-drying it when there was a knock on the door. I opened it to see my lunch, brought by a girl in a traditional maid's outfit who pushed the trolley in. I tried to make conversation, but she didn't seem to hear me, and I wasn't exactly surprised.

They obviously didn't want me to socialise until they were sure I wasn't out to make trouble, and in a way I was glad because I didn't want to get to like these people. I pulled out the copy of *Cosmo* that I'd bought to read on the train but been too nervous to do more than flick through, and read it while I tucked into the prawn salad and crusty bread with gusto, then put the trolley outside the door, and sat back to wait. If this was working for a living, then I was all for it.

By the following morning I wasn't feeling quite so sanguine. To be honest, I was getting downright nervous, and not for the obvious reason. What if Liberty was right about my list of taboos reducing my value? What if no one wanted me, and my big scoop turned out to be a damp squib? Dickie was such a gossip that I'd never live it down and the fact that I'd been prepared to do it in the first place wouldn't do my reputation any good either. I knew journalistic morals all too well. If I pulled it off I'd be acclaimed as a bright new star. If I didn't, I'd be known as a pathetic little tart with ideas above my station for the rest of my very limited career.

I paced across to the window, staring out at the blue sky and hating the sunshine I'd normally have been out there basking in. It was such a gorgeous day that the guests were probably all out windsurfing or something, or at least I hoped that they were. Believing that had to be better than the other option; that no one fancied me.

Then there was a knock on my door, and I hurriedly opened it. It was Imo, but she wasn't her normal casually elegant self. She was wearing a maid's outfit, but it was nothing like the one that the maid who'd brought my meal had worn. Instead, it was a minuscule black dress, out of which her breasts bulged as if threatening to overflow with each breath. Her skirt was so short that I could see her stocking tops and the cliched outfit was finished by a frilly white apron and matching cap.

'Well?' she demanded, and I knew the girl inside the clothes hadn't changed. 'Rupert told me what happened yesterday.'

'Oh,' I muttered, starting to feel sick. I didn't like the sound of Rupert telling all, and I'd just noticed that she'd got another uniform draped over her arm so I wasn't interested in hearing what he'd told her any more 'It was good,' I conceded, then nodded at the uniform. 'Is that for me?'

'Unless you think Rupert would look better in it?' She giggled, then gave me a detailed list of instructions that left my jaw somewhere round my ankles, and left, still giggling.

I stood staring at the door, wondering for the first time if I could really go through with it, but still curiously relieved that someone wanted me. Then I reminded myself that every two hundred and fifty quid I earned was two hundred and fifty quid off my overdraft, and picked up the crotchless knickers with their attached suspenders and slid them up my legs. I already felt cheap, but, to my surprise, I liked it. The sensation intensified when I fastened the seamed stockings into place and pulled the dress over my head, feeling the tarty nylon settle against my skin. The bodice was incredibly tight, and pulled in more tightly still by the wide elasticated belt, and it took me a minute to adapt my breathing.

I stared at my reflection in the mirror, knowing it was just as well that I couldn't breathe too deeply. One false move and my boobs would fall out, which was just the effect that the outfit had been designed to give. Cheap sex, on offer to the highest bidder; that was it, and I was shocked to find that I quite enjoyed the effect. The frilly white apron with its heart-shaped bodice drew even more attention to my already well-displayed breasts, and they threatened to pop out altogether as I pinned my hair up, then fastened the white cap with its froth of lace on top. I looked what I was – an animated sex toy, and I felt a pleasant tingle of anticipation between my legs as I headed towards the hotel proper.

Finding my client's room was easy because the rooms were all meticulously labelled. He was in the ocean suite, and I tapped on the door, called 'Maid service,' just as I'd been told to, then picked up the absurd feather duster that waited beside the door and went inside.

This had to be another test. Liberty Hall knew how much I liked being in control, so she'd deliberately put me in a situation where I'd lose control to see whether I'd bolt. I swore that she'd be disappointed there, with any luck as disappointed as I was surprised by what happened when I opened the door. I'd expected to be grabbed straight away, but the room seemed to be empty. I flicked at a polished wood table with the feather duster, swearing I'd kill Imo if she'd set me up. Then I heard bath water gurgling down a drain, and worked it out. Any minute now he'd come in, probably naked. He'd see me, and . . .

The 'and' was what I was there for, but I couldn't say that I was looking forward to it. Then the door opened, and I saw him. He's one of those politicians you seem to see every time you turn the TV on, without actually being able to put a name to, let alone say what he believed in. One of those grey, faceless men who lurk behind the scenes, pulling the strings, far too clever to go on the record about anything. A real pillar of the establishment, but right now all he was wearing was a short towel, and the only pillar I could see was an entirely different sort.

'Who told you to come in here?' he barked, and for a ghastly moment I wondered if this was Imo's idea of a practical joke. Then I looked at his erection, which was growing steadily redder and harder and remembered my script.

'I'm sorry, sir, but I've got to service the room.'

He smiled and moved towards me. I edged uneasily towards the door, just as I'd been told to, but he beat me to it, and turned the key in the lock before I could bolt. Not that I'd been planning to, because Imo had told me that our esteemed minister's big turn-on was the sort of little slut who'd argue at first, but deep inside was gagging to be used like a cheap whore.

I couldn't say that I was exactly gagging for it, but neither was I about to tell him to find someone else to play his pathetic little games with the way I'd normally have done. I was being paid, which made all the difference. Not just was it different, it was turning me on almost as much as my apparent fear was him. My nipples felt rock hard as I retreated until he had me pressed against the wall, and my pussy was getting wet and sticky as his breath drifted across my face.

'So here we are,' he murmured, running a well-manicured hand down my face, then inside the neckline of that straining dress. 'Just you and me, and you're here to service me, right?'

'I'm here to service the room, sir,' I corrected, trying to ignore the feeling of his hand in my bodice. This was wrong. It broke every rule I'd been brought up by. It was also so exciting that my legs were trembling.

'You're here,' he snarled, and I didn't feel like laughing any more, 'to do whatever you're told. Bought and paid for, just like everything else round here.' He pinched my nipple for emphasis – hard. I yelped and tried to pull away, but there was nowhere to go.

'Please, let me go,' I whispered, not sure if I was acting any more. Part of me wanted to run, the rest actually wanted to be helpless. Maybe I even wanted to be 'used' as he'd no doubt put it. Certainly I don't think I could have left even if he had suddenly let me go.

'You're here,' he repeated as if my pleas were turning him on, 'not for your brain, or your conversation, but for this!'

His knee forced my legs apart, his free hand darted beneath that skirt that was more of a frill than any real protection, aiming straight for the slit in my knickers. Two thick, fleshy fingers buried themselves knuckle deep in me, and I had to accept the unpalatable fact that his little game was working for me too.

'Please, sir,' I said weakly, knowing I was blushing.

'Shut up, you little bitch!' His mouth fastened on mine, but it wasn't like any kiss I'd ever had before.

Normally, men at least pretended to feel tenderness before they fucked you. This was bruising, biting, more like an animal on heat than a human being. I tried to bite him back, instinctively fighting him, feeling the excitement build until it cramped my belly. His knee ground against my crotch, and the fingers inside me stilled.

'Little hell cat,' he grunted as he lifted his mouth from mine and grabbed my hands, twisting them behind my back. 'I'll show you who's master here.'

He grabbed the towel from round his waist, and used it to tie my hands together. I struggled a bit more, then let him win just as my instructions had said to. I kept begging him to let me go, but he didn't answer. His cock just got harder and redder and wetter and I got more and more excited. I'd always been sure that I wasn't into being tied up. Now I knew I'd been wrong about that, too.

Once I was trussed to his satisfaction, he dragged me across to the dressing table. It was an antique, like everything at Liberty Hall. Oak, high-topped, with a triple mirror that currently reflected my flushed face and his triumphant smile as he reached round and yanked my bodice down.

His face was getting redder and redder and I knew I was giving him what he wanted and felt an incredible sense of power, which was daft, considering that I was helpless. He flipped my skirt up and slapped my buttocks, then jerked the knickers down, baring my bum.

'There's nothing you can do to stop me.' His voice was husky, his face such a dark scarlet that I wondered if he'd have a stroke before he could come. 'I can do whatever I like with you, and I will.'

I planned to say 'as long as it involves a condom' because I might temporarily be a whore, but I wasn't stupid, but he'd moved away before I could do more than open my mouth. I wondered about running for the door, but I might just manage to escape and lose both the cash and my story. Besides, he wasn't the only one who was getting off on this scene, so I looked at my reflection, savouring my alleged debasement, and felt exhilaratingly aware of my power. My breasts were bare, lifted and displayed by cheap, scratchy black nylon that made the contrast between tanned flesh and hard red nipples seem more erotic still. From the waist down at the front I was decent enough, but the rear reflection was something else entirely. The knickers nestled just beneath my buttocks, lifting them the way a bra does breasts, and my seamed stockings were still incongruously straight. Then he was back, and how I looked didn't matter.

There was no foreplay, no pretence at gentleness. He just shoved his latex-covered cock up me and began to pump. To and fro his hips went, and I knew he was going to come. I moaned pitifully when his hands fastened on my breasts like two vices, and not all of it was faked. The bastard would come, but what about me? I wasn't stupid enough to expect him to care about my feelings, but I'd expected him to notice me, and I got the feeling that he wasn't seeing me at all. His body slammed into mine, as he muttered, 'This'll show you, Margaret. You think you're too good for me, but you're mine now, aren't you?'

I knew that the scandal from that would add at least a grand to what I could ask for my article, and I concentrated on that comforting thought while he grunted and groaned and worked at me. Finally, he came in a long shuddering rush, yelling 'Margaret' again and again.

Right, I thought as he pulled free, that's that done. I didn't feel how I'd expected to feel. No sense of triumph, no sense of revulsion or shame, just a strange emptiness. I'd been fucked by a man I neither knew nor liked. I'd also earned myself two hundred and fifty quid and that was all there was to it. I began to straighten up, but he had other ideas. He gripped my bound wrists, holding me there while he jerked the condom off, tied a knot in it and threw it at the bin.

'You're such a snooty little bitch that you won't even come when you're told to, but you're damn well going to come,' he snarled. 'Before I let you out of here you're going to be screaming at me to stop because you can't handle any more orgasms.'

'Sir!' I whispered, knowing exactly why Imo had left this bit out. She'd always had a sick sense of humour. There again, he wanted to make me come; I desperately wanted to come, so in the end it didn't really matter.

'Turn round,' he ordered, and I didn't get much choice in the matter. He'd been a promising athlete when he was young, and had boasted in interviews about how fit he'd kept. He might be a politician, but that was one thing he hadn't been lying about. He tucked his hand under my bum, and I was airborne, landing on the bed with a thud that knocked the breath out of me.

'Keep your legs spread,' he ordered.

I obeyed, gulping when I realised what he was planning. On the dressing table lay a silver-handled brush. It had a long thick handle, elaborately chased with engraving, and I didn't have to be either Einstein or a seasoned whore like Liberty Hall to know what was about to happen. Sure enough, six inches of cold, hard silver handle was shoved inside me.

'Leave me alone,' I whimpered, acting for all I was worth.

'I'll make you want me,' he promised and crouched astride me on the bed, his flushed face rammed against mine. His flaccid cock pressed against my belly, growing less flaccid with every second. I wondered what sort of twisted psyche he had, then suddenly I didn't care any more. All I cared about was giving the performance of a lifetime, buying into his fantasy and using it to fuel my own orgasm. I turned my head away and let my hair fall forward to cover my face, making the most of my ability to cry at will, smirking when he softened.

'Just relax and I'll make it good for you,' he coaxed, and I almost came on the spot with the thrill of it. Having this powerful man at my mercy was already much better than good, and the thought of hearing him make his resignation speech after my article was printed was the icing on the cake. I was trembling by then, my body gathering itself to come, but I couldn't afford to forget my job, and that made it sexier still. I was being about as bad as it was possible to be, and he was getting off on it every bit as much as I was.

'You're hurting me,' I whimpered, relieved when he undid first my belt, then that tight bodice. He tore the dress off and dumped it on the floor, leaving me naked except for a pair of knickers at half mast, torn stockings, high-heeled shoes and a silver hairbrush stuffed in me.

'Relax,' he coaxed, back in his kissing babies persona, 'and I'll make it all better.'

He began to kiss me again, as gentle now as he'd been rough earlier. I lay deliberately still, which wasn't easy, because he was damn good at what he was doing. His tongue darted into the hollow of my throat, then he reached down and began to work the hairbrush to and fro. At first I tensed, then, gradually, I began to enjoy it. I'd masturbated with a dildo before, but I'd never felt anything like this.

The brush was rough and cold and slid in my wetness as he pushed it in and out. I bit my lip to stop myself whimpering with pleasure or asking for more, but I knew he'd win, and I reckon he did too. His mouth fastened on my nipple, suckling it savagely, his teeth nipping at the sensitive skin. The hand that wasn't brush-fucking me slid upwards, delving among my pubic hair until he found my clit. I whimpered when he began to stroke it, wondering if this Margaret knew what she was missing.

'There,' he breathed, briefly lifting his head from my breast. 'That's not so bad, is it?'

I didn't answer, but he knew he'd won, and I didn't care as long as he gave me what I was increasingly desperate for. For a middle-aged man he'd got impressive stamina. He was already hard again, but his earlier furious urgency was gone. He seemed quite happy to stroke and kiss and caress me, always working that brush inside me and rubbing my clit with a painstaking gentleness that wasn't quite enough to let me come. I moaned and raised my hips, remembering how he'd pounded into me before and hoping he'd do it again. I'd still got the unsettling feeling that he was playing out a scene that he'd played a hundred times in his imagination, and I was just a warm-bodied substitute, but I was long past caring who he thought I was, or that he was paying for this. My body was tensing round the brush, my cunt oozing with every thrust and nothing else mattered.

'Please?' I hadn't meant to give him the satisfaction of hearing me plead yet, but when he smiled triumphantly I was glad I had. He was getting his money's worth, and I'd ruin him for it later, and beat Liberty by enjoying what was supposed to turn me off and maybe even scare me off too.

'Stay still,' he ordered, and I didn't even think about arguing, although my arms were sore from being pinioned behind me.

'Won't you let me go?' I asked, buying into his game. 'I want to,' I paused, realising that this Margaret wouldn't use crude words or make demands for sex. 'I promise I won't struggle,' I amended hastily.

'No,' he whispered, giving me an excellent view of his stiff cock as he held it to my lips. 'Lick me dry,' he ordered.

I did, tasting the latex and spermicide, but not caring. I wanted to come, and he was a means to an end. Later I might feel shame or remorse about what I'd done. For now I was the amoral little madam that my father had always claimed I was, and all that mattered was the pleasure that this man could give me.

'I know,' he said suddenly, and I realised he was seeing me at last, and revelled in it. He lay down again, undid my hands briefly but kept a grip on them which meant I couldn't have escaped if I'd wanted to.

'Clasp them above your head,' he said, and I obeyed unquestioningly.

I'd never been into bondage, and I still wasn't turned on the way Imo had described being by it. But he wanted it, and I wanted to come as much as he wanted to make me come so I didn't feel helpless or degraded; just very, very aroused. He tied my wrists again, then lay on top of me and pulled them down until they were wrapped round his shoulders and we were held together in a mockery of a loving embrace. I'd been sure he'd replace that damn brush with himself, but he didn't. He eased the brush until only its narrow tip was inside me and began to rub his cock against my now rock-hard clit, laughing when I moaned.

'You want me, don't you? Go on, tell me how much you want it.'

'I want it!' I tried to sound as if his wiles had overcome my scruples, which wasn't easy when I was feeling so smug. He might be powerful, but he was as ruled and fooled by his cock as the next man, and right now I was the only one who could give him what he wanted.

'Oh, God!' I gave it my all, and not just because I wanted that two hundred and fifty pounds. 'Please, I've got to come. I'll do anything you want if you'll only let me come.' I writhed against him, then my groan wasn't acted. He whipped the hairbrush out and then he was inside me, stretching me wider than I'd ever been stretched before.

I moaned, then his mouth came down hard on mine, and I couldn't breathe properly, let alone protest. His hands massaged my back and buttocks; the suspenders bit into my thighs as I wrapped my legs round him to encourage him deeper. My hips were jerking frantically against his body, and he was driving home, seeming to go further inside me with each stroke, his balls swinging against me. He gripped my buttocks, encouraging and directing my movements, and my hard nipples grew harder still as they rubbed against his hairy chest.

My belly tightened; my head lashed from side to side. I muttered and moaned, pleading incoherently, but we both knew that I didn't want him to stop. My stomach tightened, my clit felt unbearably sensitive and my pussy was getting a wonderful seeing-to. Then I was coming and coming, pounding his back with my bound hands as I urged him on. He grunted, arched his back, and the composed, powerful politician came inside me for the second time in less than an hour.

He didn't pull away as quickly this time, which didn't surprise me. I was almost thirty years younger than he was, and I was shattered. We lay together, his cock gradually shrinking inside me, for what must have been at least ten minutes, then he untied me without looking at my face.

'I'm going to have a shower. Be gone when I come back,' he snapped.

And that was it. He walked away, I got dressed in the remains of the maid's uniform, and went back to my room. I retreated to the bathroom and locked the door, then sat on the loo seat while I wrote down everything that had happened. Then I had a long shower, taking the matching silver brush that sat on my own dressing table into the cubicle with me, wondering what the heck I was doing. I knew I shouldn't be so turned on, but I was, and I came three times more just from that brush and the memories. Then I relaxed enough to wonder if I'd done enough to be kept on, and, if so, what I'd be expected to do next.

I'd never expected to enjoy being what they call 'a working girl', but I had, and I hoped that the minister would send for me again. Even if he didn't, there were plenty of other guests and who knew what they'd want me to do? All I knew was that it would be something they couldn't get outside Liberty Hall. Something I'd be paid to provide them with, some little perversion that would provide me with meat for my articles even if I didn't enjoy it. But I wasn't as sure that I wouldn't enjoy it as I'd once been. I wasn't even sure of myself any more, but I knew I couldn't leave yet.

I stared at the iron bedstead, remembering how intense the sensations had been when I'd come while the minister had gripped my hands, and wondering how I would feel if I was tied to it and really helpless, not the play acting that had so unexpectedly turned me on. My overused and sore sex tightened at the idea, and I considered masturbating one last time, then slid naked between the sheets feeling well fucked and very tired. I didn't realise that I was already different from the girl who'd arrived at Liberty Hall the day before. She wouldn't have been looking forward to being a whore for reasons that didn't involve making her fortune and her career. Only I wasn't her any more. I was ashamed to realise that I was looking forward to it – but not ashamed enough to consider pulling out.

4

I was so shattered that I didn't wake up until it was almost dark. I don't think I'd have woken then if I hadn't heard heavy footsteps on the polished floorboards and realised that there was a man in my room. I lay still, keeping my eyes closed and my breathing as relaxed and even as I could, praying that whoever it was would think I was still asleep, and wondering what he was playing at. The contract I'd signed the day before had made it clear that I wouldn't be expected to do anything I hadn't been briefed about beforehand. I could refuse to do anything too, on the understanding that Liberty Hall could terminate my contract if I did. But I wasn't stupid enough to expect anyone to play by the rules any more than I intended to, so I wasn't really surprised that someone had got hold of a duplicate key and unlocked my room.

He was heading for the bathroom, which seemed to rule out his being a burglar. Not that I'd ever thought that he was. No self-respecting thief would ignore all those well-heeled guests in favour of a glorified maid's room, so he must be searching my room. If I'd been him I'd have made a leisurely search while I was busy with the minister, but maybe something had happened that stopped him. Or maybe this visitor wasn't official, in which case I was potentially in far more trouble than if he had been.

Liberty had limits, but someone who'd already committed burglary was far more likely to hurt an inconvenient witness. I've never been into pain, so I kept pretending to be asleep, hoping that he wouldn't decide to investigate the hot water tank where I'd tucked my notes and escape clothes between the heavy layers of lagging. I couldn't see why he should, but I couldn't see why he should be in my room at all, and I was starting to feel so nervous that it was hard to keep my breathing steady. The footsteps paused in the door-way, while, I guessed, their owner checked that he hadn't disturbed anything that might give the game away. Then they came closer to the bed. I tensed, swearing that I'd go for him before he could do any-thing to me and to hell with giving the game away that I might be more than I seemed. He might sound big, but I was mean, and determined, not to mention terrified when he stopped right beside my head. I sat up, grabbing the duvet and the bedside light switch and wishing I was the sort who wore nightclothes.

'What the hell do you think you're playing at?' I spat when I got a good look at him, revising my options rapidly because there was no way I'd be able to over-power him.

This laddie looked as if he belonged in a back street with a length of four by two timber in his hand rather than this poshest of posh hotels. He was powerfully built, and his face was hard and brutish, dominated by expressionless dark eyes and a thin mouth that looked as if he didn't make a habit of smiling as if he meant it. He was wearing the tightest and darkest blue jeans I'd ever seen, topped with an equally tight white T-shirt, and he was staring at me as if I was a pin-up picture. He didn't say anything, and my temper really flared. I let it have free rein, because I'd just realised that I was fairly safe. A rapist would have grabbed me by now. Therefore he wasn't one, and I didn't care about Liberty

Hall's rules; this wasn't in my rule book and he wasn't going to get away with it.

'Get out!' I snarled, and reached for the table lamp, trying to decide whether to aim for his head or his groin.

'Now now, don't be like that.' For such a thuggish looking man, he had an astonishingly soft voice and it did something to me that no one else had ever managed.

It scared the shit out of me. The combination of that voice and those eyes made it clear that this man hadn't heard of the civilised rules that I pretend to live by. He'd do whatever he wanted to with and to me, and for a second I wanted to do whatever it was too. Then my common sense cut in, and I glared at him.

'Don't you fucking well tell me what to do. Give me one good reason why I shouldn't call security right now!'

'Imo wondered why you hadn't come down to supper, so I said I'd check that you were all right.' That wasn't a particularly good reason, but it was enough to stop me yelling. He wanted to scare me, so I wasn't going to let him know he'd succeeded.

'I'm Lance,' he went on. 'I've got the room opposite yours. You hadn't locked your door, and didn't answer it when I knocked, so I thought that I'd better check that you were all right.'

It sounded plausible enough, but I knew I had locked the door. I didn't believe the rest of his explanation either, but I couldn't ask what he'd been doing without revealing that I'd known he was there and not done anything to stop him right away.

'Why didn't she come herself?' I asked instead.

When he smiled, I wished I hadn't asked. It sounds stupid to say that a smile could be frightening, but this one definitely was. It was too knowing, too calculating, too anticipatory. It made it clear that something was happening to Imo right now, something that he'd like to do to me as well. Only I wouldn't enjoy it, and I knew that me not enjoying it would only add to his fun.

'She's a bit tied up right now,' he drawled, then stared straight at me. He had the weirdest eyes, so dark that you could hardly tell the difference between his pupils and his irises. Even when he wasn't threatening me he was, if you see what I mean, and he simultaneously attracted me and gave me the creeps.

'I wouldn't have expected someone like you to come here,' he said, and my suspicions turned into certainties.

'Why not?' I drew on the benefit of my misspent youth to sound as innocent as I wasn't.

'From what Imo's told me you strike me as the last person in the world who'd take a job like this without an ulterior motive.'

'So do you,' I retorted, because I couldn't imagine him giving up control of anything. His stare intensified, and I began to wonder if I'd pushed him too far, then he smiled.

'But you'd be wrong. It's the perfect job for me, Tess.'

He stroked my bare shoulder too gently for comfort. If I'd been feeling charitable I'd have said that he was treating me like porcelain. I'm not that sort, so I'll admit that his touch left me shivering. Somehow, I knew that if I gave him an excuse he'd not just hurt me, but enjoy doing so. I wanted to order him to get out. But if I did that he'd know that he'd managed to scare me, and you must never let a bully realise that so I just smiled at him hopefully, enigmatically.

'I collect people the way a butterfly collector collects insects,' he continued happily.

I shivered, imagining being pinned to the iron bed like a butterfly in a collection, with him exploring my body with those strong, ruthless hands. Being tied up for Rupert was one thing. He'd view it as a game. I wasn't sure what Lance would see it as, but I knew I didn't want to find out.

'I like finding out what makes people tick; what they'll do and what they won't do.' His smile hardened. 'And what happens when they do what they always swore they wouldn't and find they enjoy it.'

'Everyone needs a hobby,' I said, then abandoned bravado and wrapped the duvet round me. 'Now, if you'll excuse me, I'd like to get dressed.' Even a girl who'd chosen this job without an ulterior motive would have limits, and I'd just reached mine. The duvet might cover me, but it still felt as if he could see through it.

'And mine's a particularly nice one,' he went on, without moving an inch, and it was all I could do not to shiver again.

It might be nice for him, but I was pretty sure it wasn't nice for his victims, and I knew damn well that he suspected me. I also knew that if he'd got proof he'd have done something by now. As long as I kept my cool he wouldn't get any proof either, because I hadn't done anything wrong – yet. Those notes I'd made about the minister would be hard to explain, so maybe I shouldn't have hidden them so carefully. They were bound to look suspicious if they were found, but he hadn't found them. He was just trying to get me jittery and off guard, and he was doing all too good a job of it.

'So what do you do here?' It felt weird to be making polite conversation with a sociopath, but I wasn't moving until he'd gone. I knew it was daft to feel self-conscious when I'd just stripped off for that politician without a qualm, but Lance was different, and not just because he wasn't paying me.

'I make people's dreams come true. Some of them turn out to be nightmares, but that's life for you, isn't it? Still, you must be hungry.' His voice didn't change as he made what could only be called a threat. 'I'll wait outside while you dress, then we can have supper together and get to know each other better. I'll be writing some of the scenes you'll play out, so I need to get a flavour of your personality.'

'Scenes?' I asked, and wished I hadn't when his smile widened.

'The games that the guests come here to play. We're here, as I said, to make their dreams come true. Would you like to see how we do it?'

I didn't want to spend a second more with him than I had to, but arguing would only make him suspicious so I had to agree. I was pretty sure that he'd searched my room before I'd realised he was there, more certain still that Liberty Hall hadn't authorised him to. As yet, she didn't suspect me, and I didn't want her to start having doubts, which meant I had to be nice to Lance.

'It might be fun.' Too much enthusiasm would be suspicious too, but surely polite curiosity was OK? Even if it wasn't, the more I knew about what really went on in this exceptionally private hotel, the better equipped I'd be to make my exposé really sensational, so I'd got to take a few risks.

'Then I'll wait outside.' He got up at last and prowled across to the door like a stalking puma. It closed behind him and, in an unexpected touch of chivalry, he locked it again. If I'd been a heroine in a gothic novel I'd have let out a gasp, maybe even a deep sigh.

'Oh shit!' I muttered instead, then got up and opened the wardrobe, and pulled out one of the short sleeveless shift dresses that my contract had said I'd be expected to wear whenever I was on hotel premises. It was pretty enough – white, scoop neck, stopping a few inches above the knee. Sort of posh institutional, which summed the whole place up, but Lance wasn't like that.

I didn't know what Lance was, and part of me wanted to run away from him while I still could. The rest wanted to find out, and maybe play his games, but I told it to shut up while I concentrated on this new set of problems.

What had he been doing in my room? What did he want with me? I knew that I didn't want anything to do with him, but I'd still have to be nice to him. That didn't start with keeping him waiting, so I had a quick shower, pulled on bra and briefs, then slid the dress on. I tugged a brush through my tangled hair, added a touch of lip gloss and mascara and then I was as ready as I was ever likely to be so I reluctantly opened the door.

Lance was leaning against the wall outside, waiting for me. He smiled when he saw me, and I felt colder and more shivery still. 'Ready?' he asked, and I nodded. He didn't speak again as he led me down the passages I was getting familiar with, then out into a pretty, planter-bestrewn courtyard. Across from that was a long, low building that might once have been a stable.

'The health club,' he explained when he noticed me looking at it. 'I run it.'

'When you're not making people's dreams come true,' I said cheekily.

'What are your dreams?' His smile was just as unnerving when I wasn't naked and vulnerable, but I still wasn't letting him know he was getting to me.

'To be rich and famous.' Stuff working with kids or saving fluffy bunnies or all the other goals that wannabe beauty queens simper about. I've tried being a poor nobody, and I don't like it.

'Nothing else?' he asked, and I considered panicking, then told myself not to be stupid. There was no way he could read my mind, so he had to be trying to get me off balance, and I didn't intend to let him.

'Not really.' I expected him to push it, but he just opened the front door of the health club, then led me down a corridor marked STRICTLY PRIVATE.

'We'll have a look at the facilities before we eat.'

I nodded, and began to wonder if I'd been overreacting because Imo might have asked him to check on me. She so enjoyed teasing me that it'd be entirely in character, but he'd lied about unlocking my door, so I couldn't afford to let my guard down yet.

The facilities were as plush as the rest of the place. There was a pool, a well-equipped gym, a sauna and steam room, then another door marked PRIVATE, which he unlocked and ushered me through. It opened onto a narrower corridor, with doors set either side, close enough together that the rooms had to be pretty small. It was also incredibly quiet. So quiet I realised, as my nerves not just came back but brought all their friends with them, that this whole area must be soundproofed. I could only think of one reason why someone would go to that much trouble and expense. And that reason left me remembering Rupert's warning, and wishing that I'd had the sense to insist on Imo being there when I had Lance's grand tour.

'These are the special treatment rooms,' he explained as he produced a bunch of keys. I nodded, because my mouth was too dry to manage words. I had no reason to believe that he'd do anything to me that I didn't want him to, but something about him gave me the creeps. Then the door swung open, and I knew my instincts had been right.

The room was about the size of a doctor's examination room, or a decent-sized store cupboard. I'd only thought about doctors because of the black leather upholstered bed in the centre of the room. It belonged in a surgery, one of those couches where you can tilt the

front and rear sections up and down to make examin-
ations easier. Not that the girl on the bed was in any fit
state to be examined, because Lance hadn't been lying
about one thing. Imo was so thoroughly tied up that
there was no way she'd be able to move, let alone check
on anyone. A monitor like one of those gadgets you use
to listen to sleeping babies rested by her bed; connected
to a pad beneath her. At least that meant that nothing
would be allowed to happen to her, but realising that
didn't make me feel any better about what I was seeing.

'Have a closer look,' Lance murmured, and pushed me
gently through the door.

I looked, looked away, then looked back just as
quickly, hardly able to believe what I was seeing. Imo
was swathed in strips of what looked like oiled silk, as
tightly bound as an Egyptian mummy. Her breathing
sounded so loud in the quiet room that I knew she was
either terrified or really turned on. Knowing her, quite
possibly both. Coils of fabric were wrapped from the tips
of her toes to just below her shaved sex, pressing her
legs tightly together. More cloth covered her belly, flattening it, leaving her breasts free, but they hadn't
escaped Lance's ministrations either. The silk pushed
them upwards more effectively than the most expensive
bra could have managed, and her nipples were pinched
by tiny, silver clamps.

'What have you done to her?' I whispered as Lance
walked across to the examining couch. Imo turned her
head as if she sensed movement, and I realised she was
blindfolded with more of that silk. A ball gag filled her
mouth too, making her about as helpless as it was
possible to be.

'You don't need to whisper,' Lance explained
urbanely. 'She's wearing ear plugs, so she won't know
you're here, or what's going to happen to her next. We

can do anything we like to her, and she won't be able to stop us.'

'God,' I whispered, imagining being that helpless. It didn't do anything for me, but seeing Imo like that definitely did. I knew I should look away, but I stayed where I was, with my back pressed against the door and I was breathing almost as fast as she was while he removed those wicked little clamps. She moaned against the gag when he massaged her abused nipples, and I knew she'd be in agony as the circulation came back.

'How long has she been like this?' I asked, wondering if I should run and get help while I still could.

Imo might be into pain and humiliation, but this had to be too extreme for anyone to enjoy. Only this was Liberty Hall where nothing was too extreme, and even Lance wouldn't kidnap the boss's daughter, would he? Looking at Lance I had a horrible feeling that he both could and would. For all I knew he had, but he answered as casually as ever. 'Since this afternoon.'

That meant she'd spent about four hours totally helpless; unable to see, hear or move. If I made a move out of turn I could join her, and I wasn't important enough for anyone to care about, so it could last a lot longer. I apologised mentally to Imo for leaving her to her fate, then realised I didn't have to worry too much about her after all. Lance had begun to rub her breasts with the smooth, confident strokes of a highly trained masseur. Her next moan had a definite tinge of pleasure, and she tried to raise her body to force more of her breasts into his hands. As she moved I saw something between her legs, something that was held in place by those bandaged thighs. Something that gleamed white with the secretions that meant that, impossible as it seemed, Imo was enjoying herself.

'Don't worry.' I don't know whether Lance had read

my mind, or if my reactions were that obvious, but he was smiling at me as if I was a not very bright kid. 'She's enjoying it. Look, I'll show you.' He indicated a chair set close to the bed, and I sat down on it without considering arguing.

'She's lost it now, all right, so she should be in paradise,' I said with black humour, then realised what I'd done and pulled back, determined not to fall under Lance's creepy spell.

'She is, but she's not here just to enjoy herself.' Lance lifted one hand from her breast, and pulled that white thing from between those constricted thighs, then held it up so I could get a good look at it. 'It's a three-pronged probe,' he said, unnecessarily.

I just nodded. I'd never seen one before, but I'd read about them. It had a slender wand at the back that would slide into the tight sheath of her rectum, a thicker probe filled with what looked like little balls, and a short, beak-like knob at the front which would press against her clit. I clenched my buttocks, imagining lying for hours with that rammed up you, not knowing when or if your tormentor would return or what he'd do to you when he did. To my horror, it did something for me. It didn't turn me on the way that it obviously did Imo, more gave me a sick little thrill as I imagined doing it to someone else.

'It's remote-controlled, and I've set it to switch on and off at random intervals,' Lance said, interrupting my little fantasy before I could develop it. 'She's due for another orgasm now. Would you like to do the honours?'

'No!' I exclaimed, then added more temperately, 'It's your scene.'

'But you'd like to watch, wouldn't you?' That wasn't really a question, and him being right didn't make me like him any more.

'Does what I want matter then?' I countered, already sure that it didn't. Could this be another test, aimed at finding out how kinky I was? I had said that I'd do anything except that little list of 'won'ts' that didn't seem anything like such a good idea now I was in the seclusion of Liberty Hall. I might as well have put flags round my private taboos and invited Lance to come and break them, but it was too late to change things, so I'd have to make sure he didn't find an excuse to get his hands on me. Part of me wondered who I was trying to kid, because these people didn't need excuses. This was private property, and so well guarded that I wouldn't have a hope in hell if they wanted me in Imo's position. Realising that scared me, but bravado kept me going.

'I don't mind watching,' I said, and found it hard to breathe when he looked at me again.

I know that doesn't sound like much, but I knew that he knew that I didn't mind at all. Just like he knew I'd got a knot in my stomach at the sight of Imo so helpless. I'm not a lesbian, but I was starting to wonder if I might be into domination. Lance obviously was, and there was no way that I wanted to be his slave, but this was different. I wanted to watch whatever he did to Imo, and I didn't much like myself for it.

On the other hand, I didn't really have much choice. Besides, it wasn't as if Imo would know what I'd done, and she probably wouldn't care if she ever found out that I'd been there. I had a sneaky feeling that knowing she'd been watched would make it better for her, and I didn't think that was just me trying to justify myself. She talked about her sex life often enough, but she'd never mentioned stuff like this. That was a shame after all the time she'd spent trying to shock me, because this would have done it, but she couldn't know what she'd done, let alone enjoy it. She didn't even know that I was there as she moaned and wriggled, her moans taking on an edge of pain when Lance refastened the clamps. All she could do was feel, and even that feeling was restricted to the two zones that Lance had chosen; her small, pert breasts, now with monstrously reddened and swollen nipples, and her groin. All that she was, all her bright brain and cash, didn't matter any more.

'It'll hurt for a while.' Lance might have been a lecturer giving a dull tutorial for the hundredth time. 'The circulation's come back now, so the constriction will be all the stronger. But, gradually, the pain will turn to a warm, throbbing feeling. Have you ever tried it? No, I forgot. You're not into pain, are you? Of course, you wouldn't have experimented.'

'That's right. Just a simple vicar's daughter, that's me. What'll you do to her now?' That focused his attention back where I wanted it – on Imo.

'Bring her off. It's about time.'

'You'll finish it?' I asked, feeling a curious mixture of relief and disappointment.

'Finish? It's only been four hours. A mere –' he consulted a chart that hung at the foot of the bed. '– five orgasms. By the time this scene is ready for the guests, it's got to last at least eight hours.'

'Oh.' I knew he was smirking at the shock I'd tried so hard to hide, but I'd run out of things to say. People actually paid to be utterly helpless and degraded? No wonder Imo so often said that people were odd, and she had to be one of the oddest. Her whimpers were already dying away, to be replaced by a new tenseness, as if she was waiting for something.

'Let's see what she can manage this time.' He crossed to the sink, rinsed off the sticky probes, then set the cold tap running, waited until the water must have been icy cold, and held the vibrator beneath it.

I was glad I was sitting down so he couldn't see me shaking, because that thing would be really cold when he reinserted it. Cold and hard and unlubricated. Not that its being dry would matter. Imo's thighs were so sticky that it'd slide in easily, but the idea of that cold anal probe sliding up inside a hot, narrow passage left me feeling distinctly odd. I was trying not to think about it when he handed the probe to me and then fastened broad leather straps round Imo's breasts, thighs and knees, and adjusted the bed until she was almost vertical, with her head dangling towards the ground. She whimpered as the straps pressed the clamps against her painful-looking nipples, and I wondered what she was thinking. Was she scared? Excited? Longing for what happened next or wishing she hadn't started it? There was no way out for her, which led me to another question. 'I thought you B & D types always had a control word?' I couldn't see how Imo could signal that she'd had enough, but knowing that she had a way out would make me feel less guilty about enjoying watching her.

'What's the point?' Lance asked with a smirk. 'If you can stop it it's just a game, and nothing like as much fun. Reality's where it's really at.'

I could see that, and I'd never seen anything more real than Lance and his warped little mind. But he was occupied with Imo, which was how I wanted him to stay, so I nodded and settled for watching while he slid that probe back into position. It took him a few seconds to get it angled right, then he gave one sure thrust, and Imo's body arched.

'No!' I heard her scream against her gag, but Lance didn't care.

'The cold must add an interesting sensation. Let's see what happens if we do this,' he murmured as he picked up a small remote control unit. 'Anal stimulation first, I think. It'll be sharper when it's untouched by pleasure.'

I wanted to protest, but I was too scared that he'd start doing this sort of stuff to me. So, with another mental apology to Imo, I nodded and watched him turn the vibrator on. He didn't move it in and out of her. He didn't even bother to touch her, although there was a compelling eroticism to her plight that would have aroused a saint. It had certainly turned me on, although I'd been sure that no woman could be turned on by such a scene, and I knew I wasn't the only one. Lance's erection shoved against the loose cotton chinos, but he didn't do anything about it. He didn't speak, let alone move. He just watched Imo trying to pull her body away from the intruders and, like me, he must have known that she hadn't got a hope. Between the silk that cocooned her like the butterfly Lance had spoken of in its chrysalis stage and those leather straps she could have been used to define the word 'helpless'.

Gradually, the note of her whimpers changed, and so did her gestures. She stopped trying to force the cold probe out of her body, and started pushing herself down against it and trying to fuck it.

'Now we increase the stimulation.' Lance seemed as cool as ever, and I began to wonder if he was human as he flicked another switch and the buzzing noise got louder still. 'The vibrator against her clit is running now,' he explained unnecessarily.

It began to move up and down as well as vibrating, and Imo's moans grew louder and more desperate. Her head thrashed from side to side as she struggled to work herself against the vibrators, fighting the straps that cut into her. A dark flush spread across her ears, then down over what little I could see of her neck. Finally, the wave of colour reached her breasts, which seemed to get harder still, pushing up against the black leather straps that made such a stark contrast with her white skin.

'She'll come in a minute,' Lance observed, and held his finger just above the third switch. My thighs clamped together so hard that it hurt, but I still didn't say anything. I don't think I could have done. All I could do was watch while Imo's movements became more and more frenzied, waiting for the moment when she lost control.

It came sooner than I expected. Her scream forced its way around the gag and her body contorted, straining against the straps. Her buttocks thrust against the leather couch until the silk shone with fresh moisture. Her hair swung to and fro, her normally tidy Dutch doll bob wildly dishevelled as she gave herself over to the feelings. Her breath came in heaving gasps as her body began to still. Then Lance hit the third button.

'This one's rather clever,' he drawled. 'Not only does it vibrate, but the little balls inside move at the same time. It usually gets good results.'

It might usually do, but I could have sworn that Imo was too tired to feel anything. She screamed a protest against the gag as Lance turned the switch on the anal probe to maximum, but he didn't give a damn. He'd decided that she was going to come, and to hell with what she wanted. Maybe he never cared what anyone else wanted. It was hard to tell, hard to do anything except watch and listen with growing horror as Imo's exhausted body was forced towards a second, stronger climax. Tears dripped from beneath her blindfold, adding fresh tracks to the stains on her cheeks, and Lance's smile widened.

'She's beautiful like this, isn't she?'

I could only nod, because I knew he was right. I'd never seen a woman look so helpless before, and there was something incredibly sexy about her vulnerability. Something that was making my knickers cling to my wet and sticky sex and had got me so turned on that my nipples were almost as erect as Imo's were becoming. Gradually her sobs changed note again, and Lance smiled and went on with his lecture.

'It's strange, Tess. People always think they've gone beyond pleasure, but there's another barrier beyond that. Once you're through that barrier pain and pleasure mingle and mutate until they become the same thing, and the sensation's so intense that you get addicted to it. But you wouldn't be interested in finding out about that, would you, Tess?'

I couldn't force words past my dry lips, but he didn't seem to expect me to. Instead, he adjusted the switches with minute care, then went on. 'When she comes this time, she won't know whether it's pleasure or pain. Her rear passage will be sore, her clit far sorer, but it won't make any difference.'

He was right. Imo had stopped sobbing now, stopped making any sounds except for her harsh breathing. Her body no longer worked itself against the intruders. Instead she lay still and tense as if she was waiting for something, or as if she was too scared to move any more.

'Soon,' Lance whispered, moving to stand beside her upper torso, 'she'll really feel it.'

Then it happened. A single scream ripped past the gag as her body arched upwards. I didn't know whether it was pain or pleasure, but I'd never imagined anyone could have such an intense climax. And still Lance wasn't finished. He waited until she lay still, then removed the clamps from her nipples and leaned over her, stroking one abused breast while he gently sucked the other. She whimpered softly, seeming beyond screams of protest, beyond anything except exhausted obedience.

'The third climax –' he lifted his head just long enough to smile at me and explain '– will be the strongest of all. Turn all the controls up to maximum.'

I knew I should have protested or insisted on leaving, but I just flicked those damned switches. Imo's body gave another jerk as the clitoral attachment went into overdrive, but she didn't scream. She seemed to have accepted her fate. Who knew – maybe she was getting a kick out of it? One thing I was sure of – she was going to have that third orgasm whether or not she wanted it.

It took almost a quarter of an hour of agonisingly patient stimulation before she gave another keening cry, then thrust her breasts into Lance's waiting grip, and now the tears were soaking her cheeks. Lance waited until she was finally still, then, without any apparent hurry, turned the vibrator off, but left it inside her. He raised the bed until she was upright, then unfastened the straps, and turned her onto her belly, adjusting her head until it was turned to one side. She lay as limply as a rag doll, and I wondered if she'd passed out.

'Next time,' he said, apparently as unmoved as he'd been all along, 'I'll fuck her arse. She won't know when that's going to be, or how long she's been tied up, or when I'll release her. All she'll know is that the next climax will be more extreme.'

'Of course,' I agreed, too overdosed on what I'd seen to consider arguing.

'Did that turn you on?' His attention was focused on me now, and I didn't like it.

I nodded anyway, because there was no point lying. Whatever Lance was, and the first word that came to mind was 'psychopath', he knew too damn much about women's minds and bodies for me to get away with anything except the truth.

'Would you like it to happen to you?' He shook his head before I could frame an answer. 'No, that isn't your scene, is it? You'd prefer it like this.' He lifted me off the chair, sat down himself, then arranged me so that I was sitting astride him. Then he freed his erection from his chinos, shoved my skirt up, jerked my knickers to one side, slid two fingers inside me to test my wetness, then pulled out a condom and put it on. 'Put your arms round my neck,' he ordered.

I should have argued, but I didn't want to. I wanted what he was giving me – a good, hard uncomplicated fucking, so I moaned encouragement, driving myself down on him.

'Ah, you're a noisy one,' he said, as if I were a lab specimen, but I was too turned on to care. He stood up with me impaled on him like one of those butterflies I'd thought of earlier pinned to a board in a collection, and pulled Imo's ear plugs out, laughing when she turned her head blindly. 'It's not your turn again yet, Imo, but we'll let you listen while we have our fun.'

I felt utterly humiliated when he sat me on the couch beside Imo's head where she could hear every slurping movement as Lance fucked me, but not humiliated enough not to moan and cling to him. He didn't touch my breasts, didn't stroke my clit or need to. He just used me as if I was a sex doll, and it felt incredible. I was so turned on that I came as fast as he did, not caring that Imo would hear every whimper and plea and moan.

As soon as he'd finished he pulled out of me, tugged off the condom that glistened with my juices and dumped it beside Imo's head where she'd be able to smell us. Then he put the ear plugs back into Imo's ears and tucked his penis away. I slid off the table, rearranging my soaking knickers, hardly able to believe what I'd done. When he spoke, I knew he had to be a mind reader.

'I bet you never expected to do that, let alone enjoy it. And this is just the start, Tess. Now, let's have dinner.'

5

What happened after that was a real anticlimax. Lance unlocked the door, and I followed him back into the plush parts of the hotel that Liberty Hall wanted the world to see. We didn't mention what had happened while we ate dinner in the sunny courtyard that still retained its warmth even now that the sun was setting, and that made it all the more surreal. Lance talked most of the time, and I listened with horrified fascination, knowing I wouldn't be able to write even half of it up because no one would believe me. Even if by some miracle they did, no one could publish it under the current obscenity laws! Hearing him explain the job that was also his passion was horrifying, but it was fascinating too. And knowing that the things that he was describing with such relish could happen to me if I put a foot wrong added an extra frisson that made me far quieter than usual.

'Well,' he said as the clock on the tower chimed ten. 'You need your rest. You're going to have a busy day tomorrow.'

I wasn't tired. I was far too keyed up to feel anything except nervous anticipation, and too determined to stick it out to listen to the voice in the back of my mind that kept telling me to get out while I still could. But I intended to take precautions. Dickie had to know what was going on, because someone would have to come to the rescue if I got caught. No one in their right mind would call that greasy tabloid hack a knight in shining armour, but it was him or nothing, so I'd take what I could get.

'Are you looking forward to it? Or have I scared you off?' Lance asked, and I knew it was time to strike back.

'Look.' I stood up to make sure he realised that he might be able to intimidate everyone else, but I was different. 'You haven't scared me and you won't manage to, no matter how many kinky stories you tell me.' That was a lie, but I think I fooled him. 'I'm here because I want to be.'

'What about tonight? Did you want that as well?' His smile made it clear that he knew I was lying, but I was too glad he wasn't pushing it to argue.

'I don't know. It was very intense.'

For some of the time I'd wanted to run and scream, although at other moments I'd been tempted to help him, but I'd been held captive by his charisma. He wasn't my type, but I hadn't argued when we'd fucked. I don't think I could have argued with him any more than Imo could have done, and I wondered what she was doing now. Was she asleep? Could you sleep when you were trussed up like a parcel, with a three pronged vibrator rammed into your aching body? Even if you could adjust to that, how could you relax enough to sleep when you didn't know what would happen to you next? She wouldn't even know Lance was in the room until he touched her again, and I couldn't afford to think I might be in her place someday, or I'd bottle out.

And I had no intention of pulling out, and it wasn't just because of the money any more. I wasn't sure that I liked what I was finding out about myself, but I had to know what I really was, and how Liberty Hall had dragged herself from an orphanage to become the ruler of a growing empire.

The obvious answer was by first acting in porno films

and then being mistress to every rich man she could find, but I had a feeling it wasn't that simple. Imo had been born when Liberty was barely out of her teens, and Imo had never made a secret of the fact that she didn't know who her father was. She tried to make a joke out of it, looking at actors and other bigwigs and trying to work out which one was Daddy, but she wasn't the only one who joked about the stuff that really hurt, so I'd seen through her long ago.

She didn't actually like men, any more than I did. Maybe that was why she didn't have a problem about using them. But that didn't make her a victim. She and her mother were the furthest things from victims that I'd ever met. If anything, the guests were *their* victims. One word from Liberty would destroy them, so no wonder she seemed to be above the law. I wanted to be too, so I'd got to make a success of this.

As long as I played by her rules I was safe, and I'd always been good at appearing to keep the rules. It's safer than outright rebellion and if all else fails you can usually frame someone else. I know that's not nice, but I've never pretended to be nice, and this private diary is the one place where I can be honest about stuff, so I always try to be. I'd enjoyed watching Lance work on Imo. I'd do it again if I got the chance, maybe even help him, but I definitely did not want to be in Imo's place, or not much, anyway. A tiny part of me might want to know how it would feel to be so helpless, but the sane majority of me would run screaming from it.

But for once I didn't want to think about sex, because I had to concentrate on my next move. I had to get out of the hotel long enough to ring Dickie. I had to admire a woman who could flaunt her past with such self-confidence that she'd call her hotel after herself and damn anyone to comment on what she'd once been. Did

I fancy her as well? I'd always been sure that I wasn't like that, but watching Imo tonight had left me with an uncomfortable suspicion that I could have been wrong.

Not that it mattered if I had been, because nothing was going to happen between us. All that was about to happen was me going over the wall, in best Colditz style, and heading for the phone box I'd spotted on our way up from the station. It was taking a risk, but ringing from the hotel would have been a far greater risk. Anyone could listen in, and I wasn't stupid enough to think that they wouldn't. Or maybe I was. In hindsight, I should have arranged codes and stuff before I'd gone undercover, but I hadn't had much time and I reckoned that was deliberate too.

Liberty had done all she could to make sure that I couldn't break her rules, but I was cleverer than she'd realised, or maybe just luckier. I knew who to contact, and I intended to contact him tonight, so I faked a yawn, said goodnight to Lance, and headed for bed. After I'd heard his footsteps in the corridor and the clunk as he locked his door, I climbed through the ground-floor window, glad that I'd kept those jeans and dark sweater hidden. All the clothes they'd provided were light, bright colours that would have stood out a mile and the last thing I needed was to be caught by security.

It seemed to take for ever to sneak across the grounds, but my watch said it was only ten minutes. The little gate in the wall that I'd noticed when we walked up the drive the day before was almost overgrown with ivy, but after the practice I'd had in the graveyard it was easy to clear it away, and picking the padlock was child's play. I know good little vicar's daughters aren't meant to know how to do stuff like that, but the groundsman who gave me my first fucking at boarding school didn't just teach me about carnal pleasures, so I had that door open in under five minutes. Five minutes after that I was in the call box, right on schedule for my midnight rendezvous.

'Well?' Dickie demanded. 'What's happened?'

'You think I'm stupid, don't you? What's the point of me writing my piece if I tell you what's going on?' If I said too much he'd be able to double-cross me, but if I didn't say anything he might dump the story altogether, or even tip Liberty off and drop me right in it. That meant I'd better tell him something tantalising but non-specific. 'It's scary stuff. Dynamite.' I shivered as I remembered how helpless Imo had been. 'There was this girl, trussed up like a mummy with a triple-pronged vibrator –' I heard him panting as I gave him an edited version of what had happened, and finished smugly. 'And you'll get the really good stuff once I'm out and clear.'

'And they don't suspect anything?' Dickie sounded almost as excited as Imo had been.

'I don't think so, but if I don't ring you each day . . .' I couldn't think of a way to finish that didn't sound ridiculously melodramatic, but he finished for me.

'You want me to ride to the rescue? Save you from their evil clutches?'

I longed to wring his neck for laughing at me, but I needed him, so I had to stay polite. 'Something like that. Look, I've got to go. I'll ring you tomorrow.'

'Right, and be careful.' He sounded worried, which was so unlike him that I started worrying. Had other people tried this and failed? I couldn't see the tabloids letting a scoop like this go, so they must have done. What had happened? Had they vanished? I tried to convince myself that that sort of thing didn't happen these days, but I couldn't make myself believe it.

The bit about evil clutches was uncomfortably close

to the truth too, although Lance wasn't exactly evil. He was curious, which was somehow worse. He'd wanted to see how far Imo could be driven, and his claiming that Imo had volunteered, which I was inclined to believe even if I was discounting everything else he'd said, wasn't much help. I wouldn't have volunteered, and I had a feeling that my being unwilling would be the icing on the cake for him.

I closed my eyes, resting my head against the cool plexiglass of the phone box while I thought about the worst case scenario. I didn't want to end up locked away behind a soundproofed door and I didn't have to. All I had to do was walk down to the station and catch the night milk train, and I'd be safe. It wasn't as if I'd even have failed, because I'd already got more than enough of a story to earn my fee.

But would I really be safe? What if Lance came after me? What if I went into my rooms at college one dark night to find him waiting, just as he'd been there when I woke tonight? All it'd take was one jab from a syringe and God knew where I'd be when I woke up. I tried to convince myself that I was being melodramatic because I was tired, which I suddenly was, but I still couldn't shake the feeling that I was heading for real trouble. I considered my options for a good ten minutes, then sneaked back up the hill and into the hotel. I've never been a quitter, and of course, I was cleverer than the rest had been. But I'd definitely be on my guard.

I suppose I should have tossed and turned all night, but I slept like a lamb, and only woke when someone tapped on the door. I got up and pulled on the cotton robe they'd provided before I unlocked it, surprised and relieved to see Imo, looking almost her normal immaculate self. She had dark shadows under her eyes though, and judging by the way she was walking, she'd be sore for days. She also had an air of suppressed triumph, like a tomcat after a really successful night on the tiles.

'Hi,' I said, wondering how much she knew about how much I'd seen and done, and how she felt about that knowledge. If I'd been her I'd have been one massive blush, but she just grinned.

'I thought I'd show you that I'd survived. Lance said you were worried.' She pushed past me with the tray, put it down on the bed and helped herself to a croissant. 'Sweet of you, but it was great,' she said round mouthfuls. 'Mind you, it was extreme, even by his standards. He claimed you inspired him!'

I took a mouthful of orange juice while I tried to work out what the right answer was to that comment. 'You knew?' There was no tactful way to ask whether she really had agreed to what had been done to her. If she hadn't, then cash or not, story or not, I'd be out of there like a rat down a drainpipe.

'Did he take me prisoner?' Imo giggled. 'Bind me then have his wicked way with me, despoiling my innocent virgin flesh? Not likely. He said he'd had this idea for extreme sensory deprivation. I volunteered to try it out, because we've got to get it right before we offer it to the customers. Market research and all that. I didn't know the details beforehand, but that was part of the fun.'

I'd been sure I was as liberated as they come, but I now knew how much I'd got to learn. 'But you're all right?'

'I ache all over, but it was worth it. And you? Not too shocked?'

'If you say a word about me being a vicar's daughter,' I said tightly, because that was one running joke that had never been funny.

'No.' She finished the croissant, licked her fingers,

then hugged her knees, watching me with a friendly curiosity that was a million miles away from the way that Lance had studied me. 'But Lance is right. I wouldn't have expected you to enjoy watching or fuck him like that, or do any of this.'

'Shows how little you know me, doesn't it? Anyway, I need the cash.' That should be enough of the truth to satisfy her, and I wasn't sure if I wanted to ask why she'd suggested I did it if she'd been so sure that I'd be out of my depth. Had it been her idea of a joke? If so, I felt better about what I was doing to her mum, so I decided to believe that it was, and changed the subject back to what still fascinated me. 'What did it feel like?'

'Being totally helpless? Haven't you ever tried it?' Imo sounded surprised.

'You know me. Just a simple vicar's daughter.' I used that hated fact for my own ends, savouring the irony.

'But you liked it when the minister tied your hands yesterday, didn't you?'

I had liked it, and I was curious about what it would feel like to be really helpless, but I wasn't ready to try it yet, so no way was I answering that. 'What's on today's schedule?' I changed the subject again.

'You won't believe it. Some people are really weird!'

I decided not to point out that, coming from a girl who got off on being trussed up like an ancient Egyptian corpse, gagged and blindfolded, then repeatedly fucked, that was the pot calling the kettle black. Instead, I read the notes in the envelope that rested on the tray, and decided that she was right. Some people really were weird, and one of them, quite possibly, was me! But compared to the rest of the inhabitants of this place, I was a paragon of normality.

'Think you can do it? Mother thinks it'll be an extra

thrill for him, so there'll be a bonus for you if you pull it off.'

I could see that me being who I was would be the crowning glory of this little scenario. Just the thought of what my Dad would say if he ever found out was enough to turn me on. That wasn't saying much, because I seemed to be getting aroused more and more easily these days. Practice makes perfect, I guess.

'Yeah. Why not?' I shrugged and ate the rest of my breakfast. I knew I'd need all my strength, and besides, I was hungry.

An hour later, showered, my hair washed and dried, I was back in that white uniform shift and heading into the hotel proper. This time my destination was one of the towers, which would suit my next client nicely. If he'd been born in a less civilised age they'd have locked him in a dungeon and walled the door up to make sure he couldn't escape. Unfortunately, we live in the 21st century, so they've made him a bishop. One of the right-wing ones, into hellfire and damnation, which made what I was about to do all the sweeter.

'Room service,' I called as I knocked on the door. His eyes widened as he opened it, and I knew he'd recognised me.

'Tess!' he gasped, and I smiled.

'At your service, your Grace.' I know all the proper titles and how to behave with important people like him. Being a vicar's daughter has some advantages, including one I'd never expected. As he stared at me, I swear I could see him thinking how shocked Dad would be. Just as Liberty had calculated, that was adding to his fun.

'Only Liberty could do it,' he said reverently and gestured me inside.

His suite was better than the room I'd been in yesterday. He'd got a posh living room with a cross hanging in one corner. Through the open door I could see a bathroom leading off a bedroom, but that wasn't what I was staring at. There was a wooden chest full of sex toys in the centre of the carpet. Everything I'd ever heard of, loads of stuff I hadn't. He must have been considering his toy collection when I'd arrived, because a thick dildo and a black play suit rested on the floor beside it.

'Is that for me?' I asked, because one of us had to say something, and the bishop seemed to have lost his voice.

I picked up the play suit when he nodded and took it into the bathroom. I'd done a striptease for Rupert, but the bishop was a very different matter. As far as he was concerned, I was fallen and wicked, and I planned to be, in spades! It didn't take long to pull the lycra sheath off and drop it in a heap along with my bra and knickers. Then it was a matter of wriggling into that outfit. It too was lycra, but that was where any resemblance ended. The play suit had no crotch, and only cut-out slings for my breasts. Two shoelace-thin straps fastened behind my head and, although I say it myself, I looked pretty good in it. I hadn't sunbathed much that summer, so my skin looked very white against the black.

I adjusted the straps until my breasts bulged suggestively, and rubbed my nipples until they stood up. Bright red nipples and pussy would have emphasised my depravity nicely, but I hadn't brought my lipstick with me, so I had to do my best with what I'd got. I borrowed his comb and dishevelled my hair until the curls were even wilder than usual, and I looked as close to one of the models from *Playboy*, or something harder, as I could get. Then I walked back through that austere bedroom and posed in the living room doorway in the oldest posture of all: one hip forward, hands beneath boobs, lifting them up and practically shoving them at him. One fallen woman, reporting for duty.

'Come here.' His voice was shaking, and I'd never felt so powerful. This was Dad's boss, for God's sake, although that was a funny thing to say in this context. God would be as shocked as my father by what was about to happen. Or maybe not – I've always suspected that He was broader minded than his ministers wanted us to believe. Otherwise, he wouldn't have made sex so infinitely variable and fun. But that wasn't the point right then.

The point was that all those sex toys were waiting to be used, along with the uncomfortable-looking chair that had been pulled to face the most comfortable armchair in the room, where the bishop now sat. He was still wearing his cassock and dog collar, just as I'd always seen him, but it didn't put me off. I sat astride the cane chair, leaning my breasts on the back of it, and making sure he got a good view of my sex.

'What do you want first?'

I didn't know how hookers talked, but if they were being paid by the hour chances were that they were practical about it, so I'd be the same. I already knew that the bishop didn't want to be touched. He just wanted to give orders and watch the results. That was fine by me. I got the pleasure; and having him watching me was a real turn on. Assuming that his career wasn't finished totally by what I'd write about him, it'd be worth a tense weekend at home to sit in Dad's church and stare at the bishop while he preached. He'd feel me watching him and remember just as I would, and imagining his panic left me so wet that I hurried to obey him when he spoke.

'The black dildo.'

He didn't believe in starting small, did he? That big black beastie was a good ten inches long, and an inch and a half wide. But this was what I was being paid for, so I crouched in front of him, opened my mouth, licked my lips, then began to give the dildo head, kneeling where he could imagine it was his cock if he wanted to. Judging by the sudden bulge in his cassock he did want to, so I licked and sucked for a good five minutes, giving it all I'd got, and he wasn't the only one that my little display was turning on. By the time he barked, 'Enough,' I was creaming myself.

'Kneel on the chair. Put the dildo down and . . .' he was too delicate to finish, but I knew what he wanted. I'd mouth-fucked it, and now he wanted to see the real thing. I put the dildo down on the chair, then stood astride it, holding my lower lips open and giving him a real eyeful as I slid my body downwards. I let it tease my entrance while I did the old moan and groan in ecstasy bit, and not all of it was faked.

My moisture was like an oil slick on the seat as I eased myself down until his toy was right up inside me, then began to finger my clit with one hand. I stroked my breasts with the other hand, just as I'd have masturbated at home, and I didn't block him out or want to. I was getting off on the look in his eyes, knowing that this was a man who was supposed to be chaste and spiritual.

'Not enough,' he jerked the words out, and I stopped dead. That wasn't easy, when my body was gathering itself for an orgasm, but I couldn't afford to forget that I wasn't there for fun. 'Get the vacuum pump.'

I'd never tried that, but after what I'd seen and enjoyed last night why should that bother me? I fetched it, looking down at the two black rubber cups with the tubing that led to a little pump.

'Come here and bring the black toy,' he ordered, and I obeyed. 'Now kneel at my feet.'

He touched me for the first time as I obeyed, but only to arrange the rubber cups on my breasts. They fitted tightly, with cut-outs for my nipples, but he didn't manipulate them through as I'd expected.

'Get yourself ready,' he ordered, and I took that to mean rubbing my nipples until they jutted out, held upright by the rubber that felt cool against my skin. 'And the rest.'

I put the dildo back in, feeling it held snugly inside me by the carpet that pressed against me, and longing for him to start. I didn't have to wait long, but I still yelped when he did. It didn't exactly hurt, but the air left the cups as he pumped, leaving my breasts tight, hard, bulging, and more sensitive than they'd ever been.

'Masturbate,' the bishop snarled, his normal oily charm gone.

One well-manicured hand worked the pump until my boobs felt as if they'd explode. The other was beneath his cassock. I could guess what he'd be doing, and it just spurred me on. I slid my hand downwards, following it with the other one. One pushed down on my pubes, opening me up, the other found my clit. Predictably, it was hard and wet, and I made the most of it. I increased the pressure at the base of my belly, just as he was tightening the rubber cups around my breasts. I kept the sensation just below pain, but the ache in my stomach was growing remorselessly. I licked my lips and raised my body, feeling the dildo slide inside me, reminding me of the way that Lance had slid the previous night. Only this time I could set the pace, and I did, savouring each thrust and each sliding stroke of my finger over my wet clitoris. I wanted to come, but I knew my job. The customer was king and he'd got to come first.

He was panting hard and red faced as he thrust up the skirts of his cassock. Beneath it he was naked except for his socks, and his cock wasn't the best I'd seen in the last few days by a long way. Not that I cared because it wasn't coming anywhere near me. He was paying to watch me wank, and I was giving him a real show. I moaned, not as loudly as Imo had the night before, but quite loudly enough to satisfy him, then I forgot all about him and went for it. The pressure on my breasts was turning into something glorious and my cunt ached for more of what I was giving it. I speeded up, wriggling my bum as I worked, driving myself onwards, then I gripped my mound hard, forcing myself apart so I could pinch my clit tightly as I rubbed and rubbed. All the while the dildo left me gloriously full, and my hard aching breasts made it perfect. I wanted to topple forward when I came, longing to close my legs and intensify the sensations until I was screaming. But I didn't because I wanted to see what he was doing far more to prove who was really in control.

I stared at him, storing every tiny detail. He was wanking in perfect synchronisation with my movements. His cock grew harder and harder then, seconds before I couldn't hold back any longer, he groaned and shot semen over my face. I opened my mouth to taste it, and the wickedness of what I was doing made it perfect. I came, yelling my pleasure as my body twisted and convulsed, even enjoying the pain as my frantic movements made the rubber cups of the vacuum pumps bite into my breasts.

'That will be all, thank you, Tess,' he said and turned away, just as he'd often done when I'd brought him and Dad coffee after he'd taken Confirmation services at Dad's church.

I stumbled to my feet, letting the dildo fall on the

floor at his feet. The sweat- and semen-stained play suit followed it, and I walked proudly into his bathroom, washed myself clean, got dressed and let myself out. He didn't say a word to me, or even seem to notice that I was going. All he seemed to care about was the dildo that was generously smeared with my juices that he now sniffed as if it were expensive perfume. The dildo that, from what Imo had said, would join his impressive collection.

I headed back to my rooms, wanting nothing more than a bath. After that I'd write up my notes, and then I'd have to have a real think about my future. Each day I stayed here increased both the risks and the potential gain. I was learning so much, and not only was I enjoying it, I knew I was good at it. These rich powerful men, who'd pay so handsomely for the use of my body for a few hours, were like lambs to the slaughter. Even if I didn't write this story, what I was seeing and doing here would give me contacts that'd open any door I wanted, and without the scandal of starting my career with this sort of exposé. Maybe I shouldn't have been considering double-crossing Dickie, but it wasn't as if I owed him anything. He didn't give a damn about me, any more than I cared about him. The only person who really loved me was me, and I save my loyalty for the people who love me.

6

I didn't leave, of course. Instead I had another bath and wrote my notes up, then had a well-earned nap, and spent the afternoon playing tennis with Rupert. I went to bed with him that night too, for some nice, friendly vanilla sex. No commitment, or any of that romantic rubbish, just some gymnastics that left us both more than satisfied. That set the pattern for the next few weeks and, gradually, almost imperceptibly, I began to change. I can't say that I stopped being shocked altogether, but it definitely took more and more to reduce me to the disapproving silences that Imo had always enjoyed provoking.

And Imo wasn't the wildest girl I met there by a long way. Gradually, as people began to relax around me, I met some of the others and even, in a strange, wary way, made friends with them. Not in the way that I had with Rupert, where we seemed to understand each other instinctively, but I definitely became a bit more than a colleague to the others. There was wild, curly haired Cara, whose statuesque black beauty reduced every man who saw her to awed silence, and whose dirty laugh and evil sense of humour made her great, if shocking company. Danica was an elegant Hungarian girl, who looked as if she'd been born to wear tight uniforms and thigh-high boots and order people around, but in real life wouldn't have said boo to a goose. Sam and Chris were bodybuilders who swung both ways; good-looking in the burly sort of way that had never turned me on, but still a good laugh and a constant source of scurrilous gossip.

The one thing they all had in common was a complete lack of shame about what they were doing, and as I began to draw them out – at first to add colour to my story, then, increasingly, because I was fascinated by their lives – I started to see why. Cara, for instance, had worked the streets until Liberty had spotted her potential.

'She groomed me, Tess,' she told me one sunny afternoon when neither of us were wanted. We were lying beside the pool in the area that was reserved for staff, topping up our tans and basking in the August sunshine. 'She taught me how to talk, how to walk ... how to *be*.'

'Be what?' I rolled over onto my stomach, remembering the old *Pygmalion* story and, to be honest, wondering if it could apply to me as well. Because I was all too aware that I was changing. Not only was my body sleeker and better cared for than ever before, but my attitudes were altering, and I wasn't sure if I'd want to go back to university when my time here was up, or even be able to.

My bank account was almost back in the black now, and I was only halfway through my contract. If it went on at this rate, I wouldn't be worrying about cash at all next year ... and I liked having money to spend, even if I hadn't had much opportunity to spend it recently. We lived an almost cloistered life at the Hall, although nuns or monks were the last thing that we could ever be described as.

'Be whatever the suckers want me to be!' She gave her trademark rich, dirty chuckle. 'Have you met "Mr Jones" yet?'

We all knew that his name wasn't Jones. It'd have been hard to miss one of our brightest stars of stage and screen, but he wanted to play at being just plain folks, and was paying well for the privilege, so it was no hardship for us to indulge him.

'Make me kiss your boots?' I laughed too, remembering a memorable encounter the previous day. He'd actually begged to be ordered around, and I'd enjoyed doing it too. 'God, they're weird, aren't they?'

'Are we any better?' She stretched, as unselfconscious as a cat in a sunbeam. 'You don't . . . ?'

'I don't,' I said quickly, because I knew what she wanted. She and Imo had a habit of disappearing together for long 'siestas', and if I was curious about how her jet-black body would look entwined with Imo's fair complexion, I kept my feelings firmly to myself.

I might be changing fast, but I was determined that my commitment to my list of taboos would remain as strong as ever. I felt that I'd begun to relax about them being broken recently. That as long as I didn't get caught out no one could make me do anything I didn't want to do. Even Lance had backed off, transferring his attentions to Danica who seemed to enjoy being terrorised. All in all, life was looking good as I reached for my glass of iced fruit juice and took a long swig.

'Where is Imo?' I asked, more from idle curiosity than any real need to know.

'Getting ready for tonight.' Cara's giggle was dirtier than ever.

'Tonight?' I wasn't booked for anything, and hadn't even realised that anything was up, which, in hindsight, proved that I hadn't been paying attention. The Hall had been taken over by a group of Hooray Henrys intent on having a stag weekend to break all records for raunchiness and rowdiness, and tonight was their last night. I'd enjoyed them as much as they'd enjoyed me, so being left out now stung.

'Tonight...'

Someday, I'd find a way to put a bell round Lance's neck to warn me of his comings and goings. He moved like a cat, and had that same feline ability to arrive exactly when he wasn't wanted, the way a cat can be relied to leap on you with muddy paws when you've got all dressed up and haven't got time to change.

'Did I frighten you?' His voice sounded like a particularly menacing purr, but I just shook my head and smiled at him.

'Why should you have done? Did you want me for something?'

'I'd like you for all sorts of things, but tonight I've written a very special part for you.'

I knew damn well that he was only pausing for dramatic effect, trying to scare me. He was doing all too good a job of it as well, but I refused to let it show. Instead, I kept my own mouth shut, and eventually he gave up on his favourite game and went on. 'It mightn't be your scene, of course. You with your limits...'

Between Imo and Lance, all the other 'service providers' knew about my taboos. Most of them laughed at them, but not Cara. She'd told me to stick to my guns, and she was leaning forward now, obviously ready to stick up for me. Not that I needed it, of course, so I kept looking at him, then, when it was clear that he wasn't going to answer, asked, 'Why not tell me and let me make my own mind up about it?'

'It's a mediaeval banquet.' I'd like to be able to say that I'd faced him down and won, but I reckon he'd just got bored with his game. 'Beautiful maidens, dining off gold and silver trenchers, until the guests rebel and carry them off to the dungeons, and ravish them.'

I laughed. I couldn't help it because it was such a cliche. Every torrid historical romance ever written seemed to have that sort of scene, which didn't alter the fact that, back when I'd been a teenager, it had been one of my favourite fantasies. It still was now, and the nerves that had started twanging when Lance had mentioned writing a scene just for me eased.

'You've got a dungeon, then?' If I got a look at it, it'd spice up my story no end, so saying yes would be business as well as pleasure.

'With all mod cons.' Lance nodded, without a trace of irony. 'Complete with cell complex, and a torture chamber.'

'A torture chamber?' My flippant mood vanished in record time, because I knew Lance all too well. He'd just love to get me chained to a rack; or maybe a cold stone wall. Then he'd cut my clothing away, a piece at a time, and then . . .

I shivered despite the hot day, because those images belonged in a nightmare rather than a fantasy. It was up to me to make sure that they stayed there, and that meant never giving him any cause to suspect that I was up to no good, or that he could cow me the way he seemed to cow the others.

'Sounds fun,' I said casually.

'I thought you'd see it like that. So if you two lovelies would like to report to make-up and costuming? It's gone four now, and getting you ready will take time.'

That was something else new, but I was long past being surprised by the care that Liberty devoted to making every detail of her guests' fantasies become enticing reality. Instead I nodded then, once he'd gone, turned to Cara.

'Does he give you the creeps as well?' Perhaps I was stupid to reveal a weak spot like that, but she was always uncharacteristically quiet when Lance was around, and I needed to know that I wasn't the only one that he scared the shit out of.

'Look, Tess, I know you think you can handle anything, but Lance is different. You don't want to give Lance any excuses to play games with you.' Cara hadn't answered the question, but what she said was quite disconcerting enough, given that she always prided herself on facing everything head-on.

'Has he played games with you then?' I couldn't resist asking but, just as she always did when faced with a question that she didn't want to answer, Cara went temporarily deaf and gathered up her book and towel and headed inside.

'I'll just have a shower, then I'll show you where to go.' Cara was as friendly as ever, but I knew she wasn't going to answer my question, and to be honest I was relieved because I wasn't sure that I wanted to add any more fears to the ones that crept out to haunt me in the middle of the night.

So I had a shower myself, then waited outside Cara's door until she was ready, making careful mental notes as we headed for the health club that was Lance's domain, heading down the corridor that led to the sauna, and then turning right.

'Come on, come on.' The woman who greeted us was the first person I'd seen at the Hall who wasn't perfect. She was still attractive enough, but she was on the wrong side of middle aged, and carrying a few more pounds than she should have been. She smiled at us maternally, then assessed us with quick expertise before producing costumes from a massive cupboard lined with racks.

'Burgundy velvet for you,' she said, handing Cara a dress that came right out of a fairy tale, then she gave me another long, almost clinical study. 'And white for you. We'll make you into a terrified virgin. They'll like that.'

A terrified virgin. Hmm … that tallied with my fantasy almost too well for comfort, but I wasn't arguing. Instead, I slid out of my 21st century white shift and began the long tortuous process of getting dressed mediaeval-style. First I put on a tight-fitting straight shift that fell to just above my knees, then a silk undergown with tight sleeves, and then a white velvet dress with incredibly full sleeves and a skirt that must have taken at least a dozen yards of material.

By the time she'd finished getting ready I was as hot as hell and thoroughly uncomfortable, but they still hadn't finished with me. Next stop was the hairdresser who covered my wet hair with glossing and straightening serums then blow dried it until it hung glossy and gleaming in the sort of well-ordered curls I'd never known it was capable of. I'd have been quite happy for her to leave them like that, but she pinned them loosely on top of my head, then covered them with one of those pointy hats with the floating veil that you see in old *Robin Hood* movies.

'Nice,' she said, holding a mirror so I could see the effect, then she reached for a pale pink lipstick and a surprising array of cosmetics. Half an hour later I looked young, fresh and innocent, and as if I wasn't wearing any make-up at all.

Cara, meanwhile, looked anything but innocent. She was more of a queen than ever, stately and imperious, just waiting to be humbled.

'Ready?' she asked, her calm as impressive as ever. I nodded, fighting nerves as I followed her down to the dining hall where the guests normally ate.

That too had been transformed. Long wooden tables ran the length of the rush-covered floor, and a raised dais had been installed for us ladies to sit at. I said 'hi' to Imo and Danica as I passed them, and smiled at the others, who were only faces with vague names attached to them, and took my seat.

That felt weird too. I was used to wearing knickers, and the feeling of the silk chemise brushing against my naked sex was odd. Not unpleasant, not exactly erotic, just a constant reminder that beneath all those layers I was more naked than I'd ever been in public.

I won't bore you by describing the food, except to say that it was as spectacular as everything else. Mediaeval music was piped in from the gallery, for all the world as if it was being played by invisible musicians, a jester wandered between the tables where a dozen men sat drinking and laughing raucously, and a good time was being had by all. Until it started. I didn't see what began the scuffle, but within seconds a fight had erupted, and then one of the lads whose bed I'd shared the night before yelled, 'Get the women!'

And all hell was let loose. Two hefty, rugger playing lads lunged for me, grabbing my elbows and lifting me bodily off the ground.

'She's for Will!' they hollered, passing me along the line as if I'd been a dress-maker's dummy.

'Let me go!' I screamed, acting the part of a modest maiden for all I was worth. They took no notice whatsoever, any more than the other roisterers listened to the pleas of the other girls.

I was slung over a muscular shoulder, my head dangling down, giving me an excellent view of a good set of buttocks, well displayed by tight fitting hose. Whoever had got me was masked, wearing one of those leather hoods that I'd always associated with torturers. I could smell him – hot and sweaty and aroused – and I knew I smelt the same beneath the expensive perfume.

'To the dungeons!' the groom-to-be yelled exultantly as we reached the hall with its elegant reception desk. He felt along the panelled walls, pushing and probing. In best Hollywood fashion, a section of panelling slid aside to reveal a steep, dark flight of stairs.

It took a while for my eyes to adjust to the lack of light and, by the time I could see clearly again, we'd reached the bottom of the flight of stairs and walked into a scene that was straight out of my most-cherished teenage fantasy: a long, narrow corridor, lit by torches thrust into sconces, with cells opening off on either side, each blocked off from the world by heavy, nail-studded oak doors that were so thick that they'd muffle any screams. No one in the hotel above would know that we were here, or what was happening to us. Hell, I couldn't kid myself that they'd have cared even if they had. I'd known I was on my own ever since I arrived here, and this was one scene that I was really looking forward to so I didn't much care.

The men ahead of us had already dragged their protesting captives into the first cells they'd found, but my captor kept going straight ahead, following right behind the groom for whose benefit all this had been organised. Was I there to give him some practice before his wedding night? Not that I imagined his bride-to-be was still a virgin, but my part in this was clear. I was the poor, helpless maiden, about to be despoiled, and I couldn't wait!

Really getting into my role, I began to scream and pound my captor's back, demanding that he put me down. Seconds later, he did – on a carved wooden frame in a cell that seemed a lot larger than the others we'd passed. The groom-to-be used the torch he'd been carrying to light the wall sconces and, as the room grew lighter, I realised that I wasn't lying on a frame after all

– I was lying on a rack! I began to struggle, but I might as well not have bothered. Seconds later my arms and legs were lashed to the corners of the dark wood frame, dragged so wide apart that my muscles were already aching. As a finishing touch, he pulled the headdress off, leaving my hair tumbling round my face. One virgin, just waiting to be ravished.

'Please,' I whimpered, feeling my erect nipples pushing against the layers of fabric as I thought about what might happen next.

There was no doubt about it. I was here to be ravished, which suited me just fine, but the damsel I was pretending to be wouldn't give in without a fight, so I struggled to raise my head enough to look around. Lance hadn't been kidding about there being dungeons where any normal house would have had a wine cellar, and this was right out of a B & D textbook. Chains hung from rough stone walls, a set of stocks stood in one corner, and something that looked ominously like an iron maiden took up most of one wall.

Not that I had much time to admire the scenery. Will, the groom, who, if his breath was anything to go by, was well on his way to being blind drunk, had already climbed onto the frame and now forced his lips onto mine in a blubbery, beery kiss that didn't belong in any of my teenage fantasies.

Then he began to tear at the tight laces that held my bodice fastened, swearing under his breath when he realised that they were securely knotted, before pulling a delicate knife from his belt and slicing through them. I lay very still, staring at him, horrified by how I was feeling as, little by little he cut my clothes away.

I didn't fancy him in the slightest, but the situation was something else entirely, and it was really turning me on. My breasts felt so hard and heavy that I thought they'd burst out of the tight underdress altogether, and I could feel my wetness soaking the thin cotton shift that had bunched up between my legs when they fastened me to the rack.

'Don't, please.' I panted, but I meant 'go on, go on,' and he did. First that beautiful gown was sliced into long ribbons and thrown onto the cold stone floor, then the silky undergown that had fitted like a glove was slashed at until he could pull it away from me. And then, all I was wearing was a cotton shift that covered my breasts and – barely – my groin.

'Christ, she's hot,' my tormentor murmured as he slid his hand beneath the shift to stroke my belly.

I whimpered and writhed, doing all I could to incite him to explore between my widespread thighs, then turned my head to watch what the man who'd brought me here was doing and got my real shock of the night as he pulled his hood off. The man who'd captured me was Sam, one of the bodybuilders, and he was as naked as the day he was born. He was also massively erect as he strode across to the groom.

'Bend over, Will. Put your head on her belly,' he ordered, with a note of command in his voice that even Lance would have envied.

'No!' I whispered, unable to believe how unfair this was.

This was the situation of my dreams – me as near to being naked and totally helpless as any man could wish for – and what had I got landed with just when I was up for anything? A guy who wanted a gay encounter! Because it was clear that it wasn't me who was turning Will on. Oh, I was eye-candy, and no doubt fun enough, because he kept stroking my breasts as he leaned forward across my pinioned body, but I wasn't the main attraction by a long way.

The main attraction was Sam, who was sliding a condom on, then producing a thoroughly anachronistic tube of lubricating gel from one of the carved wooden cupboards that had been fastened to the wall.

'Spread yourself,' Sam went on coolly, and this pampered golden boy, who'd got everything you could possibly want, actually whimpered with pleasure at being treated like a cheap rent boy and obeyed, gripping his tanned buttocks and dragging them wide apart.

He leaned forward, burying his head against my stomach while Sam slid first one long finger, then another up his arse. Then all I could do was watch and want while the groom got the fucking of his life. He loved every minute of it; almost as much as I hated it. Not because I cared what he was doing, but because I felt so incredibly left out. No one wanted me. No one had even noticed how close to the edge I'd been, just because of the situation. All I'd been was window dressing, presumably to stop the groom's friends guessing what really turned him on.

I tried to convince myself that it didn't matter, that I was quite pleased not to have to play this sick little game, that this way I could gather material for my articles for Dickie undisturbed by any emotionalism. It didn't help. The more fun they had, the more frustrated I became, and by the time the groom pulled up his hose and left, whooping raucously, I was close to tears.

'Are you all right, Tess?' Sam asked as he bent to unfasten me.

'Sure,' I lied, because the last straw would have been if he'd offered to bring me off. Not because I'd got anything against gays, or bisexuals, but because I'd just realised how much I'd changed.

The girl who'd come to Liberty Hall a month ago, willing to do almost anything for hard cash, would have been laughing cynically, amazed that she could earn so much for doing so little. I . . . well, there was no palatable way to put it. I was like a bitch on heat. I'd wanted to be ravished. Damn it, I still did want to be ravished, 'but not by Sam, or at least not like this.

I wanted to be irresistibly attractive, not to be gifted with some sort of mercy hump. I wanted . . . and then it hit me. What I really wanted was to leave, before anything else happened. I wanted to go back to how I'd been once, only I wasn't naïve enough to think that I could.

'Is that it for tonight?' My voice shook, but he didn't seem to notice.

'Yeah.' He grinned as he began to undo the strap that held my right wrist, then paused. 'For us, at least. Unless? Wouldn't want you feeling left out, would we now?'

'Sorry,' I muttered, gathering what little was left of my pride, hoping he'd put my blushes down to the hot night rather than what they were – the most acute embarrassment that I'd ever suffered. 'But that's not my scene. So if we're finished?'

I lay still and dignified while he unfastened me, then stood up, pulled down my shift and stalked across to the door and flung it open. Then realised it wasn't over for the other lucky cows. Judging by the yells and howls, they were getting what I'd wanted. What I still wanted, but for once I couldn't give in to the need for easy pleasure. I'd done that far too often recently and damn near been sucked into Liberty's web in the process. Why, sometimes I'd even forgotten what I was really there for: to gather material for an exposé that'd ruin this place and make me a whole load of money.

I tried to act casual as I headed back up the stairs to reception, relieved when I didn't meet anyone on the way back to my room. First job was a long, cold shower, and I stayed under the water until the last tingle of lust had been replaced by goosebumps. Then I wrapped myself in the towelling robe and sat on the edge of the bed to think.

It was time to decide: did I stay here or did I get out before anything worse could happen? Did I take the easy money I was making at the Hall or stick to what I'd always been sure were my principles? Were they my principles any more? I didn't know, because I'd just realised that I hadn't considered anything I'd been asked to do as being kinky for days, maybe even weeks. I'd just gone along with it, buying into the fantasy that I was in control. If I hadn't just had such a humiliating wake-up call I'd have stayed that way too, but now I was as wide awake as it was possible to be, and I knew I had to talk to Dickie.

For the last few weeks I'd avoided taking any risks by sneaking out of the Hall to talk to him, although I had managed to text him a couple of times when I'd managed to get a signal on my mobile, to tell him not to send out a search party. This said, it probably wasn't a risk any more. To involve me in a scene like the one I'd just endured, Lance must be sure he'd got me well and truly under his thumb. That just showed how wrong he'd been, and I intended to make him realise quite how badly he'd underestimated me.

The bastard had set me up – deliberately. He'd probably been wetting himself laughing at the idea of me all geared up to lose my virtue only to find that I was nothing more than window-dressing. He'd have really got off on the idea of me asking Sam to bring me off, but I'd spoilt his game then, and I'd spoil it again now. It was high time that I got back to the real world, and that meant getting out of the Hall.

Moving quickly, before I could lose my nerve, I

unpeeled the lagging round the hot water tank in the airing cupboard of my bathroom, relieved to find that my black jeans and jumper were still where I'd hidden them after my last nocturnal outing. Putting them on helped, and by the time I'd sneaked out through the ivy-covered gate I was starting to feel like me again; and even to feel smugly sorry for the poor suckers who were still caught up down in the dungeons.

I was the one in control here, even if I had been stupid enough to forget it for a while. I could end their games any time I chose. I could even bring the law down on them if I wanted to. That was probably expecting too much, given all Liberty's contacts, but I could definitely put a dent in Liberty Hall's cushy world, and after what Lance had set me up with that night, I intended to.

Dialling the number I'd memorised was the easy bit. Waiting while it rang and rang tied my nerves in knots, and hearing Dickie sounding sleepy and cross when he finally answered didn't help either.

'Who is it?' he demanded ungraciously.

'Tess. Tess Morgan, at Liberty Hall,' I elaborated when he didn't seem to remember who I was.

'I thought you'd gone native.' He didn't bother to ask how I was, and it was all I could do not to scream at him that he should try doing what I'd been doing and see if he could keep a proper emotional detachment.

'No, but I've been busy...' I trailed off tantalisingly, and sure enough, he took the bait.

'With what?'

'Come on now, Dickie, I'm not daft. I'm only valuable as long as I know stuff you don't. And the price has gone up.' Perhaps I was taking a risk, but no more of one than I was taking by being at the Hall anyway. Or perhaps I wanted to test him and find out where I'd make the most money before I decided what I did next. I couldn't deny that the idea of 'going native' had its temptations, but I was too scared to consider it seriously.

Not of what they might do to me any more, but of what I was doing to myself. Because I'd really enjoyed being fastened to that rack and stripped, and if Rupert suggested a bondage session again I knew I'd jump at it. What I didn't know was whether I'd like myself afterwards. I definitely didn't like myself much then, and Dickie didn't help.

He slimed on about how I'd got to remember the risks that he was taking. I pointed out that they were nothing compared to the risks that *I* was taking, and eventually we settled on a compromise that favoured me. Fifteen thousand pounds – and I'd have earned every penny of it.

'But it's got to be good stuff,' he warned, and I grinned savagely.

'Believe me, it will be.'

'Like?' He sounded as if he was getting off on his imagination. I'd had enough of being a sex aid to last me a lifetime.

'Listen, Dickie.' I tried to stay patient. That isn't easy for me at the best of times. 'I wasn't born yesterday. If I give you the information now you'll go for a scoop and leave me up to my neck in shit.'

'I wouldn't do a thing like that,' he protested, but I wasn't convinced.

'If I don't tell you, then you definitely can't, can you?'

'You'd better not be threatening me. If you did, I could finish you,' he snarled, and I lost my temper. I was risking, if not life and limb, then that so-called fate worse than death for him, and all he was doing was giving me grief!

'Go to hell, and you can stuff your exclusive where

the sun doesn't shine! If you don't want it, hundreds of others will,' I snapped and slammed the phone down.

I didn't bother to go through the standing and staring routine while I tried to decide whether to head for the station or go back to the Hall the way I'd done last time I'd phoned him. There was no point. I knew I couldn't leave yet, even if I couldn't understand why staying and proving myself mattered more than common sense and self-preservation. I did know that the longer I was away from Liberty Hall, the greater the chances of someone wondering where I was. So back up the hill I trudged, suddenly bone-weary and for once not thinking about sex. I got through the gate just fine, and pulled the ivy back into place, then began to sneak towards my open window, breathing more easily with each step.

'You're out late.'

I was on the concrete path outside my window and about to climb in when the silky voice came out of the darkness. At first, I was too busy not screaming to come up with any sort of an answer. Then I realised that Lance wasn't going to grab me and managed a weak, 'I couldn't sleep, so I thought I'd see if a walk would help.'

'Indeed.' He sounded more amused than angry, so I still had a chance of getting away with it. 'Guilty conscience, perhaps?'

'Why should I have? I've got a lot to think about, especially after that orgy scene you put me in.' If you're lying, always drop in a truth occasionally. If you make it an intimate confession people think you're open and honest and never realise what a devious cow you really are. Always works for me. Or at least it had until then.

'You didn't enjoy it then?' The bastard knew I'd hated it, but I was damned if I was going to add to his fun by admitting it.

'Does it matter? I'm here to make their dreams come true. Any fun I get is a bonus, isn't it?'

'Purely business?' he suggested. I nodded, then remembered that he couldn't see my expression and agreed sulkily.

'So no hurt pride?'

'Not really.' It was time for another truth. 'I was a bit shocked, but it's no skin off my nose if the blushing bridegroom's a closet case.'

'I can almost believe that, but only almost.' Lance sounded more like a snake than a human, and I knew I hadn't managed to fool him. 'Why did you keep those clothes? You know it's against the rules.'

'I know, but I needed to feel like me. All this control really gets on my tits.' I shrugged, and sat on the low wall as if I didn't have an urgent need to be somewhere else. 'Are you going to tell on me?' I wasn't sure what I'd do to stop him, or what I'd do for him if he didn't, but I acted as if I was sure he wouldn't.

'That does sound plausible. I would expect you to rebel.'

'Yeah, well.' I shrugged, then repeated the question that really mattered. 'Are you going to tell on me?'

'What'll you do for me if I don't?'

'Sorry, I don't do blackmail.' I retorted with defiance that came partly from natural bravado and partly from the knowledge that I was in quite enough shit already without giving Lance a hold over me. I knew I'd broken one of Liberty's rules, but it was only a little one, and if I got fired the decision of whether to go or stay, double cross Imo or Dickie, or both, was out of my hands, which would almost be a relief.

'No.' Lance touched me, his hand surprisingly smooth for such a big, rough-looking man. 'I don't expect that you do. You like getting your own way, don't you, Tess? In fact, you're a manipulative little bitch.'

I didn't bother to say how dare you, or any of the rest of the protest crap, because I knew he was right. I knew where I wanted to go, and I'd do almost anything to get there, and no one would think twice about my determination if I was a man.

'What were you doing out here?' I'd had enough of answering questions, so I asked one of my own.

'I was on my way back from Liberty's rooms.'

I hadn't expected an answer to that question, and I didn't like the one I'd got. Why had he been there? Had he been exercising his unique skills, or talking about his suspicions? Because he wouldn't have set me up like that if he hadn't had suspicions, even if I couldn't see what I'd done to arouse them. But he'd got real cause to doubt me now, and I wondered about seducing him to distract him, but he'd take that as a sign of guilt, and I wasn't sure I could manage it properly anyway. I knew I could give him sexual pleasure, but only the way Imo had. I still didn't fancy that, and it wouldn't give me a hold over him, so there was no point.

His voice got softer still, but it still carried clearly in the darkness. 'Do you know what we'd do if we found out that you'd been lying to us?' I shook my head. Daft, I know, when it was so dark, but he seemed to pick up on it. 'You remember that list of things you wouldn't do? Anal, lesbian, pain and humiliation, I seem to recall. If I found out that you'd betrayed us, I'd break each of your taboos in turn and make you enjoy every second of them.'

I didn't doubt that he'd do it or that he could make me enjoy it at the time, and I didn't want to think about how I'd feel afterwards. I know it sounds dumb, but those limits matter to me. As long as I stick within them, I'm still a good girl underneath. Laugh all you like, but everyone has their little foibles and that one was mine.

'Isn't it a good job I haven't betrayed you then?' I said, once I trusted my voice again, glad that I was sitting down. If I'd been standing my legs would have been shaking too much to carry me which would have been a real giveaway.

'Haven't you?' I was so close to him that I could see the whites of his eyes, and he didn't seem to blink the way normal humans do. 'I know from Imo that you plan to carve out a journalistic career for yourself when you leave university. Thing is, I don't understand you, Tess, and I don't like that, so watch your step. Now, off you go to bed.' His tone reverted back to the lazy calm that almost hid what a bastard he really was. 'You'll need your sleep because you've got a really special scene tomorrow.'

'What?' I demanded. I didn't like the sound of that at all.

'Now, now, you know what curiosity did to the cat.' His laugh chilled me, but not as much as his next words. 'Do you want to find out what it does to a Tess?'

For once I did as I was told and went to bed; ran there in fact. I locked my door, then realised how pointless that was when I already knew that Lance had a key, so I shoved the armchair under the door handle to make sure that I'd have some warning if anyone tried to get in. I didn't sleep well. My bloody imagination kept turning his words into reality, and describing the dreams of what he did to me as nightmares doesn't begin to do them justice.

7

To say I wasn't at my best the following morning would be a massive understatement. My eyes were gritty, and my mouth felt as if I'd been out on a binge; a feeling that was reinforced by a pounding headache. It was hard to concentrate on anything except the nightmares that had felt as real as anything I'd done since I'd come to Liberty Hall, but I still had to act as if nothing was wrong. I was so wound up that I'd almost have welcomed details of the 'scene' Lance had mentioned to distract me, but there was no one around to ask. In a futile attempt to distract myself I had a shower, shaved all over and trimmed my bush. Then I picked up the internal phone and ordered breakfast, trying not to think about the old saying about the condemned man having a hearty one.

This wasn't hearty. I picked at the freshly baked rolls I'd normally have wolfed while I stared at the white envelope on the tray that I really didn't want to open. I was almost sure that I was being tested. What I wasn't sure of was why. Why would they send me to see so many of their highest profile clients if they'd always suspected me of planning to sell them out? And if they weren't the most important guests, what sort of people really used Liberty Hall? Maybe I'd find out today, and I could always say no and get out if what they wanted was too kinky. Either way, there was no point putting it off, so I ripped the envelope open, expecting a concise list of instructions like the ones I'd had before. All there was was a single, heavy sheet of paper with one enigmatic sentence typed on it. 'Report to the gym at ten o'clock,' it said, and I dropped it as if it was burning me.

The gym was in the heart of Lance's territory, so I'd really be walking into the lion's den. But if I didn't go it'd be clear I had something to be scared of, and Lance liked fear. Sometimes I reckoned that he fed on it, the way a vampire needs blood to survive or, more likely, my imagination was running away with me again, and I was panicking about nothing. If they had evidence they'd have done something by now. Therefore, they didn't have evidence, and I was safe. I finished the roll, trying not to think about that other old saying about giving people enough rope to hang themselves with, then went to look in the walk-in wardrobe, wondering what a good whore wore to a gym. There were tracksuits – predictably white – with leotards to go beneath them. I liked the idea of a leotard because it'd be an extra layer of defence. Then I realised that was a damn stupid idea – Lance could easily tie me up then cut it away, no doubt getting a kick out of baring my body little by little, just as they'd done in that awful orgy scene the day before.

I also realised that these images shouldn't be making my nipples peak and my pussy wet. I wasn't interested in bondage, at least not with Lance, but Rupert would be a different matter. Maybe tonight I'd drop a few hints and replay the scene I'd endured the night before; with me very much the centre of attention ... But there wasn't time for maybes. In thirty minutes I'd got to be either in that gym or out that door. I thought about the latter, but not for long.

The white lycra leotard stretched as I pulled it on, and was so translucent that the dark shadow of my pubic hair showed clearly. I wondered about shaving it altogether because it looked cheap and tarty, then realised that that was the whole point of being a whore, and left it how it was. The leotard had a low, scoop neck that meant you could see my boobs almost down to the nipples, but if the summons was genuine I wouldn't be wearing it for long. If it wasn't and I was walking into Lance's trap like a fly into a spider's web, what I was wearing wouldn't matter.

With that unhelpful thought to cheer me up, I tugged on the soft fleecy tracksuit and tied my hair into a high pony tail, then changed my mind and plaited it, pinning the braid into a knot at the nape of my neck. It looked a bit severe, but it'd be perfect for the gym. I knew I had to act as if I didn't have a care in the world and didn't expect anything to happen that I hadn't been briefed about, so hiding behind the shelter of my hair was out. It wasn't easy, but I think I did a pretty good impersonation of insouciance when, with my trainers laced up and my stomach churning, I walked across to that long, low building.

No screams of agonised pain or pleasure greeted me, and no Lance either, so my mood was improving. As I reached the gym I'd almost convinced myself that I had to be imagining things, which wasn't surprising after those nightmares. But now it was daytime, and I had a job to do, even if I didn't know what it was yet. I knew who they were right away though – England's bright shining hopes on the athletics field. Twin brothers, both tall, lean, black, and gorgeous. Both currently watching me as if they were tigers and I was lunch.

'Hi, there.' I couldn't stop my voice wobbling. I'd never expected two at once and, courtesy of the red-topped paper that Dickie wrote for, I'd heard plenty about this pair. Apparently, they did everything together, and I mean *everything*.

'Come to join our workout?' Cody asked. I knew it

was Cody, because his name was emblazoned on the tight vest that strained across his chest above equally tight and very short running shorts.

'If you like.' I tried to sound cool and collected, and not think about the obvious thing for two blokes to do with one woman. Liberty had said she'd respect my taboos as long as I kept the rules, so I should be safe enough. But what if she knew I hadn't kept the rules and this was her idea of a punishment? I didn't know that though, and if I ran I'd be admitting that I had something to be scared of, so I decided to play along. The gym wasn't locked, and I couldn't see these two golden boys risking everything by going too far, so I was safe enough.

'You must be hot in that,' Cain commented, nodding at my tracksuit. I picked up my cue and took it off, very aware of their eyes on my body.

'Nice,' Cody murmured, moving forward as Cain circled round behind me. They both put their arms round me, and there was no way I was going anywhere even if I'd wanted to. It was like being hugged by two bears. Daddy bear was behind me, and his cock shoved against my crack as if he were planning to push it up me right away. It was every bit as big as legend claimed, and the cock pressing against my belly felt bigger still.

'We're going to have fun, aren't we?' Cain slid his hands down my back, dipping inside the scoop back of the leotard to slither downwards. He separated my buttocks, moved a finger experimentally forwards.

I wasn't wet yet, and they exchanged glances over my head. Then Cody picked me up and laid me belly down on the wide beam that was meant to be used for an entirely different sort of gymnastics. It was about six feet long, and six inches wide, set six feet off the ground. My arms and legs hung down over the sides, and Cain arranged my breasts until they did the same. I began to pant, partly with fear, partly with anticipation.

'Let's warm her up.' I didn't have to look at Cody to know he'd be grinning that trademark grin that the camera and a million women loved. Most of those women would have liked to be in my place too, and I began to relax. 'Heads or tails?' he went on.

'I'll toss you for it,' Cain suggested, and I lay watching as they tossed a pound coin to decide who'd fuck me first, as if my views didn't come into it – which, of course, they didn't. They'd bought me for the next few hours, and knowing that turned me on as well.

Cody got heads or, in this case, my breasts. Cain got the bits below the waist and they took up their positions like the well-trained pair they were. Cody crouched down beneath the bar and reached up. He didn't bother to free my tits, just cupped them in those enormous hands and began to squeeze. Imagine being trapped in a velvet-lined vice and you'll get an idea of what I felt, but that was the least of it. Cain was massaging my buttocks, separating them a little more with each move-ment. The lycra was riding up as he worked, sliding into my crack until it must have looked as if all I was wearing was a thong.

'You've got a good body,' he said conversationally, then tore the lycra away.

I could feel it brushing against my thighs, but my arse was naked and all too available. Unhurriedly, he tugged my body downwards. It slid against the leather-covered beam, the remains of the leotard pulling upwards. Once he'd positioned me with my legs trail-ing over the end and my bum thrust into space, it didn't even cover my belly. Cain had moved with him, still keeping that steady pressure on my breasts, and I whimpered, as I realised how vulnerable I was. He smiled. 'Relax, honey.'

They didn't know my name. I didn't think they wanted to. As far as they were concerned I was just a body to be used, but what were they planning to do with that body? As if my whimper had been a trigger, Cody abandoned my buttocks and stroked my belly, then gradually worked his way down. One hand pressed at the top of my mound, my labia obediently opened, and a hot, thick finger slid between them. I was still scared, but I was also turned on. He grunted approvingly as he smeared my wetness forward, working it onto my clit. I lifted my hips to encourage him, beginning to enjoy myself. The sensations got better still when he slid a finger of his other hand inside me, then added a second one. Not thrusting together as I'd expected, but stretching them apart. I whimpered again, but it wasn't a protest, and I think they knew that.

'Easy girl,' he ordered, as if I was a horse rather than a human being with needs and wants and fears. He intensified the pressure on my clit and mound. I'd never felt so open, and then he added a third finger, and my whimper became a gasp. I could imagine how my lower lips would look; thin and stretched, glistening, and knowing he was as turned on by it as I was made it better still

Cain must have got bored because he'd changed tactics. He let my boobs go and began to twist the stretched fabric until it tore, not ripping it away as I'd expected him to, but making two ragged holes through which he tugged my nipples. I yelped because it hurt, and he sighed, not with lust but with a mixture of anger and disappointment.

Oh, shit, I thought, I was paid on results and I wasn't

getting them, so I'd have to do much better. Not just because I didn't want to be tossed out on my arse, but because I don't like being beaten. It was probably a stupid time to feel competitive, but it made me more determined. I moaned again, shoving my arse at Cody as Cain's mouth fastened on my nipple. He nibbled it gently, just as Cody's fingers came together, driving up inside me clean up to the ring he wore. It bit into my labia, but I was past caring. I was too aware of the fullness, and the increasing pressure on my mound and nipples.

Cain was gripping my other breast now, twisting the nipple, his fingers mimicking the movements of his mouth. Cody's fingers were working inside me, and I knew I was going to come. My belly contracted, and I felt the wetness gushing out until it must have pooled on the leather. Then I was in the air again, still with those fingers shoved inside me.

'She's almost there.' Cody sounded as if he'd been discussing the readiness of a roast chicken, and I moaned as the glorious feelings began to fade. He carried me held out at arms' length in front of him, with my arms and legs dangling over his arm. I tried to rub myself against his wrist to get me over the edge, and he shook his head mock-reprovingly, then laughed. 'You'll get it soon enough, honey. We've never had any complaints, have we, Cain?'

I didn't think they would have done, but I'd got other problems. In the corner of the room was a pile of exercise mats. Cain was lying on them, as naked as the day he was born, his erection like a rock within the latex sheath that looked incongruously white against his black flesh. Cody lowered me onto him, settling me so I was kneeling astride him. He slid inside me, and I groaned with pleasure. I'd thought the fingers were good, but he was so big that if I hadn't already been so wet and stretched I'd have been heading for the door before he did real damage. As it was I took deep breaths and stayed very still while my body adjusted.

'Still too tight,' Cain grunted and stopped moving. Behind me I heard a ripping sound, as if something was having cellophane stripped from it, and I knew I was in big trouble. I should have expected it really. Lance had set this up, and Lance knew exactly what my limits were. He was also the sort of depraved bastard who'd enjoy pushing me past them while he lurked somewhere out of sight, watching without having to take responsibility for what was happening.

Cool gel touched my buttocks. Cody was working it well in, sliding his finger round my bottom hole, and I knew I was right up the creek without a paddle. If I refused them they'd complain, and I'd be thrown out, but right now losing my job was the least of my problems. I wasn't sure they'd believe that my protests weren't part of my act. I couldn't really blame them, because Liberty wouldn't send them someone who wasn't prepared to play whatever games they wanted to, would she?

I didn't know what to do. Cody was at least as big as his brother, and one of those broad, hot fingers I'd felt inside me so recently was pushing just where I didn't want him to go. Any second now it would get inside, and I just knew it'd hurt like hell.

'I can do better than that.' Funny how you can feel so scared and still sound so calm. Only it wasn't funny. None of it was. I was way, way out of my depth and getting deeper with every second. .

'Yeah?' Cody's finger was still pushing lightly against my anus, but it hadn't gone any further. That meant I was still in with a chance, but I'd got to make it good.

'I give the best head ever.' When his finger moved I knew I wasn't doing well enough, and prepared to bolt. Then my panic eased enough for me to realise that it was moving away from me, not inside me.

'You reckon you do, do you?' He laughed, low and throaty. 'That's not what we ordered.'

'Nope, but it's better.'

I'd been right. That bastard Lance had set me up, and I'd be lucky if I got out in one piece. The twins were bigger than me by a long way, and the gym was so quiet that there had to be no one around. Even if there had been, they wouldn't have helped. After all I'd seen in the last few weeks, I wouldn't have helped a girl I saw running screaming either. I'd have thought it was a game, just as the unholy twins obviously thought my resistance was. They were both laughing, and I remembered how many men got off on fantasies of overwhelming a woman's resistance with their prowess.

'If you don't like this better, you can play your game afterwards for no extra charge.' I took a chance and straightened up to reduce my accessibility, feeling Cain move inside me until I couldn't see how he could get any further in. No way could I take two that size, so I'd have to be good. Only good wasn't the right word for it, was it?

I cupped my tits in my hands, knowing Cody was watching over my shoulders. Slowly, hopefully, lasciviously, I rubbed them together, massaging my nipples as I began to ease my body up and down on Cain. He was so big that I was sure I would be ripped apart. He was also smiling broadly as he started to pant, and I knew he wasn't used to girls taking the initiative. Judging by the size of him he'd have a hard time getting laid at all; hence the visits to Liberty Hall, where they could do just what they liked. Only today they were going to do what

I liked, so I abandoned my tits and reached behind me for Cody's cock. It was as slick as his brother's, and I gripped it with one hand, cupping his balls with the other, and began to rub. Not hard or hurried, but as if I was so sure of myself that the idea of being scared hadn't occurred to me. Each slow up and down movement was mimicked with my pussy on Cain, and when they began to pant in unison I began to believe I'd get away with it. I'd begun to enjoy myself too. I was feeling stuff I'd never done before, and it got better still when Cain gripped my hips and began to thrust. Each stroke brushed against my G-spot, and I felt myself dripping on his belly. My hands tightened on his brother as I moaned, not because I was scared or wanted him to stop, but because I wanted more.

'More, harder,' I said when he didn't take the hint. He whistled. 'You mean that?'

When it was over I would be sore, but right then I'd never been more sincere. 'Yes! Yes!' I yelled, then yelled again because the bastard had slid out from under me. His brother pulled his cock away and reached in his discarded tracksuit bottoms for the coin he'd used earlier.

'Heads or tails?' he said again, and I knew I'd won. I didn't move, just stayed crouching, head raised and ready, buttocks thrust in the air, waiting for them to decide who got which entrance. Cain got heads and knelt in front of me, pulling the condom off. I could smell myself on him, but I was past caring. Behind me Cody pulled my buttocks wide again, and I was shit scared for a second, then relieved.

Cody thrust up inside me while Cain shoved himself down my throat until I swear it felt as if their cocks met in the middle. It hurt again, but not for long, because Cody slid his hand round to my belly, then slid his fingers lower. Two fingers held me stretched open, two more closed round my clit, squeezing, gently, gently. Cain's hands were on my shoulders, supporting me and holding my face pressed against his cock, which left my hands free. I reached up and began to massage his balls, trying to keep the same rhythm that they were setting. I was drowning in sensation; buried in it, overcome by pleasure. They were so big, so hard. I could taste my lust and Cain's lust, feel him contracting in my mouth, just as Cody was inside me, and it felt brilliant.

'Come now!' Cody's voice was unrecognisable – harsh and aggressive rather than the easy charm his fans adored. His hands tightening on my clit, he gave one enormous thrust and his cock swelled until my yell of pleasure as all the feelings came together had more than an edge of pain to it. Cain's come flooded my mouth, dribbling out of the sides, but I kept sucking and working my hips, determined to fuck them so thoroughly that they wouldn't have any energy left to do anything else.

Cody fell forward, pinning me down, Cain let me go, his head thrown back as he pumped again and again. Then he too slumped forward. I couldn't catch my breath, let alone ask them to move so that I could breathe, and it seemed forever until they pulled away.

'Well?' I asked, determined to show them – and Lance, whom I suspected had watched everything, although I couldn't see him, or any sign of cameras – that I was the best. 'Was I worth it?'

Even flaccid, Cody was bigger than most men. He eased himself out of me with a care I appreciated, then said. 'You were worth it. And next time ...'

He didn't need to finish. Next time, they wanted to fill my pussy and arse at the same time, but there wasn't going to be a next time. I was getting out of here, but I wanted a few words with Lance before I went.

Once I'd got my breath back, I pulled the remains of the leotard over my head and handed it to Cain as if it was one of his precious trophies. The soft fleece of the tracksuit felt like sandpaper against my overused sex as I got dressed, but I didn't care. I'd got away with it, so I smiled up at them, not bothering to try to hide my triumph.

'Next time will be better still,' I promised, and walked out of the gym, swinging my hips, as if I was ready to do it all again. Sure enough, Lance was lurking just outside the door. 'You fucking set me up,' I snarled, and he produced another of those reptilian smiles.

'Would I do a thing like that?'

'We had a deal!' Maybe I shouldn't have yelled at him, but I'd really lost it. 'I signed a fucking contract.'

'You did, didn't you? And I suppose you're going to claim you're keeping your side of the bargain?' He took my arm and drew me into a small office, leaning against the door and leaving me with no way out.

'Of course I am.' I took a deep breath, then let fly. 'If you reckon I'm doing anything I shouldn't then go to Miss Hall and prove it. If not, back off. I'm not interested in you or your sick little games and you can't blackmail me into anything because I haven't done anything.'

'Are you sure about that? You've never looked at that iron bedstead in your room and wondered how you'd feel if you were tied to it, then stripped slowly naked while I watched and told Rupert what to do to you next?' Damn the man, because that image had been the most erotic of the ones that had haunted my dreams recently. I didn't say anything, and he didn't seem to expect me to. 'What if they had gone on today? Would you have stopped them?'

'Yes,' I declared, but I wasn't as sure of that as I should have been. 'I've got my rules.'

'I know you have,' he agreed disconcertingly quickly. 'You think you're liberated, Teresa Morgan, but deep down inside you're still a virgin.'

'Believe me,' I shot back, 'after what just happened I'm anything but that.'

He stared at me through narrowed eyes, then pulled down my track pants. I should have screamed, should have argued and struggled, but I didn't. Not because I wanted more sex. After what had just happened I couldn't imagine being turned on again for weeks. I let him because he was looking at me. I know that sounds crazy, but those dark, dark eyes stared into mine and I felt mastered. There was nothing I could do to stop him doing whatever he wanted; nothing I wanted to do either. I don't know whether it was hypnosis or the strength of his character, but I just stood there while he put his hands on my crotch, then whistled.

'Lie on the couch.'

I wanted to protest, but I couldn't find words.

'You're no use to us if you're sore,' he said, with the first signs of impatience I'd seen from him.'

'Oh, of course.' Sarcasm came easily when I was so relieved. 'I didn't think you'd got a better nature.'

'I know you aren't that stupid. Now, take those track pants off and lie down.' He turned his back on me as if my obedience would be automatic, which it was. Now that the combination of adrenalin and orgasm had faded, my pussy ached like an overexercised muscle, which I guess it was. 'On your belly,' he ordered, and I rolled over slowly, instinctively covering my buttocks with my hands.

'I said I wouldn't use you –' he moved my hands away, and I believed him, then went rigid again when he finished meditatively '– yet.' He put a jar of cream down beside my head. It smelt great; not musky but clean and lemony. 'Now I'll sort you out.'

He moved away. I heard water running, and when he came back he had a bowl of gently steaming water and a couple of flannels.

'I can manage,' I protested, but I didn't really mind being overruled. Rupert had told me that Lance had trained as a masseur, and I'd seen his skill with Imo. Now I was feeling it first hand, and he was as good at that as he was at the rest of his little games.

He washed me clean all over, and I mean all over, working a flannel up inside me until every trace of the twins was gone. Then he rinsed his hands, scooped up a dollop of cream and began to rub my back. There was nothing remotely sexual about that massage, just a warm, relaxing, soothing feeling as he worked every kink out of every muscle. When he told me to roll over I let my thighs flop apart, too tired and relaxed to care what he did.

'See,' he murmured, sounding more amused than ever. 'Obedience has its own pleasures, doesn't it? It's all right, we won't rent you out again for a few days.' He slid well-greased fingers inside me, rubbing that magic cream in. I sighed and squirmed against his hand, too caught up in the sensations to care about the crude way he'd described my temporary profession, and he actually laughed. 'You'll enjoy anything, won't you, Tess?'

That was where I should have reminded him of those limits, but I was too sleepy. I was almost sure I heard him say 'and when I've finished with you, you're going to', but I was so close to the edges of sleep that it could have been a hangover from the previous night's nightmares.

8

I was still naked when I woke, but Lance had covered me with a blanket, which I reckoned was a good omen that his setting me up with the twins had been nothing more than one of his twisted games.

I pushed myself to my feet, expecting the movement to hurt, but was surprised at how good I felt. After the workout I'd had with the twins I'd been sure I wouldn't be able to walk straight for weeks, but I was nothing more than stiff and achy; the way you get if you suddenly decide to take up jogging after a Christmas spent doing nothing more strenuous than reaching for the choccies or the remote control. Better still, Lance had said that I wouldn't be rented out for a few days, so I'd got a breathing space.

Time to think, time to plan. Time to plan how I'd get out before Lance set me up again, because I mightn't get away with it next time. But why had he done it, and how could I use it? Could I ask to be released from my contract because of what had almost happened? That'd drop Lance right in it with Liberty, which really appealed to me, but I had to admit that part of me didn't want to leave. I'd got money now, for the first time in my life, and I wouldn't have minded earning some more, because none of what I'd had to do had been that bad.

'Oh, no, Tess,' I muttered as I pulled on the track suit and headed for the door. 'Don't fall into that trap. It hasn't been that bad *yet*, and money really isn't everything.'

I've always been sure that it was, but maybe the do-gooding types who'd tried to feed me that sort of opinion all my life had had a point for once. I could still remember the feeling of that thick finger prodding my arse. My muscles tightened automatically, sending a shot of pain through me that was matched by my gloomy thoughts. But it hadn't happened, and I wasn't stupid enough to wonder how it would have felt, was I? Imo had claimed to enjoy it, but I wasn't Imo. I didn't want to become like her either; so hooked on sensation that I'd crave it the way an addict does a fix. That was another good reason to get out right now, but I intended to leave with a bang. I'd drop Lance right in it with Liberty, then leave with my head held high, my wallet bulging, and my cover intact.

Getting out like that was definitely a good plan, but I hit a snag when I tried to put it into practice. Liberty was up in London at some fancy charity do, and wouldn't be back until the next morning. I could have done without that, but it wasn't a major disaster. I could just as easily leave in the morning, and I'd be seven-and-a-half grand to the good whether or not Dickie's paper decided to buy my articles. If they didn't, and I wasn't sure they'd risk printing even a toned-down version, there were enough foreign papers that would. I knew I was looking at a twenty- to thirty-thousand profit on a month's work, so I was feeling pretty pleased with myself as I strolled back to my room.

By tomorrow night I'd be in another hotel somewhere a long, long way from here, but it wouldn't be as posh as this one. I couldn't aspire to this sort of luxury for a few years yet, but I would some day, and this place would have given me my start.

'Tess?'

If it had been anyone except Rupert I'd have pretended

that I hadn't heard him, because the last thing I wanted now I'd made my mind up was to talk to someone I was about to betray. But Rupert was different, and right then I fancied him more than ever. His floppy fair hair was damp and his sweaty T-shirt was clinging to his chest, as if he'd just run a half-marathon. He was carrying a tennis racket in a press, and I wondered if he'd really been playing tennis or if he'd found another use for his racket. That broad, leather-bound handle was just the right width to stretch a girl, and if he then crouched between that lucky girl's thighs and licked her she'd be in heaven. I knew Liberty Hall must be getting to me, because I wanted to be that girl.

'Having dinner?' he asked, and I abandoned my plans for a nice safe solo meal ordered from room service and smiled at him.

'Why not?'

'I heard about you and the twins.' I went red, though I never usually blush, and he changed the subject with his usual grace. 'You'd better watch Lance. I think he's up to something. He keeps asking me about you, but I haven't got anything to tell him.'

'I know he's up to something, but thanks for the warning. You've been great.'

I tucked my hand through his arm, knowing I'd miss him. Maybe I could keep in touch with him, assuming he'd want to see me after I'd betrayed him. I tried to convince myself that I was being melodramatic again, but I still had a nasty taste in my mouth so I let him do most of the talking while we ate melon, followed by fresh lobster and a wickedly rich chocolate mousse that I'd never have dared touch without the workout that the twins had put me through.

'Are you enjoying yourself?' he asked as he licked his

spoon clean with x-rated sensuousness that was all the more erotic for being completely uncalculated.

'I don't know.' It was weird that I felt the need to be honest with him. That's not normally one of my weaknesses, but this was the last time I'd see him so it didn't count. 'I'd have run screaming if you'd suggested any of it when I arrived.'

'I know the feeling.' He stared at me, but I had a feeling that he was seeing something very different. 'I almost left a hundred times in my first summer. A lot of people don't make it past the first day.'

I nodded, glad of the information that'd make my sudden departure seem all the more plausible. If I wrote the story cleverly enough maybe they wouldn't realise it had been me who'd grassed them up. Perhaps I could do an 'as told to', slanting it from a bloke's point of view, writing about me as if I'd been an unseen watcher.

'And Lance.' It was Rupert's turn to shake his head. 'The way his mind works.'

'I know, but he was almost nice to me today.'

I remembered how good his hands had felt, and wondered if he'd massaged Imo like that after that marathon session I'd watched all that time ago. Soon, all this would just be memories, like the moonlight on the sea, or the soft wind that ruffled the fairy lights that were strung through the branches of the trees that surrounded the terrace. Soon, I'd forget it all, only I had a feeling that it wouldn't be that simple. I wasn't sure vanilla sex would ever be enough for me again. I'd lived on the edge now, and I was surprised to find that I liked it there. I was still more surprised by what I was considering doing, or to be exact, inviting Rupert to do to me.

'Penny for them?' he asked, taking my hand.

'Just thinking.'

'About your bed?' He lowered his voice mischievously, and my half-made plans got more tempting still. 'About what would happen if you woke one night to find me in your room?' His voice got lower still. 'With iron manacles to match the bedstead? Would you fight me, Tess? Would you struggle while I tied you up? Beg me to stop? Or would you enjoy it as much as I would?'

I wriggled on the seat, trying not to think about the images his words conjured up, and he sighed.

'But Lance put you out of bounds because you're sore.'

'There are other ways. Anyway, I'm not that sore.'

Maybe I was being stupid, but this was my last chance to find out what bondage was like. Oh, I knew I could find some bloke who'd tie me up easily enough. The Internet is full of chat sites for people with those sorts of needs, and any university town attracts the broad minded, but I wanted Rupert to do it. Stupid as it sounds, I trusted him. Besides, he wanted to do it to me, and maybe letting him play out what seemed to be his pet fantasy would make me feel better about betraying him.

'Would you struggle?' he asked again, and for once his blue eyes were serious.

'Try it and find out.' That was as clear an invitation as he was getting, but he changed the subject, so I didn't know what he'd do.

Instead, we talked about the real world that seemed such a long way away from this quiet hotel; about his film career, and my ambitions to be a journalist, films we both liked. He was convinced that he'd be the next George Lucas or Stephen Spielberg – but isn't every kid at film school?

'I'm going to bed,' I said when the clock in the tower chimed ten thirty, sorry to leave him, and a little hopeful. Would he come to me like a thief in the night? If so, what would he do? Would I fight him? Would I be able to?

I tried to make my mind up about that while I had a quick shower. Then I rubbed more of the lemon-scented cream that some kind soul had left on the side of the bath into my aching muscles and slid naked between the white cotton sheets, leaving my door unlocked to make it easier for him. For a while I lay alert and expectant, tensing at every sound, expecting the sash window to be slid upwards at any second. Then the day caught up with me and my eyelids grew heavier, and closed altogether.

At first, I was sure it was a dream. The slow, lazy kiss that left me panting for more, followed by the soft silky cloth that gagged me couldn't be happening. Then I began to wake up and I knew it was real. For a second I panicked, then, as my eyes adjusted to the darkness, I realised it was Rupert. He was dressed just as a cat burglar ought to be, in a tight black polo neck sweater and even tighter ski-pants that displayed a bulging erection, but his fair hair gleamed in the darkness and so did his teeth when he smiled. He flicked the bedside lamp on, and I moaned when I saw the bag beside his feet. Not much sound came out – a bit more than round Imo's ball gag, but there was no way that my protests could be heard. Only I wasn't going to protest, was I? Because the last thing I wanted was to be rescued. I'd wanted this ever since I'd seen Imo helpless; and after that humiliating orgy, I was desperate not just for physical pleasure but to know that I was desirable without having to play someone else's games for cash. His smile widened as he reached for one of my wrists, and I knew he understood. It was going to be the best yet.

I lashed out at him, but it was only a token gesture so it was easy for him to snap the iron cuff round my wrist. It was padded with something that felt like velvet so it didn't hurt. I knew I'd soon be helpless, and that really turned me on. Soon, he'd be able to do anything he wanted with and to me. He could make me come until I was begging him to let me rest; or not let me come at all, and there'd be nothing I could do to stop him. He smiled, obviously savouring the sight of my cuffed wrist, then pulled the single sheet I'd slept under back to waist height. Then, slowly and deliberately, he fastened the other cuff round my left wrist, and looped a length of chain between them. Grinning, he fastened that round the bedpost until my arms were raised above my head, but still quite comfortable.

'Soon, you'll be completely helpless,' he murmured, and nuzzled my neck, working his way down, first to my breasts, then to my belly, planting gentle, sucking kisses on every inch of flesh.

Maybe I should have fought harder, but it felt so good, and it was only a game, so I let him pull the sheet back, expecting to feel his tongue curling round my clit. He licked my inner thighs until I was moaning, and enjoying the muffled sounds that were all that made it past the gag as yet another sign of my vulnerability. Then I let out a real yell. Not only had he stopped, but he stood up.

'You're not helpless enough yet.'

He locked the door, pocketing the key to emphasise how in control he was, then did the same with the sash window. He smirked as he reached into the bag again and took out something I'd only ever read about. A spreader bar, I think they call it. A length of wood with cuffs at either end and a sliding mechanism so you can alter the distance between the cuffs. Once the victim is fastened into it you can keep their legs close together or pull them apart, changing their posture like one of those bendy dolls kids used to play with.

As he held it under my nose, I saw that these cuffs were velvet-lined as well. They'd also got dozens of tiny rings set all round them, presumably so you could fasten extra chains and adjust your helpless plaything's position. Obviously, they were part of his working kit, and I wanted him to work on me. I also knew that he was giving me a last chance to pull out, but I didn't want to. It wouldn't be much of a game if I made it too easy though, so I drew my knees up to my chest, tucking my feet under me. I could just about sit up, and the tug of the chain as I moved my wrists reminded me that I was, technically at least, helpless. One good kick in the groin would have sorted that out, but I had other plans for his groin, so I didn't try it.

'You're going to be helpless,' he repeated and pushed me back down again.

At any other time I'd have told him that he should find a better scriptwriter before he started directing, but I'd got other things on my mind just then so I just lay there, staring up at him, drowning in lust. He reached for my ankle, tugging it free. I put up a token protest, then lay meekly while he bound my other ankle and adjusted the bar until my legs reached the corners of the bed. My thigh muscles protested at the exertion so soon after the twins' games, but not painfully enough for my moan to be anything more than part of the fun.

Once I was helpless enough for him, he stood back and studied his handiwork. I shivered as I remembered what Lance had said about ordering Rupert to tie me up then directing his every movement. But Lance wasn't there. Rupert was, and he was smiling at me, so I was worrying about nothing. All I had got to do was relax, and it'd be every bit as good as I'd expected the night before to be.

I lay there, savouring being so defenceless and exposed, waiting for him to do his worst. I didn't have much choice really. I could still move my legs, but I couldn't close them, and he hadn't finished yet. After careful consideration he looped another chain round the spreader bar, fastened it to the end of the bed, then stripped off, and slid onto the bed beside me.

I could smell him, I could see him, I could definitely want him, but I couldn't have him unless and until he chose. I had a feeling that he wasn't going to choose for a long time and swore that the next time we played this game he'd be helpless and I'd be firmly in control. Then I remembered that there wasn't going to be a next time. This time tomorrow I'd be in a hotel somewhere a long way away from here, writing the articles that were going to make me famous; and for a second I regretted what I was planning to do.

'You're beautiful,' he said, and spread my tangled hair over the pillow until I looked like the virgin sacrifice that I wasn't. Then his fingers began to trail over my body, never staying long enough anywhere to let me come, always teasing, always tantalising. He pinched my labia gently, and I moaned, thrusting my mound at him to try to encourage him.

'Not yet,' he whispered as he turned the light off. 'We've got all night, and you're not escaping me that easily.'

I'd never felt so warm, so wet, so hungry. Then all I felt was the sort of terror that almost had me wetting myself. The main light had come on, leaving me blinking, and a cold voice said, 'actually, she isn't going to escape at all.'

It was Lance! And I was helpless, and feeling a real

fool. I hadn't checked the airing cupboard to make sure my bundle of notes was safe the way I usually did whenever I'd left my room. I'd been too tired, too lulled, too sure that I'd won, too engrossed in thinking about Rupert and turning our shared fantasy into reality to take proper precautions. Now the notes were in Lance's hand, and I was in deep shit and getting deeper by the second.

'Would you like to explain these?' he asked.

Rupert stood up, not seeming to care that he was naked. His erection jutted in front of him impressively as he faced up to Lance, and I hated the thuggish man all the more for depriving me of it. 'Suppose you explain first. I locked that door!'

'But I had a key, which is just as well really.' He waved my notes like a detective in a TV thriller when he's explaining how clever he's been at the end. 'Or did you know about these, Rupert?'

'Knew she kept a diary?' I began to hope I'd get away with it when he gave a short angry laugh. 'Of course.'

'Did you know she's got a contract worth fifteen grand to write all about us for a sleazy Sunday paper?'

Rupert swung round to stare at me, his erection deflating visibly. 'Is this true?'

'Of course it's true,' Lance answered for me. 'She's been sneaking out at night too. I wasn't sure why when I spotted her the other night, but now we know, and we have to work out what to do with her.'

'Leave her for Liberty to deal with.' Rupert was avoiding looking at me as he got dressed, and I knew he wouldn't help me. Why should he when I'd have dragged his reputation through the mud with all the rest? Anyway, I'd never have been daft enough to think that he cared about me just because we'd fucked a few times, any more than I cared about him. All right, maybe

I was lying about that. I did care about him, in a funny sort of way, but I knew I had no right to expect him to feel the same way about me.

'Who do you think ordered me to keep an eye on her?' Lance laughed and ran a finger down my face. 'She's been selling us out all along, and before you say it, Rupert, there can't be an innocent explanation. If there was she'd have given it to us by now. Look at her – she's not protesting her innocence, is she?'

I couldn't. For one thing I couldn't speak, and besides I hadn't got a good explanation. I just lay there; staring at him with what I hoped was more defiance than fear and wishing I could close my thighs. Lance looked me up and down, his smile turning cruel, then reached down and, with no semblance of passion or affection, slid three fingers into me. I tried to pull away, but I was as totally helpless as he'd no doubt planned for me to be all along. I don't think Rupert was involved in that part of his plan, but I knew who'd given him the idea of tying me up, and made sure he had all the equipment and the perfect opportunity to play his games. I'd been played for a sucker, and my hurt pride added to the mixture of fear, shame, and a faint hint of a dark excitement that I refused to admit might grow into pleasure.

'She's wet,' he murmured, glancing at Rupert speculatively. 'Wet and ready, and we can take advantage of that, can't we? And you can film it all.'

'And you'll...?' Rupert didn't finish, and I began to feel very small, very scared, and very, very sick. Rupert was an unashamed hedonist who seemed capable of enjoying anything, but he was looking at Lance with fascinated horror.

'It serves her right,' Lance said coolly. 'Don't worry, you won't be expected to participate. Just film it.'

'All right.' Rupert seemed to relax. 'As long as Liberty approves.'

'Approves?' Lance laughed and came towards me, this time holding a thick length of black cloth. He handed my notes to Rupert, who flicked through them then put them down, shaking his head sadly. But Rupert was the least of my problems as Lance fastened the blindfold, then went on. 'She's set it all up, filming and all. She has plans for this little bitch, and so have I!'

Just film it, I thought while Lance unfastened the chains that held my cuffs to headboard and footboard. Film what? And what would they do with that film, and how could I have been so bloody stupid? Quite how stupid I'd been was brought home to me when Lance bent me double, fastening the wrist cuffs to the ankle cuffs. When he'd finished with me, I was curled into a fetal ball, with my buttocks jutting upwards, open and vulnerable. I expected him to touch me again to ram that point home, but he just opened the door and wheeled in one of the enormous wicker laundry hampers the hotel used for the mountains of dirty linen it generated. With Rupert's help, he stuffed me inside it. The lid was strapped down, and I felt it begin to move.

We were heading down the hall, I guessed, determined to think rather than give in to my growing panic and give Lance the satisfaction of hearing me sob and plead. Along the corridor, a bumpy trip down the stairs, then over a hard surface that might be concrete. That meant we were going to the gym, with those anonymous soundproofed rooms and that doctor's chair that'd make me even more vulnerable than I already was. But we didn't make the right turn that would have taken us there. Instead, we carried on down the path, and I remembered the other outbuildings. I'd meant to find out what they housed, but I'd had to be careful not to ask any questions that might make anyone suspicious. Fat lot of good that had done me! That brave list of the things I wouldn't do echoed round my mind and I knew Lance would revel in putting me through them all.

I bit down hard on my gag, determined not to make a sound that Lance could correctly interpret as a sob or a scream for help, or a plea for mercy, trying to think of a way out. Nothing had come to mind by the time that the jerking, jolting ride ended. They didn't bother to let me out. I don't know how long they left me there. It could have been minutes, could have been hours. Wherever I was, it was disorientatingly dark, and I couldn't hear the clock on the tower that had always marked off time for me before. Sensory deprivation, I think they call it, and it was incredibly effective.

I began to shake, and long for a loo, but there was nothing I could do about it. Tied as I was, I couldn't pound on the sides of the crate for attention, and I wasn't sure I wanted them to notice me if I could have done. I struggled to think logically, and found an explanation that made sense. They were waiting for Liberty to get back, so I still had a slim chance of escape. They'd got no proof of what I'd been planning to use that diary for and, while hiding my notes in the hot water jacket was odd, it wasn't a crime. Most importantly, I was her daughter's friend. Surely all that would count in my favour? I wasn't all that sure, but it was the only hope I had, so I clung to it, listening to the thud of my heartbeats in the silence, trying not to think about what could happen.

It felt like forever until I heard footsteps again, this time two sets – one of them a woman's, judging by the click of high heels. The straps were undone, the lid lifted, my blindfold removed. I blinked, almost blinded by the sudden light as Lance lifted me out of the basket.

I hoped he'd let me go when he reached for the cuffs, but all he did was unfasten the loops so that I could straighten up.

But I couldn't, which was another humiliation to add to what I already knew would soon be a long list. I was so cold and stiff and cramped that he had to manhandle me to my feet. He rubbed my body with the same gentleness he'd shown what I guessed must have been the day before, because it must have been after midnight now. Then he guided me across to a seat, and I got my first good look at my surroundings. There were four cameras fastened to the wall, angled to focus on another iron-framed bed like the one in my room. This one was king-sized and covered with a fur throw, and I didn't need to be the next Einstein to know that I'd be chained to it for the filming Lance had threatened. On one side of the set was another doctor's couch of the sort Imo had been tied to, but I was sitting on one of those canvas folding director's chairs.

I tried to kick Lance when he knelt between my open thighs, but I might as well not have bothered. A couple of clicks, and the spreader board was fastened to the chair legs. Just in case I'd had any illusions about escaping he attached more chains to my wrist cuffs and looped them round the arms of the chair. Finally, when I was about as helpless as it was possible to be, he attached one of my wrists to the wooden arm of the chair, unfastened the chain that had been between them, and repeated the gesture with the other wrist. Finally he took the gag out of my mouth, the swivel chair that had had its back to me swung round, and Liberty Hall spoke for the first time.

'Well?' she asked quietly. She was wearing a red velvet evening dress that had to be a Chanel original. A choker, set with what had to be genuine diamonds, encircled her slim, elegant throat and I'd never felt more small or vulnerable.

'I haven't done anything,' was all I could think of to say, and it was true. I should have added the word 'yet' but that was just a technicality.

'What are these for then?' She didn't sound angry as she held my notes up, and that made it scarier still.

'I always keep a diary. Ask Imo. And while you're at it, ask him –' I decided to go for righteous indignation and diversionary tactics and jerked my head at Lance '– what the fuck he thinks he's playing at! He's been out to get me ever since I told him that I wouldn't play his sick games.' I almost mentioned that he'd burgled my room before we'd even been introduced, but if I accused him of that, I'd have to explain why I hadn't complained at the time and that wouldn't go too well with my pose of outraged innocence. 'He tried to set me up with the twins today, which was well out of order. We had a deal, remember? No anal . . .'

'. . . No lesbian, no pain, no humiliation,' Liberty finished passionlessly, and I knew my excuses weren't going to wash. 'I seem to remember that the deal also said that you would keep our affairs confidential. Shall I check the contract in case I've made a mistake?'

'No,' I conceded, then rallied. 'But I haven't told anyone anything.'

'Then Dickie Lawrence is lying? You're not his plant inside my hotel? He didn't get you to sign a contract?' She picked up a sheet of paper from the table beside her.

Oh shit, I thought as I recognised the contract I'd signed, and that word summed up Dickie too.

'He didn't betray you.' She reached for a glass of what looked like iced mineral water from the table beside her.

My mouth felt dry and tasted so foul after the gag that I'd have sold my soul for a sip, but she didn't offer it to me. She just took a slow, lazy mouthful, savouring it as if she knew exactly how I felt and wanted to emphasise the gap between us, then went on. 'But he couldn't resist telling his editor about the big scoop he'd got lined up. His editor's wife is a friend of mine from the old days, and she persuaded him to find out more. She told me tonight. I spoke to the chairman of Consolidated Press, then to Dickie himself, and here we are. So?'

'I didn't have a choice.' Surely she'd understand that when she'd been poor herself once? 'I was short of cash, and he came to me.'

'You approached him,' she corrected dispassionately, and I knew that wouldn't wash either. 'He told me all about it, eventually.'

I didn't like the sound of that 'eventually', and I didn't fancy finding out what it meant the hard way, so I shut up before I risked annoying her any more.

'Well?' she repeated, then sighed. 'You're a greedy little slut, Tess. You'd do anything to get what you want.'

'And you're so different?' I'd sworn to stay proudly and prudently silent, but her cold assessment got to me. 'I've done nothing that you wouldn't have done if you'd been in my position.'

'But I'd have made sure that I didn't get caught. I'd have done whatever it took without complaining or indulging in lists of things I wouldn't do that aroused people's curiosity.' She glanced at Lance, who smiled vindictively. 'But the result will be the same, Teresa.'

People only ever call me 'Teresa' if I'm in real trouble, but I'd never been in trouble like this before, or been this scared.

'We gave you a chance to run, but you didn't take it. You were so sure that you were cleverer than we are, and now you know the truth. You weren't clever at all, and now you're going to pay the price and learn what you really are.'

9

I didn't bother to answer. There was no point, because I knew that nothing I could say would change her mind. Liberty watched me with the sort of dispassionate curiosity that the more cruel game show host displays towards the contestants for a while longer, then went on.

'Remember that little list? You're going to experience it all.'

'You wouldn't dare. You can't afford the scandal.' She might be powerful, but no one was above the law. Or was I deluding myself yet again? I had a horrible feeling that I was; and it grew stronger still when she smiled.

'Really? When you've been filmed enjoying every second of your alleged "ordeal"? If you go to the police, or publish one word about my hotel the video of what we're about to do will be turned into a website. Pay per view, naturally, which should please your mercenary nature. Just think, men all over the world could wank while they watched you being punished. I expect they'd enjoy it far more if you struggled. We could charge a premium rate for it. Women would enjoy it too, of course, particularly with the content I have in mind. And believe me, women can be far crueller than men. We can prove it to you, if you like.'

'What about Imo?' I clutched at the last straw I'd got, but Liberty pulled it away.

'We're not going to tell her anything about this. As

far as she's concerned, you've left the Hall, no doubt due to your revulsion when you discovered Lance's plans for you.'

So Imo wouldn't be able to help me, assuming that she'd want to once she'd heard what I'd tried to do. I closed my eyes, wishing I could close my ears as well when Liberty went on. 'We'll start with humiliation, and just a soupçon of pain to let you know what's to come. After all, we wouldn't want you disgracing yourself in front of the cameras, would we?'

I didn't bother to answer, and I kept my eyes closed when Lance knelt in front of me again. Pathetic, I know, but I couldn't face seeing his intent expression, knowing he could do whatever he wanted with me. He clipped a longer length of chain between the wrist cuffs, then a matching one between my ankles. Only when I was trussed to his satisfaction did he unfasten the spreader bar and the chains that held my arms to the chair arms, and yank my wrist chains until I opened my eyes and stood up.

'This way.' His smile was as twisted as his nature. 'I'll enjoy this.'

'Good for you! I won't.' I did my best to sound defiant, but it wasn't very good.

'You will in the end. You'll cry and scream and protest at first, just like they always do, but it doesn't matter. The studio is soundproofed, and everyone here has far too much to lose to waste time feeling sorry for you. We like our lives, and we don't –' his hand darted between my legs, twisting my labia until I abandoned the last of my pride and screamed '– like cheap little whores trying to muscle in and wreck things for us!' He shoved me through a door, into a spartan but functional bathroom, then gestured to the loo. 'Use it.'

I'd have liked to have spat in his face, but I needed to

pee so badly that even him watching me couldn't put me off. I sat, pressing my knees together in a futile attempt to protect myself while I did what I had to do, then he grabbed my leash again.

'Don't you want to know what we'll do next?'

'I'm sure I'll find out soon enough.' I might have been helpless, but I was damned if I'd add to his pleasure by pleading. Then I realised I'd already done that by defying him and lashed out at him, almost as angry with myself as I was with him.

'Go on, fight me. You can't win,' he sneered.

I certainly tried to. I kicked, I struggled, I yelled, but I might as well not have bothered. He just dumped me flat on my back on that black leather-covered doctor's examining table. I landed so hard that the breath was driven out of me so I couldn't protest or struggle while he fastened leather straps across my breasts, belly and hips.

'First humiliation and a little pain, then the main course,' he said cheerfully.

And the main course would be anal sex, only it wouldn't be proper sex, because he'd force me. I knew that he could make me enjoy it, and that made it even worse than if I'd been able to convince myself that I was enduring whatever happened next in order to survive. I hoped he'd get it over with quickly, but I should have known better. There was a soft whine of compressed air, and the bed tilted backwards until my head pointed towards the floor. Just to emphasise how helpless and available I was, he eased rubber-covered pillows beneath my hips until my arse was raised a good six inches off the bed. I kept my mouth shut, waiting for the inevitable, and his smile widened.

'Not yet,' he said, and disappeared into the screened-off area. When he came back, he was wheeling a stand piled with medical-looking equipment, and all my pride and defiance vanished.

'No!' I screamed, not caring that the other people in the studio turned to look at me.

'You've got to be clean before we film you,' he said reasonably. 'Who knows what could happen otherwise? It wouldn't be nice for the cameramen, would it?'

'Please?' I'd sworn not to plead, but this was different. This was a bag of water hanging from a stand, with a long tube leading from it. A tube with a nozzle that Lance was now greasing.

'This first pint is soapy, to make sure you're clean, so I don't expect you'll enjoy it. But soon you'll discover how little difference there is between pleasure and pain.' He spread more of the gel he'd used on the nozzle round my crack, working it sadistically slowly into the ring round my anus. His fingers pressed against it, then moved away seconds before I was sure he'd shove home, leaving me whimpering with terror that was laced with a warped, twisted feeling that I didn't want to admit could be lust.

'The human anus is a wonderful piece of design,' he explained as he worked. 'It'll stretch to at least an inch in diameter, usually far more. That means you'll be able to take this, and everything else you're going to take tonight without any damage. Would you like to be gagged?' His voice never wavered from that conversational tone that made it worse than if he'd gloated openly. 'It'll stop you being able to upset yourself by pleading and make you feel more helpless. Lots of women find they enjoy it. No? Well, don't say I didn't give you the choice.'

I didn't answer, but I soon wished I had, because all the pride in the world couldn't stop my scream when he slid his little finger past my reluctant sphincter. I clenched my muscles and tried to resist him, but the combination of his slippery finger and all that gel made it impossible. He slid inside me the way that a hot knife does through butter, and he'd been right about two things. It did hurt, and it was humiliating.

'Don't make such a fuss. I'm not hurting you yet.'

'You are,' I whimpered, biting my lip to stop myself crying. The physical pain wasn't half as bad as I'd expected it to be, but it was how I felt inside that really hurt. I didn't want this, but I knew that wouldn't stop him making me enjoy it, and part of me was already enjoying the helplessness. He slid his finger free, pushed it in again, repeating the gesture until there was no resistance, then added a second finger.

'Do you still want to plead for mercy?' he asked, but I shook my head. All I wanted was it over with and me a long, long way away from Liberty Hall, and I wasn't stupid enough to believe that was going to happen soon.

'No? Then let's get on with it.' He reached for the nozzle, easing it between the fingers that held my sphincter open. I tried to clench myself to stop him, and he stopped. Not because he'd had an attack of conscience, because he hadn't got one. I was pretty sure he'd just come up with a refinement that'd make it worse for me, and his next words proved me right. 'Of course, you need an audience for it to be really humiliating. Rupert?'

Rupert appeared, looking more workmanlike than I'd ever seen him. He was festooned with bits of equipment, and was still avoiding looking at me.

'Rupert hates having this done to him. You didn't enjoy many of my little games, did you, Rupert?'

Rupert shook his head, his full lips tight with revulsion. He seemed fascinated by the floor, but I didn't expect Lance to let him get away with that.

'Watch this.' Lance's tone hadn't changed, but his smile was definitely nastier. 'What do you think would happen to your career if she was allowed to publish her article? Respected film directors don't make porno movies, do they?'

Rupert looked away, and I knew I'd lost my last flimsy chance of an ally. 'It's just not my scene,' he muttered sullenly.

'It doesn't have to be. All you have to do is watch. If you like, you can try to console her when she sobs.'

I swore I wouldn't give the bastard the satisfaction of hearing me sob, but I felt like crying all right. I'd never thought that Rupert and I had the hearts and flowers and everlasting love bit, but we'd had some good times together, and I'd trusted him, moron that I was. Now he was staring at me as if he'd never seen me before and didn't much like what he was seeing now. 'Why, Tess?'

I didn't bother to answer. He wouldn't understand, and I didn't dare open my mouth in case I started screaming, because Lance was easing that nozzle into my arse.

'It'll hurt more if you struggle, and I didn't think you were into pain,' he warned, but I just bit my lip harder and kept right on fighting him.

It did hurt, and I reckon he enjoyed every second as he slid first the nozzle, then the tube inside me. It took what felt like for ever, but at last it was in, and Lance moved away. 'Almost ready,' he murmured with a menacing smile.

I swore at him and tried to push it out, determined to stop him somehow, then stopped dead. As the liquid began to flow, my gut was cramping in a way that was frightfully unnerving. I knew exactly what would happen if I managed to force that tube out. I'd soil myself, to use the polite phrasing, and I wasn't adding to the humiliation by co-operating with any more of his little plans.

'Take deep breaths and it won't be so bad,' Rupert whispered. I glared at him, wishing I dared open my mouth to swear. But if I did I might start screaming and not be able to stop, so I bit my lip. The cramps kept growing, and I reckoned it couldn't make it any worse, so I gave it a try.

It was hard to concentrate on my breathing rather than the soapy water that seeped into me until I was sure I'd burst, but I managed it somehow, and found that Rupert had been right. Gradually, the agonising cramps lessened, and so did the feeling that I'd burst at any second. I began just to feel full, and think maybe it wouldn't be so bad. Then, as if that bastard Lance knew the first terror was fading, he increased the flow rate.

'I'm sure you want this over quickly, don't you? And we can't keep the others waiting.'

I watched the water bag the way a rabbit watches oncoming car headlights, only I didn't have the option of running away. But I wanted to. The cramps I'd had before were nothing compared to what I felt when the liquid flooded my rear passage. My belly was thrust up against the straps by the pressure, and I damned my determination to keep my pride and screamed, trying to curl up against the incredible, humiliating fullness, but too tightly bound to manage even a wriggle.

'It'll take about five minutes to fill her.' Lance wasn't talking to me, which made me feel more used and humiliated still, as if I didn't matter to anyone any more. 'Then we take the tube out, put a butt plug in, and make her hold it for another five. That's the first wash out, then we'll rinse her out.'

'Please, don't do that!' Sod pride. Survival was all that mattered now. Maybe someday I'd get my revenge, but even survival was currently looking like a lot to ask. 'I'll do anything you want. I won't write anything, and I'll play any of your games, just take that tube out.' I'd never been more sincere. My stomach felt as if it was about to explode. I couldn't see how anyone got off on this!

'You still don't understand, do you?'

I began to cry because I understood all right, and his passionless explanation brought the reality I'd been trying not to think about home to me.

'You've got nothing to negotiate with, because you're already going to do anything we want, Tess. We don't have to care about you, and we don't. We will punish you, and you will enjoy it all, sooner or later, because we'll keep working on you until you do. Someday you may come to me and ask for this, just as Imo does.'

I closed my eyes, trying to pretend that it wasn't happening. But I could still feel the water running into me, and imagination made the bag grow bigger and fuller with every second. In the end, it was easier to watch the water in the bag drop as my belly got more and more distended and know that each inch the water level fell was an inch closer to it being over.

Rupert made soothing noises and stroked my hair, which was a fat lot of good, but at last the bag was finally empty. Lance pulled the nozzle free, then, before I could damn what was left of my pride and dignity and let the water flood out, shoved a butt plug up my arse. I howled because it was hard and cold and wide. Another wave of cramps hit me, and I sobbed and screamed.

'She can't take this,' Rupert pleaded.

'Of course she can. She's just a little exhibitionist. If she makes too much fuss, I'll gag and blindfold her.'

I shut up, because not being able to see what was happening would make this impossible to handle.

'See? There'll be another two waves of cramps, then we'll let her expel it, and rinse her out. Then she'll have an orgasm.'

I couldn't imagine anything less likely, but I wasn't risking opening my mouth again in case he put his threats into practice. I just lay there, wishing that I could curl up and die. The two waves of cramps he'd prophesied tried to tear me apart, but I kept my sobs and snuffles quiet rather than annoy him. What felt like hours later he undid the straps, picked up the chain that dangled between my wrists and led me to the bathroom. He turned me to face him, then jerked the plug out. I clenched my buttocks, desperate to avoid adding to my humiliation.

He knew that, of course, so he kept me waiting for what felt like for ever until he gestured me to the loo. The soapy water poured out as soon as I sat down. It was an incredible relief, and I didn't care that Lance was watching. I made it last as long as I could, but he was wise to that little trick as well. Another jerk on my chain brought me back to my feet, and then it was back to the examination couch. I didn't bother to struggle while he refastened me. I hadn't turned into some ecstatic submissive, but I knew it'd only add to his fun if I fought him. Besides, they hadn't hurt me yet, and I wanted it to stay that way. I knew that pain lay ahead, as part of my punishment, but the longer I put it off the better.

'This time,' he repeated as he regreased the nozzle and hooked up a fresh bag of water, 'you're going to come. If you don't, we'll keep doing this until you do, and there are mixtures we can use that make the soap look soothing. Do you understand me, Tess?'

I nodded, and closed my eyes while he repeated the routine of inserting the nozzle in my arse. It went in more easily this time, and didn't really hurt, which was one thing to be grateful for. I tried to convince myself that meant anal sex wouldn't hurt either, but I wasn't daft enough to believe it. This was a nozzle, barely an inch wide, and I'd felt Lance inside me before. He was at least three times that, and not into being gentle.

The water began to flow again, and I tensed, waiting for the cramps to start. I must have looked surprised when they didn't, because Lance went back into explaining mode, as if he were one of my lecturers.

'Two pints of water this time, nice and warm and soothing. See, Tess, it doesn't hurt, does it?'

I didn't answer, but he was right. It didn't actually hurt, but I felt very full, very humiliated, and very, very scared. Then Lance began to massage my belly, and the feelings magnified tenfold.

'The nerve endings are very sensitive when you're this full,' he explained, and I knew he must have seen my eyes widen. I hated my lack of control almost as much as I hated him.

I already knew how sensitive those fucking nerve endings were, because it felt as if all the weight in the world was pushing down on my mound. My sex was heavy and congested, the rear passage, stuffed with the tube and water, pushed against it until my clit was shoved forward, and still the water kept going in.

'See, she likes it, so it isn't really a punishment at all. Does that help your tender conscience, Rupert?'

Rupert turned and walked away without saying a word. I bit my lip, because the bastard was right, and Rupert seeing it was the ultimate humiliation. Or at least I hoped that it was, but I had an uneasy feeling that Lance had only just begun. I didn't want to come, but my body had other ideas, and Lance was good at his sick trade. The cramps hit me, less strongly this time, but he kept rubbing my belly and by the time the last drop of water had drained from the enema bag I knew he was right. I'd never wanted an orgasm less, so I clenched my buttocks against the butt plug when he tried to replace it, trying to make it hurt and dull the feelings, but he just smiled.

'I won't put it in if you don't want me to. But if I don't, all the water will flood out when you come, and everyone will know what a dirty little slut you are. Maybe I should get Rupert to film that too? It'd make a wonderful scene...'

I co-operated after that, trying to pretend it was just a porno movie I was watching, or a book I'd got really caught up in. All Lance did was massage my stomach. He didn't touch my clit, or my breasts, didn't penetrate me, or need to. I had a plug shoved up my arse, my belly was so full that every touch was magnified a hundred times, and the bastard was winning. My nipples were hardening, and my breasts were growing warm and heavy.

Then my stomach contracted, not from an enema-induced cramp, but from the familiar pre-orgasmic spasms. He pressed down hard on my mound, and I screamed. My arse tightened round the plug, the tremors transmitted to my sex through that thin internal wall that felt as if it'd tear at any second. Then it all came apart, and I was crying as the combination of the pleasure and the humiliation and the fear of what was to come came together in one titanic orgasm.

He didn't bother to wait until I'd finished sobbing and shaking before he undid the straps, carried me to the loo and jerked the plug out. Warm water cascaded between my legs, and I cried all the harder as the pleasure was replaced by the sick knowledge of what I'd done.

'See?' he murmured. 'Humiliation can make you come. Want to guess what comes next?'

I didn't need to guess. Now I was clean the next stop on his tour of my inhibitions would be the thing I'd managed to avoid in the gym. There was nothing I could do to stop him and, after what he'd just done, I knew I'd enjoy it. Stupid as it sounds, that was the scariest thing of all. I was too frightened to struggle when Lance wiped me clean, then picked me up again. He hooked my chain round the top of the shower support, tucked my hair into a shower cap and washed me down, rubbing soap in with a vicious pleasure when he saw my breasts respond. By the time he'd finished, I was panting and close to another orgasm, too blinded by my tears to see anything.

'Not yet,' he whispered. 'Not for a long time, in fact.' He didn't bother to unfasten me as he rubbed me dry, then covered me in baby oil until my skin gleamed. 'Must have you looking your best for the cameras,' he said cheerfully, then began to brush my hair out with long smooth strokes that didn't help the tingle between my legs.

If I'd been the good girl that I'd always been sure I really was, none of that would have turned me on. But it did, and he knew it and enjoyed it, and that knowledge made it more humiliating still. It got worse when he led me back into the studio, and a girl hurried towards me, carrying a tool box full of make-up. She looked at me, not with surprise or horror, but with the same passionless practicality that Lance displayed towards his victims.

'The tear stains'll take some covering up,' she said after she'd taken a good long look at me.

'Just do it. She has to look as if she's begging for it.'

I wasn't, but I was past pleading for it not to happen.

It was going to happen, and I would enjoy it, and there was absolutely nothing I could do to stop them.

'Lie down, and spread your legs,' Lance ordered after he'd led me across to the iron bed I'd noticed earlier.

I obeyed, feeling the cuffs tugging against my ankles as I reached the limits of the chain. I'd expected him to chain me spreadeagled the way they did in the books I'd once thought erotic when I'd masturbated while I read them. Instead, he refastened the spreader bar, extending it enough that I knew how helpless I was, but not enough that it really hurt. Then he lifted it up into the air. I slid down the bed, gliding over black satin sheets, grabbing the headboard with my bound hands to stop my hips slamming against the heavy iron foot-board. Lance didn't seem to notice how uncomfortable I was, or maybe he just didn't care. He tugged and moved me until my hips were lifted off the bed, my legs vertical. Then he fastened the spreader bar to two hooks that hung from the ceiling, positioned rubber pillows beneath my hips, and looked at my hands. My arms already ached from grabbing the bedstead, but he obviously liked what he saw.

'That position displays her breasts well. We'll have her like that, shall we?'

'You'd better use a bit more chain if she's going to be there a while, but it looks good,' the girl agreed. 'Do you want her blindfolded?'

'No. It's got to be clear who she is and how much she wants it.'

I tried to lash out with the chain that held my wrists when the girl came closer, but stopped dead when Lance slid his finger between my buttocks.

'I could always wipe the oil off,' he murmured, and I abandoned that idea and lay like a doll while he fastened the cuffs to the bedstead. Then he removed the chain between them, and the girl put make-up on me. The silly cow actually held a mirror up so that I could see the results; as if I wanted to, but I had to admit that she was good at her job. All traces of the tears were gone. I looked flushed and wide eyed, but I couldn't have told whether I was scared or really turned on, so there was no way I'd be able to claim that I hadn't wanted it to happen. I'd taken the job, signed a contract saying that I was available for unspecified personal services, and there'd been no mention of my exclusions in that contract. I might as well accept it. I didn't have a leg to stand on.

Lance nodded approval, and the girl scuttled off, leaving him to arrange my hair on the pillow round my face. Then he produced a college scarf, and I gulped, knowing I'd be finished at university too if they ever heard about this. The tassles brushed against my nipples, but he made sure that they didn't hide anything. Then Rupert reappeared, carrying a black box with a length of wire attached to it. I started panicking about what sort of sex toy it would be, then realised it was just a microphone with a battery pack.

'The tape's thirty-five minutes long,' he told Lance, 'and I've set up two blondes and two redheads. It's all right.' He grinned at me as if I wanted to be there. 'You won't be the centrepiece in an orgy. There are two two-thousand-watt lights, and two five-hundred-watt lights to highlight your face.'

'Sure. You'll want to get my best side, won't you?' I tried to sound defiant, but it was getting harder to do anything except lie there and shiver. I knew what would happen, and I hated it, so why was it turning me on as well as terrifying me?

'Do you have one?' Lance asked, then elaborated with

sadistic pleasure. 'We'll tape it on five fixed cameras, then pick the best shots for the final cut of the video.'

I'd worked that out already. The cameras surrounded me, positioned on tripods at the head and sides of the bed. Another one dangled from the ceiling, leaving me feeling as if I was being watched by five enormous and temporarily sightless eyes.

'And Rupert will have the steadicam ready to zoom in for all the close-up shots. You'll be able to see it all on the monitor.'

I hadn't noticed that before, but now I couldn't see how I'd missed it. It was a dirty big screen – at least forty inches across. Only it wasn't the screen that was dirty, it was me. I was about to star in a porno movie, and no one would believe I hadn't done it from choice. So much for being a daring undercover investigative reporter!

'Are you ready?' Lance asked, and Rupert nodded.

'Just need to do sound tests.'

'Come on, Tess, moan for the cameras,' Lance smirked.

If I'd had any sense I'd have done as I was told, but then if I'd had any sense I wouldn't have been naked except for a college scarf, with my hands cuffed to the framework of an ornate iron bed. I definitely wouldn't have picked that moment to have a flashback to my childhood. Dad had always claimed I'd come to a bad end, and right now I had to admit that he'd had a point. I stayed stubbornly silent. I mightn't have much control left, but I could still control this, and I would, as long as I could. One way or another Lance would wring that orgasm from me, but every second I held out made me feel better and helped squash the tiny part of me that was enjoying the degradation.

'Cameras ready?' Lance asked, pausing inches away from me.

Rupert nodded, and stepped back – to make sure he wasn't in the shot, I suppose. He had a harness strapped round his waist, and now he slid a camera into the holster. It hung down, with a rod dangling from it for balance so that it stayed steady as he moved into position. Then he zoomed the lens out until the monitor screen on the wall opposite was filled by an image of two massive breasts, and Lance's tanned hands reaching for my nipples. I gulped, because his hands weren't empty. He was holding two clamps, and snapped them on both nipples simultaneously. I saw the prongs bite into my flesh but bit back the scream until he began to twist them. Then my yell must have blown the sound recordist's head off. Was this what he'd meant by teaching me to take pleasure in pain? If so, he'd got a hell of a long way to go. Tears ran down my face, but I was pretty sure they'd have been prepared for that and used waterproof make-up, so that wasn't going to save me, or even delay the inevitable.

'Moan for the camera, Tess. Make it sound as if you really want it.'

I moaned. I'd have done anything to stop him twisting those clamps again.

'Try harder. You know you can,' Lance ordered. I gave it my all, tossing my head from side to side to make it look better still.

'Good.' He removed the clamps, leaving my nipples incredibly erect, and throbbing almost unbearably as the circulation began again. 'She's decided to co-operate after all. And now the real fun's going to start.'

He disappeared but, courtesy of that monitor screen I knew that he was doing a striptease that a Chippendale would have been proud of. Presumably that was being filmed as well, to make it quite clear I'd spent my long vacation making porn flicks! First the shirt, dropped to reveal an oiled torso, then the combats, then tight black leather underpants. Beneath them he was already hard, but he still made a big thing about wanking for the camera. That was fine by me. The more he wanked the sooner he'd come inside me, and the quicker this phase would be over. Finally, he produced a condom, which was a small relief. He mimicked penetration as he thrust his hips forward while he worked it on, then stalked over to the bed, followed by Rupert with that damned camera.

The scene on the monitor changed, splitting into four; one an overall shot of me, with Lance lowering the foot rail of the bed, then lifting it away so that he could stand right in front of me, his cock pressing against my arse. I knew why all those cushions were there now. One thrust and he'd be inside me. Another of the cameras was focused on my arse, zooming in until I could see the sphincter muscles. The books were right when they called it a puckered rose, but it wasn't going to be puckered for long, was it?

I'd been so busy watching the screen that I hadn't kept a proper eye on Lance. I whimpered as cold gel touched my skin, and I saw his magnified fingers working some sort of lubricant round my hole. Closer, closer his fingers got, until I saw as well as felt the moment when one slid inside. I gasped, but it was more at the sight of my enormously magnified sphincter dilating to let him in than from any real pain. Another finger followed, both sliding up until all I could see were his knuckles, and I watched with horrified fascination as he began to thrust.

Rupert zoomed the camera towards my face for a reaction shot, and I saw the big close-up on screen. My face was flushed, my mouth open as I panted and my eyes enormous and bright, either with unshed tears or passion. I wanted to scream that I didn't want it, but I knew they'd punish me if I wrecked their recording, then do it again and again. If I co-operated at least there'd only be one video tape they could use against me.

I'd like to believe that was the only reason I played along, but the truth was a bit different. I might have sworn to hate every second, but I liked the feeling of his fingers scissoring apart inside me. Thank God the cameras couldn't pick that up. But they could record my reactions, including the moment when outrage was replaced by the beginnings of pleasure, which was quite bad enough. Wider, wider he stretched my arse. Then, just when it really began to hurt, his free hand homed in on my clit, spreading my lower lips until I could see the little pink nub magnified on the screen above me. It still glistened with the oil he'd rubbed in after my shower, and his fingers slid easily across it. I whimpered, because he'd been right yet again. He could make me enjoy this, and it'd be worse than the last time because the evidence would be there for all the world to see, and I'd be lucky if all the world didn't see it.

'Good girl. Dirty, sexy, horny, little bitch.'

That was the first time that I'd heard Lance sound anything except superior and I knew this was turning him on as well. But I didn't feel a sense of power the way I had with the minister and the bishop, just a lack of it. But that was still a turn-on in its own twisted way. I moaned, tossing my head to and fro, trying to ride his fingers, and I can't pretend it was just so he'd get it over with. He pushed his fingers wider and wider apart until I could feel him in my cunt as well as my arse, and I didn't need to look at the screen to know that I was dripping wet.

He pulled his fingers out, spread a little gel on the tip

of his condom, then positioned his erection between my buttocks. It felt much bigger than I'd remembered it being, and I began to sweat with fear. His other hand stayed on my clit, and I swore I wouldn't waste energy trying to fight him. I broke that resolution in record time, and screamed when he pushed against the sphincter ring.

The screen relayed the pitiless images as he slowly pushed home, and that hurt too. It showed my flushed face, and the sound recorders were taping every sob and scream as my arse stretched until I was sure that something would tear. I could feel him right up inside me, heavy and hard and hot. By the time he stopped, he was buried to the balls in me. He stroked my face in a mockery of tenderness, freeing my lips, which I'd been biting and sliding the finger that had been working on my clit into my mouth.

I sucked it without needing to be ordered to, tasting the oil and my own secretions, glad of something to focus on that wasn't my overstretched rear passage. All the time I was waiting for the first thrust that would turn pain into agony. It didn't come and, as my body adapted itself to the intruder, the pain began to ease. Soon, it was just an ache, a heavy, slow cramping feeling, an unnatural sensitivity.

'Clamp down on me,' he whispered, but I shook my head.

'Have it your own way.' He withdrew, then repeated the procedure, this time in a single hard stroke that had me screaming as the muscles that had almost adjusted were strained beyond endurance. 'We can keep doing this as long as it takes,' he murmured so softly that the camera couldn't hear, 'washing off the lubricant if necessary. Or you can do as you are told and get it over with.'

I did the only sensible thing and clamped down, then whimpered for quite another reason. It felt incredible, and the hand that swooped down to rub my clit again just added to the pleasure. I sucked harder on his finger, trying to block out the rest of what I was feeling. He smiled as if he knew what I was doing, and began to move. Not the sharp thrust that had hurt so much, but a slow, steady easing of his body within mine that seemed to brush against every pleasure point I'd got.

I whimpered again, and the pressure on my clit intensified until my whimpers became continuous. I was riding him now, raising my hips to meet each thrust, long past caring what the monitor was showing or what they'd do with that damn recording. All that mattered was the sharpness of the pleasure – the tightness of my rear passage round a cock that stretched me in a way that I hadn't been stretched since I'd been a virgin; the finger in my mouth that I could pretend was another cock. He nipped my clit between two fingers, his other two fingers and thumbs slid easily into my soaking pussy, and I did what I'd sworn I wouldn't and came – loudly.

I hated myself, but it didn't stop me. My bum still writhed against him. I still forced myself up from the pillows to meet his thrusts, ignoring the pressure on my arms that made me feel as if they were going to be ripped from their sockets. I only wanted to experience every ounce of sensation, and I knew he wanted it as much as I did. His normally emotionless face was contorted with lust, and his thrusts were getting harder, stronger. I was so high that I even welcomed the stretched feeling in my arse, despite knowing I'd be sore as hell later. Then he drove into me one last time, and gave a long, animal grunt as his mouth came down on mine. The hand that had been in my mouth crushed my breasts together, and I opened my mouth to welcome him, feeling him pumping inside me as he came.

Then he collapsed on top of me, his weight flattening my breasts as his body convulsed in mine and I came down to earth enough to realise what I'd done. Not only had he buggered me, they'd filmed him doing it, and I'd loved it. I couldn't even convince myself that I hadn't wanted it. Sure, I could claim that I'd been tied up and helpless, which happened to be true. But I hadn't really fought Lance, and the concept of forced sex and that massive orgasm didn't tie up.

I hoped they'd untie me – hell, that cramped laundry hamper was starting to look pretty good, but I wasn't that lucky. Lance straightened up, pulled his cock out of my arse, wiped himself across my belly, then headed off to dress. I could hear Rupert and the sound recordist discussing whether they'd got enough reaction shots, but no one seemed to give a damn about me. I just lay there – my wrists hurting until I could inch myself back up the bed, wriggling my hips like a bloody human centipede. Then I wished I hadn't moved, because Liberty Hall was there; as blonde and immaculate as I was dark and dishevelled.

'That wasn't so bad, was it?' She smiled then, without warning, stuffed another butt plug up my arse.

I didn't have even enough energy left to yell. Besides, after Lance, it didn't even stretch me, let alone hurt. It was just there, filling me. I could see from that damn monitor screen that it nestled up against my arse cheeks, its head shaped like a baby's dummy. There was no way that I could push it out, and nothing I could do except lie there as they cleared up, loaded a fresh tape and left.

I closed my eyes rather than see any more. I didn't need to look to know that my breasts were still hard, my sex still gaping, and that scarf still tickling my nipples. I didn't know what I was becoming, or what would happen to me once they'd had their fun. And I broke all the promises I'd made to myself that I'd be tough and not let them know how much I cared, and cried my eyes out.

10

After a while, I forced myself to stop crying and start thinking. Rupert had said that those video tapes lasted thirty-five minutes, and I'd already wasted about fifteen of them feeling sorry for myself when I should have been gathering my resources for what lay ahead. Two down, two to go. Ahead of me lay lesbian sex and pain, unless they decided that what they'd already done counted as pain. How I'd felt as Lance drove home in that first long agonising thrust had been more than enough pain to last me a lifetime, but would it be enough for them? Almost certainly not, but pain could be the least of my problems. What would they do with me after they'd broken all my taboos? Would I be held prisoner and used to satisfy Lance's ever kinkier desires? Or maybe sold to someone even worse? I had another sniffle at that idea, then reality cut in. That sort of scenario is great in stories, but you can't just make people vanish these days. Or at least I hoped you couldn't.

Dickie Lawrence knew where I was, but that was no help either. If Liberty Hall was to be believed, he was a prisoner too. I did believe her, and I only hoped he was suffering far more than I was. If the little sod had kept his mouth shut, I'd have been away from the Hall and safe by now. But he hadn't, and I was paying for it. Some day, I swore, he'd pay for it as well, but I had to get out of this mess first. That wasn't an impossible dream, because chances were that Liberty Hall would try to cut a deal. Her silence about me in exchange for my silence about her, and she'd have that video tape to weight her side of the argument. I could live with that, and compared to the other options it was a good one, but was I making pretty pictures rather than face reality? I didn't think I was, because Imo would wonder where I was.

But that led me to another problem. Assuming that I managed to survive this and went back to university, how would I face Imo, never knowing if her mum had told her what I'd tried to do? Damn it, I liked Imo, and I wasn't any better than her when it came to liking kinky sex now, was I? Not only had I done almost all the things that I'd once looked down my nose at her for doing, I'd enjoyed them, and being forced to enjoy them didn't make it any less fun. In an odd sort of way, it had made it more fun, just as being bound and helpless had for Imo. Yes, Imo would be a problem. Either I confessed all to her, which didn't appeal, or I'd have to pick a fight that'd leave her never wanting to see me again.

But there was a third option. I could ask for a second chance, play it straight this time, and keep earning all that lovely cash. With that damn tape held over me, Liberty knew I'd have no choice but to play her games, but would she want me to do it literally? Could I come back here again and again to fuck whomever I was told to fuck in whatever kinky scenario she and Lance devised? I shivered at that idea, and my arse contracted round the plug, which felt surprisingly good. If the cameras hadn't been there, I might have been tempted to see whether I could come like that, but they were, and I'd given them quite enough of a show already, so I tried to relax. I didn't do a very good job of it, but by the time the door opened again I was, if not actually calm, not screaming and pleading. I wasn't surprised to see Lance and Liberty. I hadn't expected a knight in shining armour to come to my rescue, because this wasn't some story. This was real life, and it was up to me to not just survive, but make the best of it.

'Even when she's sticky and sweaty there's something about her.' Liberty paused beside the bed, looking me up and down as if I'd been meat on the hook. I closed my eyes rather than see the contrasts between us. She was free, I was tied up. She was beautifully dressed, and I was naked. Worst of all, she was rich and powerful and, right then, I felt less than nothing.

'The customers like her,' Lance conceded. 'She throws herself into it, and she thinks fast. I didn't think she'd manage to avoid the scene with the twins, but they were thrilled to have had their plans changed. They'd like her again.'

'That's unusual, and could change what we do with her,' Liberty mused.

I knew they expected me to demand to be told what they'd do to me next, maybe beg for mercy and make a hundred rash promises. I didn't, but it was a damn close thing, especially when Liberty stroked my belly, recoiling when she touched the spot where Lance had wiped himself clean. Courtesy of the enema, at least it didn't smell, but there was a sticky patch of lubricant that didn't help my feelings of humiliation at all.

'So, Tess.'

She'd waited until I opened my eyes before she spoke again, and I knew that she knew just how I felt. She wasn't gloating the way Lance was, but she knew that I was about as low as it was possible to get, and she didn't pity me one little bit. As far as she was concerned, I'd got what I deserved. Who knew, maybe she was right?

'How do you feel?' she asked

'How do you expect me to feel?'

I wished I hadn't snapped when Lance raised a small whip. It had a wooden handle and nine little rubber thongs, each knotted at the end. It only took me a second to realise what it was, proving that all they say about fear improving the reflexes is absolutely right.

'Watch your tongue with Ms Hall,' he snapped, and I realised I'd been wrong about something else as well. There was someone who could control Lance, and she was right in front of me. 'Shall I?' he asked with obscene eagerness.

'One stroke. Across the breasts,' she said, and Lance raised the whip.

I held my breath. Actually, I'm pretty sure I stopped breathing altogether when the thongs came down, laying a precise pattern of red stripes across my breasts. I managed not to yelp, but only because my breath had been driven out of me by the shock of the impact. The thongs seemed to curl round my nipples, and I was only glad that the monitor wasn't relaying anything – at least my humiliation wasn't being recorded.

'How did that feel?' Liberty asked.

'It hurt like hell,' I said sullenly.

'That's not enough,' Liberty said. I kept my mouth stubbornly closed, and she nodded to Lance, who raised the whip again. This time the strokes landed across my belly, and I howled and abandoned my plans to be defiant.

'Next time it will be between your legs. So I'll ask you one last time: how did it feel, Tess?'

'When the whip landed –' I was hoping to make my fortune with words, but I'd never chosen any more carefully than I did then '– I felt as if it'd cut me apart.'

'But it didn't break the skin so it couldn't have done, could it?' Liberty pointed out with chilling reasonableness. 'But you said you didn't like pain, and I don't like being betrayed.'

'What are you planning to do with me?' I'd sworn I wasn't going to make myself any more vulnerable by asking that, but I was so scared that I couldn't help it.

'That depends.' Liberty smiled and ran her fingers along the nine raised weals across my breasts. 'What are you prepared to do for us?'

'I won't tell anyone anything you don't want me to,' I blurted.

'We already know that.' She smiled at the monitor camera. 'That tape's going to be something special. We could make a fortune from it, and we could make plenty more out of you if we wanted to. After you'd worked your way through our repertoire of tricks you'd be a household name, just as I was, but you don't want that, do you? Besides, that wasn't what I was asking. What will you do for us if we let you go?'

'What do you want me to do?' The whip came up again and I gabbled my next words, terrified of feeling those thongs across my stretched labia. 'I'll do anything.'

'Anything?' Liberty's smile seemed strange, as if she was remembering something from a long time ago. 'Suppose we untied you?' I nodded eagerly, because my shoulder muscles were cramping, and my thighs would have been aching even without the butt plug. 'Then whipped you, while you wanked with the butt plug in.'

I had a feeling that her coarseness was deliberate, and designed to rub in how helpless I was. She didn't need to, but it was flattering to think she believed I had enough fight left in me to make it worthwhile, so I tried to live up to her wrong impression.

'And I suppose you'll film it?' I said, trying to sound as if I didn't care either way.

'Would you like us to?' she asked, still with that maddening amusement.

'No! Please...' What they'd got on me was bad enough. Filming that would be the last straw.

'So you'll do it?'

'Yes,' I muttered.

'I forgot to mention that we won't stop whipping you until you've come, but that won't make a difference, will it?'

It made all the difference in the world, as she must have known, but it was too late to argue. I was out of choices, and maybe I was a bit curious too. Hadn't I just been wondering if I could bring myself off with only the plug and the feeling of being tied? And they were talking about letting me go if I pleased them, which was more than I'd dared hope for. Then, I swore, I'd find Dickie Lawrence and use all Lance had taught me to make him suffer far more than I'd done.

Planning what I'd do with Dickie helped distract me while Lance released my ankles, letting the spreader bar drop until my legs dangled over the edge of the bed. He rubbed my ankles with impersonal efficiency until my circulation kicked into life, then unfastened them. I didn't bother to fight. There was no point. They'd proved who was in control, and it wasn't me. But somehow, some day, it would be me, and surviving this would take me a big step closer to that day. Once he'd finished, he undid my wrists, but I wasn't so lucky there. He merely replaced the chain with one that was long enough to let me move my hands, then ordered me to stand up and follow him.

I stumbled and fell a few times, but he didn't help me, even when I landed on my arse, shoving the plug further up inside me. That really hurt, but I'd have to get used to pain, wouldn't I? I'd have to enjoy it if I wanted to escape worse punishment, so I was almost glad of the enema and the butt plug. Without them, I'd have been shitting myself with fear.

'Kneel astride that,' Liberty ordered.

'That' was the open-backed director's chair I'd been fastened to I didn't know how long ago. The studio set-up was curtained with heavy blackout curtains, so it could have been any time. I'd guess it was around dawn, probably of the second day of my imprisonment. Early enough that no one would be up and about – not that anyone would come and rescue me if they had been. I was out of options, so I knelt, feeling the plug shift inside me when Lance looped my chain round the back of the chair. It dropped down, dragging my hands with it until they were positioned just above my clit, which I didn't think was accidental.

'Do you want a vibrator?'

At first I didn't answer. My clit was sore and over-used, and I was tired and aching, so I'd need all the help I could get, but there were still limits. Using a vibrator, knowing they'd be watching me and seeing how I brought myself off, probably storing the details for future use, had a nasty submissive edge to it, and I didn't think I'd ever be into that. But Lance would keep whipping me until I came, and the idea of watching them watching that was far worse.

'Please,' I whispered, and bowed my head.

'Isn't that better?' Liberty sounded as if she were praising a toddler who'd decided not to have a tantrum. 'See? You can be obedient if you want to be.'

I could be, but I didn't enjoy it. I didn't think I ever would, or at least not the way Imo had, and I really envied her that particular quirk in her nature then.

She'd been in ecstasy when she'd submitted to Lance and what lay ahead for me would have been much easier if I'd had her ability to give myself utterly into his hands, but I wasn't like that. I was starting to wonder if I went the other way entirely, but I had too many other problems right then to bother wasting time worrying about that.

'What you're going to do,' Lance explained as he closed my fingers round a small, gold-tipped vibrator, 'is work your buttocks up and down while I lash you. Keep your tits resting on the chair the whole time. Oh, and we want to hear you moan.'

I'd been planning to stay silent, but my survival depended on doing exactly as I was told, so I wasn't going to be able to keep that last pathetic bit of my pride either. I just nodded, not daring to look at him while he lifted my breasts and positioned them on the cool wooden back of the chair just in case he misinterpreted my expression and either changed his mind about the vibrator or came up with something else to add to the torture.

'Her nipples are still flaccid,' Liberty pointed out.

'I know, and I don't reckon she'll be able to do it, no matter what you say.'

I knew Lance wanted me to suffer before I failed, and I remembered everything that he'd said about enjoying watching while he drove people past their limits. He was doing that to me all right now, and I was scared again. I'd been scared so much since he'd walked into my room that I should have been used to it. But this was an entirely different sort of fear. Until now, everything had been done to me. Now I'd have to do it to myself, and I wasn't sure if I could. I was sure that I didn't want to find out what would happen if I couldn't, so I flicked the vibrator on, working my cuffed wrists until I could press it against my lower lips. They were still sticky from Lance's last little game, and at first I thought they weren't going to separate. Eventually, they slid reluctantly apart, and I could feel the vibrator against my sore, dry clit. It seemed to rasp, and I didn't see how I could have an orgasm.

'And the rest,' Lance ordered, and I lifted my arse off the seat, feeling the plug begin to slide.

'It's not slippery enough,' Liberty said, and Lance pulled it free. I'd learnt enough not to move until they ordered me to so I crouched there, waiting. My tits rested on the top of the chair, my bound hands held the buzzing vibrator against my clit, and I hated myself almost more than them, because I was enjoying it.

'That's better.' There'd been a slurping sound, like a suction cup being pushed down, just before Lance said that. 'Now lower yourself.'

I did, and found I'd been right. Something was anchored to the seat with a suction cup. It was hard, cold and slick with gel. It pushed at me as I eased my buttocks down, and I wasn't sure I could nerve myself to press down those final, crucial inches.

'Now,' Liberty ordered, and suddenly it got easy. The whip slashed across my bare arse. I screamed and jerked away, dropping the vibrator. The dildo plunged inside me, burying itself far deeper than the plug had. It was wider too, and harder, and the now-familiar, vaguely uncomfortable feeling of being overfull began again. I whimpered as the whip came down again. Liberty put the vibrator back into my shaking hands and I began to wank. Up and down I jerked, trying to avoid the whip, but all I achieved was to thoroughly arse-fuck myself. The lines across my buttocks and thighs multiplied until there couldn't have been an unmarked inch of skin left, and I was long beyond worrying about pride or faking moans for them. I was crying and pleading and begging, working frantically at my clit with the vibrator, knowing my only chance of escape was to have the orgasm that they wanted me to, but not seeing how I could.

Then it began to change. Liberty came to stand in front of the chair, so close that I could smell her expensive perfume. I knew I must smell too, but it wouldn't be anything like as pleasant, because I was dripping with sweat. She reached for my breasts, rolling the nipples in her fingers, stopping when I shivered.

'Soon, you'll enjoy this too,' she murmured. I knew what she was planning, but right then I didn't care. The stripes across my arse had stopped hurting. They felt warm, achingly sensitive, as sensitive as my distended arse or my equally red clitoris. I raised my buttocks again, this time to meet the whip, wondering what was happening to me. It still hurt, but the pain was different now. Warmer, heavier, so close to pleasure that I wasn't sure how you'd define the difference.

It was dark, it was dirty and depraved, but not as depraved as what I was doing. I shut my eyes to block out the sight of Liberty's compassionate expression as the climax hit me with shocking suddenness, converting that pain to agonising pleasure. It tore at me, turning me inside out as it took me higher and deeper than I'd ever been before. I didn't care what they were doing. I'm not sure I knew they were there any more. The outside world had been replaced by a universe made up purely of sensation. And the piercing scream – part pleasure, part pain, part willing abasement – didn't seem to belong to me.

I didn't open my eyes when it was over. I don't think that I could have done. I moaned when Lance lifted me, sliding his arms beneath my abused arse, but I didn't try to fight him. Soon, I was belly down on the bed, my chained wrists arranged to one side with unexpected consideration. He fastened a leather strap around my knees and another across the top of my back, just below my breasts and, mercifully, well above the area he'd whipped, and I was helpless again. Not that it would have mattered if I could have moved. I was so exhausted that all I could do was pant for breath, the sounds so close to sobs that I wasn't sure which they were. I hurt, I was utterly humiliated, and then I didn't feel anything any more. I'd escaped them at last, even if it was only into sleep.

When I awoke, I was alone. My bum still hurt, and when I twisted my head round I could see why. It was red from a few inches above my calves to the very top of the swell of my buttocks. I couldn't see the base of the dildo, but I knew it was there all right. I knew how far I'd come as well, because it didn't hurt any more. I felt stretched, but I was getting used to that and even beginning to like it. I didn't know how long I'd been asleep, but judging by how stiff I was, it must have been quite a while.

I managed to wriggle until I was facing the door, and adjusted my chained wrists until I was as comfortable as I could get, wondering when the next act would start, and if I'd done well enough so far. I'd definitely come, just as ordered, and I'd never felt anything like it. I'd never be into pain the way that Imo was, but I couldn't deny that the experience had been something else.

'Oh, Christ,' I muttered as I realised that I'd betrayed myself far more effectively than Dickie had betrayed me. I wouldn't reject anything Liberty Hall offered me now, because I knew I'd get off on it.

So much for my precious taboos. Here I was, sticky, sweaty, stinking of my own musk, so desperate for a loo that I'd be lying in a puddle if someone didn't come soon. My throat was so dry that my breath seemed to rasp in my mouth. But I'd enjoyed it so much that I wouldn't rule anything out any more. Even that enema had had its compensations. I hadn't known that I could feel something so intensely, and the orgasm when I'd been whipped had been stronger still. So much for my limits and the good girl I'd always managed to convince myself I really was underneath. Now I knew exactly what I was, and I hated it. I closed my eyes against the tears I couldn't hold back any longer, then realised I wasn't alone after all.

'You know yourself, now, don't you, Tess?' Liberty's soft voice was the last straw. 'And that's a worse punishment than anything we can do to you. Shall I tell you what you are?' I shook my head, trying to block her out, but she was remorseless. 'You're a little bitch. Not amoral, but you're capable of enjoying anything. You've done it again and again since you've got here, and soon you'll cross your last barrier. You're doing well.'

'Leave me alone,' I pleaded.

She was only saying what I'd been thinking, but I didn't want to hear it. I've always known that I wasn't the paragon that my father wanted me to be, but I couldn't be some animal, able to be turned on by anything and everything. Only I was, and there was nothing I could do to change it. Nor was there anything I could do to stop them taking me further and further past my taboos until I made Imo look like a pillar of the Christian Union. I knew they could keep me here until I grew old and ugly or became as bad as Lance, and I'd never felt so small, or alone, or helpless.

'Would you like a bath?' Liberty asked. 'And something to eat?'

'Does what I want matter?' I asked sullenly, pretty

sure that this was some new form of torture. She'd offer it, make me think that things would get better, then take it away again.

'Yes,' she said, and unfastened me. She didn't touch the dildo in my arse, but when I sat up, expecting Lance to appear any second, she murmured, 'You can take that out now. And there's a bathroom through there.'

I still couldn't see how it could be anything but a trick, but I was too relieved to be able to get rid of that damn thing to care what might lie ahead. I tried not to look at Liberty while I eased it out, then headed for the bathroom that she'd indicated. It wasn't a spartan one like the one Lance had used when I'd had that enema, it was warm and comfortable. Better still, it had a lock on the door, and the first thing I did was lock it while I considered my options. There were no windows, so escape was out, even if I hadn't been stark naked. Running away wasn't going to be an option, but what the hell was Liberty Hall playing at?

Whatever she turned out to be playing at, I'd got a breathing space and there was a large, deep bathtub in the corner. Steaming water came pouring out when I turned the hot tap on, so things were definitely looking up. I filled the bath, tipped in a generous amount of the scented oil that sat on the side, and got in, sighing as the water soothed my aches. I still didn't know how long I'd been helpless, but that was the least of my problems.

Liberty had said I'd done well, but would she keep her word and let me go? I reckoned she would, but that still left my future. I didn't have to be a Pulitzer Prize winner to know that those articles would never be written now. To be honest, I was more relieved than disappointed. When I'd arrived at the hotel I'd been able to convince myself that I was doing the world a favour by exposing the perverted practices of the great and good. Now I wasn't sure any more. Hadn't I enjoyed stuff that was just as extreme? And now, when I faced that becoming public, wasn't I in a cold sweat? The answer to both those questions was a fervent yes, so even my limited conscience rebelled at the idea of dropping someone else into the same shit I was currently in.

So where did that leave me? As long as the paper kept to their contract the minimum five grand 'kill fee' was mine. I couldn't see them wanting any of this to come out in court, so I was safe enough there. That was the worst of my debts repaid, but what about my career? Dickie Lawrence was a notorious gossip, so I was in deep shit, without any way out. Only I had a feeling that wasn't right either, because I was missing something vital. Some piece of jigsaw that would make all the others fall into place, to use an old cliche. I stretched, looking at my wrists and ankles, then rolled onto my belly. My bum wasn't hurting, but it wasn't exactly comfortable either. There weren't any bruises, just the sort of achy feeling you get when you go for a long ride after you haven't been riding for ages.

And I'd been ridden all right. Thinking that conjured up unhelpfully vivid images of Lance easing himself into my arse, and I winced and closed my eyes as I realised all I'd done. Anal, pain, humiliation. That just left lesbian sex, so there'd be no prizes for guessing what Liberty was here for. My instincts said that wasn't all of it, but they hadn't done a good job of protecting me so far, had they? Was I wrong to trust them now? I didn't know, but I did know that putting it off wasn't going to change anything. So I got out, dried myself, wrapped myself in the largest towel, then, reluctantly, unlocked the door.

Whatever I'd expected, the smell of crisp bacon and freshly ground coffee hadn't come into it. For a second I wondered if this was some new, more fiendish torture still, and she'd eat it all in front of me and leave me starving. Then Liberty looked up from the morning papers and smiled.

'There you are. I wondered if you'd get here before it got cold. Come and eat.'

I was so stunned that I sat down without saying a word.

'Shall I play mother?' she asked, as she lifted silver covers from dishes. Beneath them steamed all the ingredients of a traditional English breakfast, and my stomach gave an embarrassing rumble. 'Anything you don't want?'

I wanted to say, yes, what's happened to me and what you're planning to do next, but I had just enough sense to keep my mouth shut and shake my head. She piled a plate high, then set it in front of me, pouring coffee from a bone china pot into an equally expensive cup. I picked up my knife and fork once she'd picked up hers. I'd never felt so hungry, and not even fear could stop me enjoying my breakfast. I think she knew that, because she didn't speak until I'd cleared the plate.

'So,' she asked, 'what are we going to do with you?'

'I didn't think that was up to me,' I said, more respectfully this time.

'It isn't, but you interest me. Why did you do it, Tess?'

I didn't pretend not to understand her question. I knew that I'd betrayed a friend and lied again and again. Even now I was more sorry that I'd been caught than that I'd done it.

'I wanted it all,' I said, knowing that if anyone would understand it would be her. 'I'm fed up with being the poorest person in my class. I know I'm not really poor, but compared to them I was nothing, and they were no better than I am. I'm tired of having to watch every penny.'

'From what I've heard, and judging by your bank account,' Liberty said mildly, 'you haven't been, have you? So, you were hungry for life, and you did what you had to.'

'That's about it.'

'What if there were another way to get what you wanted?'

'I don't know.' I had a feeling that I did know what she was offering, but it was the last thing I was expecting and I needed time to think.

'Whatever else you are, you're a natural whore.' Liberty sounded like my old careers mistress, although she'd have choked on that word, assuming she'd known it. 'You're not a submissive. I could see you hating every second last night.'

'I wished I was Imo,' I said, then wished I'd kept my mouth shut.

'Yes, Imogen.' Liberty's pleasant smile vanished, replaced by a worrying lack of expression. 'I'm not sure what to do about her. She made an error of judgement in suggesting you, but you could still be useful. She also thinks that you're her friend, and because of me she hasn't had many friends. That makes things awkward.'

'I am her friend,' I protested, then realised that I'd picked a pretty pathetic way to show it. 'I know it sounds stupid,' I muttered, staring at my grease-smeared plate, 'but I never meant to hurt her.'

'No, I don't think you did, which brings me back to your future. You know my secrets, but I have a video tape that you'd give a lot for the world not to see, so I think it's time that we compromised.'

'Meaning?' I'd spent the lowest points of last night

thinking about white slavery, so this sudden friendliness seemed too good to be true.

'We could be useful to each other once your punishment is over. You want money, I want a good, reliable girl. Our aims could match. Think of the access you'd get to the rich and powerful, without them ever knowing who you were. Yes.' I had the feeling she wasn't seeing me as she went on. 'That could add a certain cachet to it. A masked girl who never speaks; a secret to match all theirs. Think how they'd get off on wondering whose mouth was round their cock? You'd be anyone they wanted you to be.'

'Yeah.' Not only could I could see her point, it appealed to me as well. I'd enjoyed the sense of power I'd had over the men I'd serviced, and I liked the hard cash too. Even if I got a job on a decent paper straight out of university, junior reporters don't get paid a fortune, and I like nice stuff. I'm not ashamed of that, or of liking sex – even the kinky sort I'd once sworn not to touch.

'And you could be a good dominatrix, with the proper training. Would that interest you? Say if we started with Dickie Lawrence?'

'I'd have got away with it if he'd kept his mouth shut,' I muttered resentfully, before realising that wasn't the best thing to say to the woman I'd tried to con.

'Yes, I rather think you would. Which brings me back to the last part of your punishment. Would you rather be tied up and ravished, or will you co-operate? It'd take the responsibility away from you if you were tied up, and I'd enjoy it, but it's your choice.'

11

Would I rather be tied up and ravished like a character from a third-rate bodice ripper, or make love with Liberty Hall willingly? That was a hell of a question to have to answer, especially when it had come out of the blue. Once I'd have rejected the suggestion instantly, just as I'd rebuffed Imo when she'd propositioned me. After everything I'd already done, I couldn't see much point in acting outraged, because acting was all it would be. To be honest, I was curious about what it would feel like to be made love to by a woman. Besides, I'd have to do it if I wanted to survive, so I might as well get all the fun out of it that I could.

'If you're tied up –' at least Liberty didn't seem to have noticed how gobsmacked I was '– you can relax, knowing there's nothing you can do to stop me. If you decide you want to resist, I won't know whether it's a game or for real. If you're free and resist . . .' she paused delicately, but I knew what she meant and finished for her.

'I get it. If I'm free and resist, then I've failed.'

'Precisely.'

'And you'll enjoy having me bound and helpless, won't you?' I couldn't be scared when I was talking to one of my own kind, especially not when I'd just realised how much I liked her. She was only doing what she had to to survive, exactly as I'd always done. It felt great not to have to worry about morals or being a good little girl and not frightening the horses.

'I might do. Does that matter to you?'

I stared at her while I considered my answer, surprised to find how much it did. Call it professional pride if you like, but I wanted to be appreciated if I was going to give my all. Lance's detachment had hurt me almost more than what he'd done to me, but I'd broken that and made him want me. And if I could do that, then proving myself to Liberty would be, if not easy, at least definitely achievable. I suppose I knew then what my answer would be. I'm pretty sure that she did too, but she didn't say anything and, after a bit, I lost my nerve and muttered, 'Yes. It means I'm the best.'

'Indeed.' She didn't need to point out that I'd have to go a long way to beat her. I knew that already; and I intended to go the distance and learn all I could from her. 'So, which is it to be?'

She didn't wait for an answer. Instead she unbuttoned her silk blouse and dropped it on the floor as if it had come from New Look rather than some designer, while I watched admiringly. Her age was the sort of closely guarded secret that MI5 would be proud of, but her body didn't look much more than late twenties. Maybe early thirties, if you were feeling really uncharitable. You only had to look at her to know she exercised regularly, and spent a fortune on expensive creams. She was as well preserved as money could make her, and stripping off didn't seem to bother her at all, which shouldn't have surprised me after all those films. Her skirt slithered down her legs, leaving her dressed only in a soft cream silk bra and matching French knickers.

'Well?' she challenged, and I stood up, letting the towel fall, trying to match her self-confidence.

'Tie me up,' I murmured, and it wasn't a forced decision. I wanted this to happen, and not just so that I could survive. I might have been certain that I wasn't a dyke, but looking at her body, and seeing her appreciating my body in turn, was turning me on. Besides, I told myself as I headed back towards the bed, I didn't have a choice. Hypocritical, I know, but it helped me look at the bed where I'd already experienced so much without wanting to scream and run.

Someone, not Liberty, I guessed, had changed the bed linen while I was in the bath. Before it had been black satin. Now the sheets were crisp white cotton, and smelt of starch, as innocent as neither of us were. I looked at the bed, then at Liberty, then took a deep breath and lay down. At least she wasn't like Lance. She might get off on tying me up, just as I'd got off on seeing Imo so helpless, but it had to be clear that it was a game for her to be able to enjoy it. Probably, I guessed, because she'd been forced herself more than once.

'Behold the less than innocent, non-virgin awaiting her fate,' I said, in best Hammer house of horror style.

'Good girl,' she murmured. When she smiled, I'd have walked barefoot over hot coals for her. I didn't of course. I did spread my arms and legs wide in silent invitation, but she shook her head.

'This is more fun,' she said, picking up two long silk sashes from the floor. One fastened my right wrist to my right ankle, the other held my left wrist and ankle the same way. Hog-tying, I think they call it, but the result was that my thighs were bent up and outwards, with my hands resting at my side. My pussy and clit were easily accessible, and if she rolled me over I'd be crouching on the bed, with my arse in the air. I was still helpless, but it was a damn sight more comfortable than anything else I'd experienced in this room.

'You're beautiful, and you know it.' Liberty lay down beside me, still partially clothed. I felt more naked than ever as I waited for her to make the first move, and I enjoyed the helplessness. 'I can see why Imo wanted you. I wonder if that's why she brought you here? We'll have to make sure she has you, won't we?' She discussed my sexual future as if she were deciding which doll to buy her daughter. Maybe it was that simple as far as she was concerned. She certainly didn't go in for any rubbish about love, not even the basics I'd used when I'd convinced myself that my one-night stands meant that I had girl power and wasn't just being a slut. 'How do you feel about that? In fact, how do you feel?'

She answered her own question, not with words, but by running one soft, long-nailed finger down my belly, sometimes scratching lightly, sometimes caressing. It doesn't sound like much, but it felt incredible, so I let my thighs flop further apart, inviting her to do whatever she wanted. Funny, I'd been so sure that this was going to be the worst ordeal of all, but now it had started I really wanted it. I tried to wriggle my hips to encourage her fingers to wander where I wanted them most, but she just smiled.

'Not yet,' she said, and knelt between my legs. I could feel her silk knickers brushing my mound, but I knew she wasn't planning to touch me there yet. Instead, she leaned forward and began to nuzzle my breasts, tiny delicate touches that were incredibly erotic.

She knew my body, that's all I can say. With a man, no matter how good a lover he is, there's always an adjustment period while he finds out what turns you on. This was different. She knew exactly where to touch me, and she did, first with her fingers, then her lips. By the time she gave up on my breasts and slid my hands down my belly towards my mound I was wet and ready and whimpering for more.

'Please?' I begged when she paused with her mouth inches above my now swollen clit.

'Please what?' she asked with a disturbing smile.

I tried to convince myself that doing whatever she wanted me to was a simple matter of survival, and she'd probably been planning to touch me anyway. But I couldn't, and it didn't seem to matter any more. We both wanted it, so why shouldn't we enjoy ourselves? And it would impress her, which was something I really wanted to do. I'm not ashamed of wanting to be the best, and I wasn't even as ashamed of not being a 'nice girl' as I'd once been.

'I want to lick you as well.' My voice sounded unnaturally hoarse and breathy, and she raised her head and smiled at me.

'You're sure?'

I wasn't any more, but she seemed to understand that too. She shed her bra and knickers with smooth, feline grace, and I gasped yet again. I'd seen girls with shaven pussies before, but Liberty's clitoris was pierced. A fine gold ring hung from it, pulling it downwards, a ring I ached to tug at with my teeth.

'My second lover did that. He was into sadomasochism,' she explained when she realised I was watching her, holding her labia apart so I could get a good look. 'He made Lance look like Rupert. He used to put chains through it and lead me round, or fasten me to the bed and leave me there for days.' Her finger slid inside me. 'Would you like me to do that to you some day?' I nodded, almost as if I'd been hypnotised by her. 'He'd order me to suck him off, just as I'm going to order you to suck me off now.'

I don't think I'm a submissive. Maybe Liberty's right, and I'm just into sex no matter how I get it. But her words still made me shiver with delicious anticipation and the feeling grew when she knelt astride my face. I could smell her – an intoxicating mixture of expensive perfume and the subtler musk of an aroused woman. I knew she'd smell the same, without the perfume, on me.

'Whatever I do to you, you'll do to me, right?'

I nodded, and brushed my lips against that gold ring. She bent forward, running her tongue lightly across my mound. I followed suit, then waited breathlessly until her tongue darted with sure precision straight for my clit. I screamed with pleasure, then remembered my job and mimicked her, adding a little refinement of my own. Rather than aiming for her clit, I slid the tip of my tongue inside that gold ring and tugged it down, rewarded when she moaned, and her juices ran down my chin. She slid two fingers into me and began to thrust. I couldn't copy her, but she didn't seem to care. Her tongue ravaged my clit and I repeated her actions on her body. Nothing hurried; none of the wham, bam, thank you ma'am approach to foreplay I was all too used to with men. Just a leisurely exploration that was more erotic than anything I'd imagined in my wildest fantasies. I lifted my bum to meet her thrusts, feeling myself climbing towards orgasm, then remembered that I mustn't come until she was ready and took deep breaths until things settled down a bit. That seemed to goad her on, and she took one finger from my cunt and slid it, sticky with my juices, up my arse.

Once I'd have screamed and fought her. Now I welcomed the extra sensation, and it got better still when she added another finger. Soon, she was fucking me with two fingers in my arse, two fingers and thumb in my pussy, and her mouth fastened on my clit like a baby at the breast. She rolled it round and round with her tongue, sometimes suckling it, sometimes nibbling, sometimes just holding it there, always keeping me just below the point at which I could come. I whimpered, I sobbed, I gasped and pleaded, my words muffled by her sex. But I knew damn well she wasn't going to let me come before she did, and that made it even more fun.

I wished I wasn't tied, but I knew I wouldn't have felt as free to enjoy it if I hadn't been. And Liberty wouldn't have enjoyed it as much either, so maybe it wasn't such a bad thing. Maybe she saw herself as teaching an innocent? I didn't know or care. All that mattered were the sensations. I wanted her to feel what I was feeling, so I slid my tongue backwards, pushing it up inside her, flicking it to and fro. She tasted strange, but I didn't care about that either. I intended to make her come, and to hell with what she wanted. Every drop of her musk on my tongue was proof that I could win this strange battle.

I don't know how long the dance went on, with each of us determined to give more pleasure than we received. I do know that I'd never felt so high. Forget multiple orgasms, this single, long drawn out one was the business, but she knew that business far better than I did. Her fingers slid in and out of me, then, abruptly, she changed the tempo and pulled out, raising her head until all I could feel was her breath on my clitoris. Then, when I didn't think I could bear it any longer, she thrust her fingers hard up me. Her teeth closed round my clit, mixing pleasure with a faint hint of pain that added a delicious spice to the sensations, and I came like an express train.

I couldn't moan, because my mouth was too full, but I could lick and suck. I did both as hard as I could, and feeling her coming made my own orgasm better. Then she wriggled up and lay beside me, unfastened my bonds and put her arms round me. I curled up against her, listening to her ragged breathing, knowing my own was the same.

'Well?' she asked.

'You know damn well how good it was.' I smiled and stroked the breasts I'd been aching to touch for what had felt like hours.

'But were you good enough for me?'

I almost said that that was for her to say, then I worked out what she was really asking. It was up to me what I did with my body. I could become a rich man's fantasy and get rich myself and still stay me, or I could be what I'd been before – poor and fed-up. Not much of a choice really.

'I wasn't bad, but I intend to be a whole lot better. Will you teach me?'

'Judging by what just happened, you haven't got a lot to learn, but yes, I'll take you on. On the understanding –' her hand tweaked my nipple, not so it really hurt, just as a gentle warning '– that we each keep our own secrets.'

That was fair enough. We could each destroy the other if we chose, but neither of us were choosing. 'What do you want me to do?' I asked, beginning my apprenticeship.

'First things first,' she said, her businesslike tone belied by the blonde head that lay heavy on my breasts, her breath caressing my nipples. 'The twins. You intrigued them the day before yesterday.'

Had it really only been the day before yesterday? I'd felt as if what had happened in this room had gone on for ever, but I'd never realised that I'd been a prisoner that long, or that I'd stop hating the people who'd held me prisoner. Maybe I'd got that Stockholm syndrome thing, where hostages fall for their captors. It'd explain why I didn't hate Liberty despite all she'd done to me, but I didn't think it was as simple as that. We were two of a kind, and she was offering me the future that I'd always dreamed of. That meant that what had happened was just a means to an end; and I'd won! I knew that wasn't the whole truth, but it was comforting, so I decided to believe it.

'Mmm,' I whispered, knowing what lay ahead, and wondering if I'd got the guts.

'They do everything together, and what they fancy is...' She detailed it. I listened, interested, excited, and a bit scared, then nodded.

'I can do that, but...'

'But what about Imo? She doesn't know anything about this, and I think we'll keep it that way.' Liberty's blue eyes were full of understanding and a little sadness. 'She needs dreams, not like you and me.'

That feeling of being included made me feel warm and smug, and I nodded. 'Suits me.'

'I was sure that it would. But be kind to her, otherwise...'

I didn't need that veiled threat, but I still nodded. Trust had to be earned, and I was still on probation.

'Then there's Dickie Lawrence to consider. He isn't scared enough yet for this to be really effective, but you need a rest so that's all right.' She stroked my hair, then went on as if she'd been an executive detailing a training programme. 'I think it's time you learnt to dominate as well as submit. I have a feeling you'll be good at it. By tomorrow night, after he's been held prisoner for four days, he should be really terrified. And then.' Her smile wasn't soft and loving now. It was cruel and predatory and left me glad I wasn't Dickie Lawrence. 'We'll start your education and his degradation. The beginning of the woman with no name, the masked fulfiller of fantasies who never gives anything of herself away.'

'Did you plan like this for me?' I asked, unwillingly

fascinated by the cool business brain inside that incredible body.

'Of course, but Dickie's not as strong as you are. He'll be begging for mercy as soon as he sees your outfit. By the time we've finished with him he'll do anything we want him to, and you'll find that useful too.'

'And you'll film it all?' Part of me was revolted by the thought of seeing the cameras that still stared at me like huge black sightless eyes roll again. But I'd be masked and anonymous so no one could hold this tape against me, and I wanted Dickie to be as scared, no, *more* scared and humiliated than I'd been. Not nice, I know, but I'd just realised that I wasn't a nice girl in any sense of the words. What's more, I didn't care any more.

It felt weird seeing Imo again, but I can't say I felt guilty. Why should I when I hadn't actually done anything to hurt her? What she didn't know couldn't hurt her, and I liked her too much not to be relieved that I hadn't dropped her in it. For all her worldliness she was sweet, and fun. Even if she hadn't been, no way was I getting in Liberty's bad books by upsetting her precious daughter.

'How did you and mum get on?' she asked, and I knew she'd guessed at least part of what had happened. There was no trace of hostility in her manner though, so it looked as if I'd got away with that as well. That was more than I deserved so I swore to make it up to her, then had a few ideas about how to do it that left me warm and tingling.

'She and Lance said they'd finish your education before they offered you a real job,' she went on cheerfully.

So that was what they'd told her. Well, it was just as

true as my version of events and left all of us without any awkward questions to answer, so I just nodded and, for once in my life, blushed. Luckily she took that as enough of an answer.

'Haven't you come a long way, little innocent vicar's daughter?' She giggled as she fastened her stockings to a suspender belt, then picked up two long red ribbons and tied her shoulder-length bob into two pigtails. 'I never dressed like this at school, did you?'

I looked down at the short navy pleated skirt and demure white shirt that matched her own and grinned. 'My uniform was green, and Dad would have had a fit if my skirt had been this short.' If I bent over, my buttocks, now only slightly red despite that thorough whipping, and covered only by the lines of the suspender belt, were clearly visible. My stocking tops showed whenever I moved. My hair, which was tied into two schoolgirl plaits, swung over my shoulders, making me look like the classic fantasy figure.

'Funny things, men.' Imo had something of her mother's ability to read minds, and I had a king-sized crush on her mum, so loving Imo came easy too. 'The oddest things get them going. Imagine being like Lance and having to be in control the whole time.' She shivered, setting her tits bouncing beneath her shirt in a way guaranteed to distract any man. It didn't do too bad a job on me either. Men were better, but women were different and I could enjoy them both. Actually I could enjoy it all, and I intended to.

'But what if he was the helpless one?' I said, imagining him bound and helpless while I cut away his faded jeans, then slashed at his T-shirt. He'd be at my mercy, and I wouldn't have any mercy. I'd have him screaming and pleading to be allowed to come, and then I'd leave him far longer than he'd left Imo. Oh there was so much

I could do and learn and become, and I was as hungry to start as I'd once been to write those articles.

'Oh-ho!' Imo looked at me very oddly, then smiled. 'If you're into that, then sharing a flat next year could be great fun.'

'You're really into this submissive stuff, aren't you?'

'Yes,' she said simply. 'I love being told what to do, and being tied up. When Lance takes control, all I've got to do is feel and enjoy. I know he won't take me beyond my limits.'

I hadn't been so sure of that when he'd had me helpless, but I understood something of what Imo felt now, and maybe even shared it. But this wasn't the right time to discuss it, let alone to indulge in fantasies of what I could do with an eager slave. We'd got the unholy twins – Cody and Cain – to meet. This time we'd been invited to their rooms; a spacious suite at the top of the tower. They were both stark naked when Cody opened the door, and I gloated over the way his eyes widened when he saw us.

'Please, sir,' Imo said in a little-girl voice. 'We want to suck your lollipops.'

Cody smiled and ushered us inside. Cain lay naked on the bed already, his erection enormous and, I had to admit, looking very suckable.

'It's too big,' I squealed, right on cue, and Cody's smile became a smirk.

'That's not what you said last time.'

Last time they'd wanted to give it to me up my arse, and I'd been scared, but a lot had changed since then.

'Don't,' Imo pleaded. Her face was flushed, her lips slightly parted, and her breasts shoved against her tight shirt until I expected the buttons to pop off. She really, really wanted what lay ahead, and so did I.

The men were obviously revelling in it too. Cody

picked Imo up as if she weighed less than a child's doll, flipping her skirt up as he dropped her on the bed. She landed on all fours, looking round wildly. 'Not both of you together,' she squealed, and I could see the moment when the twins' plans were changed without them realising they'd been manipulated and knew just what Imo had meant – men *were* weird, and so, so gullible.

'Why not? She can suck your tits while we do it. No.' Cain's face set until he looked like one of those African tribal masks you see in the really expensive galleries. Proud and cruel and implacable, not to mention sexier than ever. 'You can fuck her while we fuck you.'

'Ooh, you're wicked,' Imo squealed, and I knew just how she felt, because I felt the same.

My juices were running, and the feelings got steadily stronger as they tore Imo's shirt open. She wasn't wearing a bra, and each man cupped one of her breasts in those big, hot hands I remembered all too well, and squeezed until she squealed.

'I'll be good, I'll be good,' she pleaded, in the sort of husky, breathless voice that belongs in a bloke's wet dream. 'I'll do anything you want me to. I won't fight you or anything. Just don't make me fuck her!' She jerked her head at me, and I realised I wasn't the only good liar in the room. She'd been trying to get inside my knickers since the day we met, but I'd have sworn now that she was as straight as they come.

'You'll do as you're told.' Cain flipped her skirt up and spanked her bare buttocks until she whimpered and wriggled.

'There's no point struggling, Imo.' I picked up my cue, somehow managing to sound scared rather than as excited as I felt. 'We'd better do whatever they want. Then maybe they'll let us go.'

If the papers got hold of this they would have had a field day but they weren't going to get hold of it, were they? That was the whole point of Liberty Hall. It was a place where the rich and famous could play out their fantasies without worrying about skeletons in their closets. It was also a place where people like me and Rupert and Lance and Imo could indulge ourselves, and get paid for the pleasure. I already knew there'd be another five hundred pounds in my bank account after this, but that wasn't the only reason I was there. I was part of the fantasy now, with the power I'd always wanted and plenty of money to look forward to, and I was loving it.

'But you're not into that.' Imo sounded so excited that I wondered if she thought that it really would be my first time.

'I'll do it for your sake,' I whispered, knowing we had to make them think they were getting something they weren't meant to. Any fool can do as they're told, but a true professional gives the punter what he really wants, even if he doesn't know that he wants it. Maybe especially when he doesn't know he wants it because Lance has a point. That moment of surprise when some-one crosses a limit is sweet to see, and I was seeing it now.

The twins were imagining having us helpless, and if not actually unwilling, in need of persuasion, and they were really getting off on it. The good boys of British sport were about to get their kicks from girl on girl, done at their command, and they weren't the only excited ones. I was close to orgasm at the very idea, and Imo's body was jerking as she watched them with apparent terror. She hid her reactions pretty well, but I knew she was coming. She'd been so turned on by the idea of fucking me that she hadn't needed anyone to touch her. Call me vain, if you like, but knowing that did things to me, and I nearly joined her.

'You've never had a girl?' Cain stared at me, and I knew we'd got them.

'Never,' I'd been had by a woman, but that wasn't what he'd asked, and I wasn't spoiling this by getting picky about tiny details.

'Cool,' he said on a long, satisfied breath. Then he and Cain swung into action, working together as smoothly as when their relay team had brought home a rare Olympic gold for Britain.

Imo's shirt was ripped down to the waist, her stripy school tie left dangling between her breasts so they could use it as a leash. They took my tie off and used it to tie my wrists to the top bedpost, leaving me crouching at the top of the bed with Imo's head between my thighs. I could see her breasts, full and heavy, and had another idea.

'Don't make me touch her,' I pleaded, and it was Cain's turn to grin.

'Christ, Cody, we've got a real innocent here! No arse, no girls ... it's time someone educated her!'

I bit my lip, wondering if he'd really fallen for it. Maybe he hadn't, but he certainly bought into it. He freed my hands and clamped them on Imo's breasts, then his hand slid beneath my skirt and straight into my pussy.

'This one's ready,' he said as he felt how wet I was.

Cody subjected Imo to the same check, assuming 'subject' is the right word for something Imo enjoyed as much as she did, and then the twins got to work. Being wanked by a bloke while his mirror image did the same to Imo was something else. They matched each other's movements exactly, and they were so good that they could have got jobs at the Hall if the world of athletics ever stopped paying the bills. Imo was soon pleading for more, and I was making a fair amount of noise myself. But that sort of vanilla sex wasn't what they were there for, so I wasn't surprised when they abandoned me and focused on Imo. Her fragile blondness seemed to intrigue them, which just proved how little they knew because she's as tough as they come. She was staring at them now, wide-eyed, apparently terrified.

'Don't hurt me,' she whispered as Cody lifted her up.

Cain lay down, and I knew he could see everything but I didn't care. He didn't bother to touch me, just watched. I watched too while Cody produced a tube of lubricant from the bedside table drawer and began to work it into the crack between Imo's buttocks. One broad hand held them apart, and the contrast of black and white skin made what was happening more erotic still. He rubbed and pushed, sliding first one, then two fingers into Imo. They went in easily, but I was still relieved I wasn't going to be taking one of those massive cocks up my arse.

They ordered me to lick each man in turn, then slide condoms onto their cocks. They stretched, translucent white over jet black, and I almost envied Imo. Then Cody lifted her again, raising her high above his twin's erection before lowering her slowly down, and I was just glad it wasn't me being stuffed that full. She whimpered as she was stretched. My cunt tightened as I remembered how that massive black erection had filled me until I'd felt as if I'd burst, but Imo wasn't fighting them any more. She just crouched above him, her face pressed against my navy gym skirt. Cain gripped her buttocks, holding them high in the air, then separated them until her rear entrance gleamed oily and vulnerable.

Cody groaned, then began to enter her. Imo's whimpers

grew louder, and both men groaned in unison as she was filled. They'd be able to feel each other, I realised as I began to stroke Imo's breasts. She stared at me, her eyes full of tears, and I knew it was hurting her. I also knew that she was getting off on the pain. I hope she was getting off on what I was doing to her as well. Her lips parted as Cody slid further up inside her. I wondered what it would feel like to kiss her, but that wasn't my role this time. My role was the reluctant virgin, but some day soon that was going to change. Cody was buried to his balls in her now, and she'd stopped moaning. Instead she lay still, as if she was too scared to move, and Cody smiled.

'Now her,' he ordered, and Imo sobbed as Cain flipped my skirt up, but still didn't struggle.

'I'm sorry, Tess,' she said, and put her mouth to my pussy.

'And her arse too. Make her feel what you're feeling,' Cody ordered, but I knew no one could make me feel that.

But what I was feeling was great. Imo worked me until her fingers were good and slippery, then eased them past my sphincter muscle, shoving two fingers up me until they were buried to the knuckles. My shock – part pleasure, part brief, sharp pain that faded almost before the sound died away – wasn't faked, and the men took that as their cue and began to move, again in perfect harmony. Imo's body rose and fell with each thrust, and her breath came in sobbing pants. I was panting too, working my hips, riding the sensation for all it was worth. She had two fingers in my pussy, her mouth was hard on my clit, and my hands on her breasts were just as busy. Cain twisted round until he could kiss me, his tongue thrusting down my throat in time with his movements as his cock moved in Imo, and the mundane world began to fade.

Imo was the first to crack. Her breasts tightened under my hands, her nipples so hard that they looked more like red marbles than human flesh. Her mouth and fingers stilled inside me as she keened, a long, wordless, inhuman sound of pain-laced pleasure. Again and again her body tightened round the twins, but that still wasn't enough for them. They jerked out of her, their bodies glistening with sweat, rolled a still moaning Imo out of the way, then grabbed me. My shirt ripped open, sending buttons pinging against the wall. I wondered if they were going to use the same trick they had on Imo, but they didn't, and I knew how far I'd come, because I was almost disappointed.

Instead, they rolled me onto my stomach and tore my skirt off, and I mean tore. I felt a hand beneath its waistband, I don't know whose, then all I was wearing was the waistband. My hands were tied behind me with the school tie, then one of them was in my cunt and the other in my mouth. I didn't know which was which and, to be honest, I didn't care. A massive cock filled me, two skilled hands worked on my clit – one holding my lower lips apart, the other stroking with surprising delicacy.

An equally large cock thrust to the back of my throat. I could taste latex and Imo and a faint hint of man-scent. I licked it eagerly, wanting what Imo had just enjoyed, and they seemed to want it too. The pressure on my clit intensified, and the thrusts got harder, more savage. One of them laughed, and the other reached for my tits, squeezing them so hard that I screamed. You know I said I couldn't get off on pain? Well, I did then! I bucked against them, not fighting them but encouraging them. I wanted more, and I wouldn't have cared if they had taken pussy and arse together, except that it would have meant there was no one in my mouth.

My breasts felt as if they were going to be ripped off, my sex was stretched so wide that I was sure I would be torn apart. The cock in my throat was so far down that I reckoned it'd meet the other one at any second, and I loved every second of it. I couldn't yell my pleasure, but I felt it all right. I ground my bum against someone's balls, felt him contract inside me, and worked harder on the cock in my mouth. And we all came at the same moment, entangled in one big, sweaty mound of pleasure.

12

I'd just about recovered from that lot by the evening, but Imo hadn't. She'd been so shattered that I'd half-carried her back to her rooms and washed her. Then I'd put her to bed, and made sure that she slept like a baby, and how I did that is my business and no one else's. All I'll say was that it was as satisfying as it had been with her mother, and much more fun now that I had an idea of what I was doing. Having them both in one day felt a bit like incest, but I'd promised to be nice to Imo, and I was.

Now I was getting dressed for another assignment. I'd never imagined wearing anything like the outfit that Liberty was planning to make my trademark, but I could see why she'd chosen it. The black leather bodysuit stuck to my skin, and I knew I'd be both hot and bloody uncomfortable, but the effect was more than worth it. It covered the whole of my body, fastened by a long zip that ran from neck to crotch, finishing in my bum cleft. It could be undone from either end, revealing as much or as little as I chose, and a zipper tag pressed against my clit, giving me a constant reminder of what lay ahead. Two more zips gave easy access to each breast, and the thigh-high gleaming patent leather boots were the perfect finishing touch.

I posed with my hands on my hips, and my legs straddled, studying myself in the mirror, wondering what Imo would say if she saw me like this. 'Please, mistress' as she grovelled at my feet, begging me to do my worst, quite probably. And I would please her, eventually, but Tricky Dickie wasn't getting off that easily. That reminded me that I'd better get a move on. At least I hadn't got to bother about my hair and make-up. My hair was sleeked back with gel, pinned into a tight plait that would tuck beneath the hood I was holding. I eased it down over my head, settling the eye holes into place, and even I was shocked by my reflection.

The outfit was so tight that my erect nipples showed clearly, and my mound jutted forward. It was obvious that my sole purpose was sex, but no one would have a clue who I was. Dickie Lawrence definitely wouldn't recognise me, and all this was for his benefit, assuming that benefit was the right word. Revenge was a better one, but it wasn't quite that either. It was more a question of teaching him a lesson that he couldn't forget or ignore, and I couldn't wait to start. He wouldn't know that he'd been locked up for four days, because it'd feel like an eternity since he'd been free. Sensory deprivation and psychological warfare were one of Lance's favourite techniques, so poor Dickie had been stripped naked as soon as he'd been snatched. His hands had been fastened behind him with thumb cuffs. You know – little loops of metal that slide over your thumbs, but are every bit as effective as handcuffs when it comes to making you helpless.

Just to ram home how helpless he was, they'd put ear plugs in and blindfolded him. Then they'd tied his legs together and shoved him in the boot of a car for the long drive down from London. The blindfold would have been removed once they'd cuffed him to the bare metal-framed bed that was the only furniture in an equally bare cell, but they'd left the ear plugs in and the light constantly on, so by now he should be really disorientated. No one had touched him yet, except to administer the enema that Lance had insisted on, so Dickie would be feeling humiliated as well as scared. With any luck he'd also be hating himself, and those who'd touched him and painfully aware of his vulnerability. I remembered how he'd be feeling all too well, but it was his fault, so I didn't waste time feeling pity or remorse.

All I was feeling was lust. I'd wondered what it would feel like to have someone totally helpless ever since I'd seen Imo looking like a mummy. Now, with Lance's help, I was about to find out. I was a bit nervous about that, because I had a feeling that Lance hadn't finished with me yet, but tonight, at least, I was safe enough. I picked up the long leather whip, tucked it into the tight belt that pushed my breasts up and outwards until I made a *Baywatch* babe look flat-chested, then strode across to the gym.

Lance was waiting for me outside the door of Dickie's prison. He studied me without any apparent lust, which didn't surprise me. What turned Lance on were human reactions, specifically fear. If he wasn't at the Hall he'd be locked up in a mental hospital as a psychopath, but I could see why people paid so much for his skill. Dickie wouldn't understand that, but Dickie should have kept his mouth shut. He didn't even have the sense to keep quiet when the door was opened. Instead, he let loose a tirade of threats, liberally laced with obscenities, which was pathetic when you looked at him – and I took a good long look.

He was hunched up on the bed, trying to cover his genitals. I couldn't see why he was bothering, because they looked shrivelled and pathetic, but I just glanced at Lance, waiting for guidance. He ambled across to Dickie, took the ear plugs out, then shoved him back onto the bed. Dickie fell awkwardly, his hands trapped behind his back.

'You've been a very naughty boy.' Lance's voice was mild, almost pleasant, but I still thought that Dickie would wet himself with fear.

'You can't do this. I'll have the law on you,' he blustered.

'I don't think so. Not when everything that happens in here is being filmed.'

'So? It'll be evidence for the trial.'

'If you want a court to see how much you enjoy being a bum boy, that's fine by me. You know all about the freedom of the press, don't you? They'd have a field day with that!' Lance reached down and began to rub his victim's flaccid cock.

Dickie moaned, and tried to push him away. That was my cue, and I was looking forward to it. I lifted the whip and brought it cracking down, just as I'd practised doing all afternoon. I didn't touch Dickie, yet, but the whip flicked round the edge of the narrow metal bedstead, and he got the point.

'No. Please, no. I swear I'll never tell anyone anything you don't want me to. I'll pay you anything you want. Just leave me alone, and don't let her hurt me.'

'No,' Lance said simply. 'You wanted to know what we do here? Well, tonight you're going to find out.'

Dickie stared at him, then closed his eyes. Not theatrically or defiantly, just as if all hope had gone; which it had, just as it had for me a few days before. But I didn't waste time feeling sorry for him. If he'd kept his mouth shut we'd both have been safe, but he'd had to boast. Even now, when fighting was useless, he didn't have the sense to do what he was told. Not like me. I'd survived and evolved, and if that meant losing a few ideals, then what I'd gained was pretty good compensation.

Now I'd take my place at Liberty Hall while Dickie was taught a lesson that he'd never forget, which even went some way to assuaging my need for revenge. Watching Dickie squirm as he unwillingly came erect underneath Lance's expert hands was only the start. Lance took his time over it, extracting every ounce of humiliation from Dickie's helpless body. But by the time he'd finished the once-shrivelled cock was red with blood; the hairy balls beneath it drawn up tight.

'Now,' Lance murmured, and I took a deep breath, fighting the excitement that was threatening to ruin everything.

According to Lance, a good dominatrix stays cool, calm and collected at all times. Her sole duty is to wring pleasure or pain from her victim; always tuning in to what that victim really wants, even if they can't bring themselves to admit it, let alone ask for it. She must never show any pleasure herself; not that I could when I was masked like that. So I broke the rules yet again and allowed myself a smirk and a little gloat as I reached into the canvas bag that Lance had brought with him. Dickie recognised the tangle of leather strips and metal rings right away, and his lips parted in a soundless gasp.

'That's right,' Lance explained helpfully. 'It's a cock harness. Once you're fastened into it we can do whatever we like to you without worrying about you coming and spoiling our fun. You'll be begging us to let you come by the time we've finished with you.'

'Please don't hurt me,' Dickie whimpered.

'Why should we want to do that? Don't worry, you'll enjoy it – eventually.' Lance's smile had never seemed so depraved, and I knew I'd escaped lightly. I'd only had my taboos broken, and even that, I suspected, had been as much a test as a punishment. Dickie was really going to suffer, and I was not just going to help inflict that suffering, but was looking forward to it.

I stepped forward and gently touched the tip of his penis. He might be scared, but he was also so hard that I was sure that he'd come then and there. That wasn't in our plans so I pinched him, hard, just below his glans. He howled, and his erection subsided, but not much, and not for long. I put a condom on him, then forced the metal rings down over his cock, not caring when they bit into him. Ignoring his groans and pleas, I fastened the straps so that his balls were separated. Then, with a touch of inspiration even Lance would have been proud of, I crouched down in front of him and took him in my mouth.

I couldn't see Dickie's face, but I knew he was watching me, and I was pretty sure that he was in agony. His balls were rock hard, his cock wept into the latex sheath, but there was no way we intended to let him come until the scene was perfect. His body writhed as he fought to ejaculate, then he gave a gut-wrenching sob and lay still.

'You got the hint in the end, I see,' Lance said, and I stood up and stepped back. 'This girl is in training,' he went on. 'She has to learn how to please a man, and I suppose you're close enough to that for her to practise on. I'm going to take her through a few techniques, and you're going to co-operate, aren't you, Dickie?'

'You can't do this,' Dickie protested, without any real conviction. It was still a stupid thing to say, because Lance's smile widened.

'Really? I seem to be doing quite well so far, don't I?'

The dialogue came straight out of a B-movie, but I was too busy watching Dickie's face to care. He looked terrified and aroused and humiliated and, most and best of all, helpless. The man who'd brought down the rich and famous with one stroke of a poisonous pen was totally vulnerable now, and hating it.

'First, she has to be able to give head. Do you think she's good enough at that?'

Dickie didn't answer, and Lance gestured to me. The whip only caught the edge of his thigh, but from the fuss he made you'd have thought it was a cat-o'-nine-tails across his cock. He screamed, curling up into a ball, but Lance caught him and held him flat, fastening his feet to a spreader bar so he couldn't escape us.

'I told you not to mess us around,' he said, with mild annoyance. 'Now, are you going to lie still?'

To give Dickie his due, he had guts. No brains, but guts. He brought his legs up and tried to kick Lance. Lance moved out of the way, and I raised the whip.

'The next stroke lands on your cock,' he said softly, and Dickie lay very, very still. He didn't bother to fight while Lance fastened leather straps round the bunk until he couldn't have moved, let alone done either of us any damage. 'Now, where were we? Ah yes, I was asking how good she was at giving head.'

'Great. The best ever,' Dickie babbled.

I knew I was good, but something told me that his praise had an ulterior motive, just like everything else he did. Not that it would do him any good, because Lance simply nodded.

'Now for lesson two. Has she got a sweet, juicy cunt?'

I handed the whip to Lance and undid the zip that ran between my buttocks until my sex was bare, and the toggle brushed against my clit. It made a nice bonus as I knelt astride Dickie, letting his metal encased cock rest just inside me.

'Is she wet?' Lance asked. Dickie nodded desperately.

'Do you want her?' Another even more desperate nod. 'Are you going to give it to her good and hard until she comes?'

Dickie didn't know what to make of that, but he worked it out quickly enough when the door opened. Rupert, his face incongruously covered by a Mickey Mouse mask, came in, wearing the harness with the steadicam. Dickie's very own porno video would show him bound and helpless as he fucked an anonymous leather-clad woman, apparently with enthusiasm. Lance could be a bit predictable, but it was a bloody good way to control someone, so I decided to forgive him this time.

'No,' Dickie protested. 'You can't do this. I don't want it . . .'

Lance didn't bother to answer and neither did I. I let actions speak louder than words and lowered myself onto him, gasping at the unfamiliar sensation of rings of cold metal in my hot sticky sex. Dickie groaned as Rupert went in for a close-up of his flushed face.

'Now fuck her,' Lance ordered. He stepped out of camera range, and I knew those words wouldn't appear on the finished production, any more than the whip that slashed across Dickie's ankles when he didn't obey fast enough.

Dickie screamed, his body jerked upwards, and he began to thrust, working his body against the leather straps. They must have been cutting into him cruelly, but I can't say that I cared. I was otherwise occupied, unzipping the cups of my catsuit and letting my breasts hang out, fondling them myself, knowing that Dickie was watching and wanting and doing everything I could to keep him erect and wring a truly mind-bending and humiliating performance from him.

I suppose that that sort of thing must be worse for a man than a woman. A woman can at least say she lay back and took it, and most of us are used to being fucked about by men long before we start having sex. This time Dickie was being taken, despite all his power. It didn't matter what he wanted; his body was hard inside mine, filling me with each thrust. He'd stay that way as long as I wanted him to and he was both loving it and hating it. The tangled emotions were tearing him apart, just as my world had been torn apart because of him. If he'd had the sense to keep his mouth shut Lance wouldn't have had an excuse to play his games, and I wouldn't have that video tape hanging over me. I'm sure you get the general picture. I hated him, and I intended to make sure he suffered.

I took my time, working myself to three orgasms before I pulled off him, ignoring his moan when the metal rings were forced upwards, biting into his swollen skin. I leaned against the wall while I caught my breath, glad of the bottle of water Lance handed me. Rupert stopped filming and changed the tape and, judging by Dickie's expression, he was starting to hope it was over. He was in for a shock though, because I knew the script, and Dickie's troubles were only just beginning.

'Now for the grand finale,' Lance said and unfastened the straps that fastened Dickie to the bed.

'No, please!' That seemed to be all Dickie could say now, just as I remembered it being all I could manage when I'd been in the mess he was in. Maybe I felt a bit sorry for him then, but it was his choices that had brought him there, so I was only a bit sorry, and mostly very, very excited. This wasn't something that had been on my list of exclusions, but I'd never seen it before, and I wanted to. I'd participate too, up to a point, but the final, humiliating conclusion would be Dickie's alone.

'Stand up. Walk across to that chair. Bend over and grip the back of it, then spread your legs wide and brace yourself.' Lance ordered, with the most sadistic smile I hope I ever see.

'You can't,' Dickie whispered and began to struggle again. It was useless, because it just gave Lance another chance to play with his second-favourite toy – the whip I'd been holding. It took three strokes of the whip before Dickie accepted the inevitable and stood, his legs splayed, his cock resting on the seat of the hard wooden chair as he gripped the chair back to support himself. His arse jutted out, the weals from the whip glowing as red as Rudolf's nose.

'Suck him,' Lance ordered.

I crouched in front of the chair and took Dickie's red, painful-looking cock into my mouth, running my tongue beneath the metal rings, ignoring his desperate whimpers and promises to do anything if we'd only let him go.

'Do you know what I'll do next?' Lance's voice was so silky that I knew he was close to the edge. Dickie shook his head, not because he didn't know, but because he was too scared to speak. 'I'm going to fuck your arse. Give it to you good and hard, like you know you want it.'

'I don't, I don't.' Dickie was crying now, but that was nothing to how he'd feel when he realised that he did want it.

'Yes, you do.' Lance retreated just long enough to get a tube of lube out, then squeezed the cold gel onto his fingers and began to work. Dickie was really pleading now and every second of it was being recorded by the dispassionate eye of Rupert's camera. It zoomed in and out, taking close-up after close-up, and I knew he'd record the moment when Dickie got it right where he deserved. So did Dickie, and he closed his eyes.

Lance slid a greased finger up Dickie's rectum. I knew

that not because I could see it, but because Dickie howled. His eyes flew open, and his whole body jerked, sending him so deep down my throat that I gagged. I gulped, gripped his balls to make it quite clear who was in charge, and began to move his cock in and out of my mouth. Dickie stared down at me, too scared to move, and Lance murmured, 'That was one finger. This time I'll use two and stretch you so you're ready for me.'

'No!' Dickie howled, but Lance laughed and did it anyway.

'If you complain again, I'll use a big butt plug instead, and leave it in for a few days. You'd need another enema afterwards, and then we'd do all this again. Let me make this quite clear, Mr Lawrence. You are going to be fucked until you come. We do not care how long it takes, or what we have to do to get that orgasm. You can co-operate now or endure as long as you like, but sooner or later you're going to come. I'd enjoy it more if it was later, but it's up to you.'

Dickie shuddered as the impact of that little speech hit him. Something in his eyes changed, and I grinned despite the cock that gagged me. Who'd have imagined that the bloke who always had to be in control was really as much of a submission junkie as Imo? Now he was going to learn that about himself, which was prob-ably the worst punishment anyone could have imag-ined. Even if no one else ever saw the tape he'd still know what he'd done, and, in the darkest corners of his soul, want to experience it again.

'And then –' Lance rubbed salt into the wound the way that only he could '– we'll show you the tape. There's already some good footage on it of you enjoying being whipped. It's so hard to tell the difference between pleasure and pain, isn't it?' His smile widened. 'Then there's you being fucked by my little friend here and, of course, this. If you ever write one word about Liberty Hall or try to contact that little bitch Tess Morgan I'll send it to every newspaper editor in the country. Your crusade for moral purity won't look very good then, will it?'

Dickie's howl was the loudest yet, and I knew that Lance must have spread the two fingers that were up his arse as wide as he could, stretching him ready for his grand entrance. Right on cue, Rupert moved in for another close-up.

'Just get it over with,' Dickie said tightly.

'Soon,' Lance promised, adding another finger to make it clear who was in control. This time Dickie didn't howl. He stayed bent over, panting for breath, his hands so tight on the back of the chair that I wondered if he'd break it. I knew this was utter hell for him, and waited for it to get worse.

I know that sounds sadistic, but it wasn't really, because I knew he'd enjoy it in the end. Lance was too good at his trade for him not to, and my future depended on Dickie Lawrence keeping his mouth shut, so I couldn't afford luxuries like pity. He didn't enjoy it when Lance finally slid a condom over his erection, freeing it from his trousers as if Dickie was some bum boy who wasn't even worth undressing for, then pressed it between Dickie's buttocks. He howled again and again, and I felt him jerk as he was penetrated, but between the gel and Lance's careful preparation it couldn't have hurt much so I didn't feel all that guilty.

'Relax.' Lance's voice was soothing and gentle, and his hands were massaging Dickie's buttocks. 'Just go with it, and you'll enjoy it.'

I picked up my cue and began to give Dickie all I'd got, cramming his balls into my mouth as well as his prick. He got harder still and, to my intense satisfaction, let out a moan of reluctant pleasure when Lance began to move inside him. He took it slowly, reaming the virgin arse as if Dickie really had been his lover, and gradually Dickie's gasps turned to groans. If he'd been able to come, he would have, but the harness meant he couldn't and now it was time for the ultimate humiliation.

Lance pulled out, waiting with Dickie's buttocks spread, his cock still nestling against the entrance to his sodomite while I got to work. Two quick jerks of the harness and no evidence remained that Dickie had been forced. Another, more careful movement took the condom off, and he was ready for his grand finale. I kissed his cock one last time, then moved back. The released cock jerked, and Dickie moaned again, his ability to think temporarily wiped out by lust.

'Give it to me,' he begged, and I knew he'd hate himself for it later.

'You only had to ask,' Lance said, and I moved back out of shot. Rupert took my place in front of Dickie, and it was his dispassionate video camera that recorded the last, frenzied coupling.

Lance made the most of it, sliding his cock lubriciously in and out while he massaged Dickie's penis, and Dickie was beyond caring what happened to him. He groaned and whimpered, arching his back to meet each thrust. Then his sperm, thick and milky white, jetted upwards, splattering against the lens of the video camera. Dickie Lawrence, champion of the so-called moral majority, had just been thoroughly anally fucked and had fucked up his career in the process. As he came down to earth, he knew it. I turned away, because I didn't want to watch the moment when the implications of what he'd done hit him. Too close to my own memories, I guess. Besides, I had urgent needs of my own that left me wet and sticky beneath the leather. I don't think I made a sound, but Lance turned round.

'You two can run along and play now. Use the gym.'

I didn't need a second telling, and Rupert was just as eager. He undid the buckles that held the steadicam harness and placed it in a corner while Lance refastened his prisoner to his bunk, leaving him with his come splattered across his belly. Then we were in the corridor, and having problems looking at each other. I pulled the hood off, sighing as I shook my sticky hair free. Being in that outfit felt like being in a sauna, but it did something for me. Judging by his erection, it did something for Rupert too, but he still wouldn't look at me.

'I'm sorry,' he finally muttered. 'I didn't know what Lance was planning when I tied you up, but . . .'

Maybe I should have made a little speech about how I understood and forgave him. Actually I had forgiven him. I couldn't do anything else really. Hadn't I just done the same thing to Dickie and got off on it? 'Done's done,' I shrugged. 'Did you enjoy watching me?'

'That's not my scene.'

'But you tied me up that night.' And I wouldn't have minded if he'd done it to me now.

'That was different,' he began, then looked at me and I knew he'd got the hint. He took my hand as we went into the gym, not just locking the door, but dragging the beam the twins had fucked me on across it to make quite sure no one could interrupt us this time. Then he looked speculatively at the apparatus.

'That'll do nicely,' he said, dragging me across to the wall bars, assuming that you can call it dragging when your victim goes willingly. He undid the belt of his trousers, and folded it across his hand.

'You're going to be helpless,' he said, just as he'd said that other night. Then he gripped my wrists, holding them above my head while he fastened the belt round them, and gave more crisp orders. 'Climb up two rungs.'

I climbed, knowing that would bring my pussy level with his cock, and he fastened the belt round the beam. My feet were supported by the bars, so it was surprisingly comfortable, as well as a real turn-on. He undid the zippers across my tits and eased them free, making a big deal out of licking my nipples. Then, when I knew I'd start screaming if he didn't get on to the real thing soon, he yanked at the zip at my crotch. Like Lance, he didn't bother to undress, but I didn't care about his lack of finesse. I wanted it as much as he did, so I wrapped my legs round his back as he buried himself inside me, gripping the bars to support myself.

His hands were hard on my breasts as he began to move, but not as hard as his cock was. It shoved right up inside me, and he moved back and forward with each thrust, setting my body swinging. I came quickly and easily, then again and again before he did. Then he unfastened me, because, unlike Lance, he's a gentleman. We went back to my room, showered together, and he asked seriously, 'What are you going to do now?'

'Not write that bloody article!' I said fervently.

'And the rest? Will you go back to university and forget it all?'

'No. I can't. I'm different now. I think I'm addicted.' That was the second time that I'd admitted the truth to Rupert by accident, but he was so damn easy to talk to. No wonder the women guests kept him so busy. He made every woman feel as if they were the most important person in his world, but for once my indiscretion didn't matter. Forget think, I knew that I was addicted, to the sex and the cash and the feeling of being in control despite what the customers were deluded enough to believe.

'Liberty thinks that I'm worth training.'

'She's right.' He stroked my thigh, not with sexual intent, more thoughtfully. 'Imo's too much of a submission junkie. Not enough of a queen bitch streak, not like you. You'll be running this place some day.' I wasn't sure whether I'd been complimented or insulted, so I kept my mouth shut, and he went on. 'And the Hall will go on.'

'And you'll come back and play the games?' I asked, hoping he would. Neither of us were into the hearts and flowers stuff, but he was a good lover, and I enjoyed him.

'I will. And you?'

'I'll keep playing the game all right.' I remembered Liberty's suggestion and smiled, because I knew the best was still to come.

13

'Go into your room and lie down,' I ordered Imo three months later.

I'd known what she wanted as soon as she'd walked into the flat we now shared, and I'd enjoyed making her wait for it even more. She'd cooked supper, washed me, brushed my hair and helped me dress for my date, all the while naked and chained and tormentingly unsatisfied. Her freshly shaved sex gleamed with her secretions as she scurried to do my bidding, and I smiled. She might think that she was desperate now, but that was nothing compared to how she'd feel when I finally relented.

Her room had a double bed in it, of course. Liberty didn't expect us to live like nuns, and we didn't, but the flat was in a quiet, exclusive block, well out of range of any college gossips, so no one ever caught us out. And Imo's room was soundproofed so that she could moan all she liked, but she wasn't moaning now. She was lying on a bed that looked as if it belonged in *Goldilocks and the Three Bears.* Only Goldilocks had never cupped full, red-tipped breasts with chained hands, let alone pleaded.

'Let me come before you go out. Please, Tess.'

'Did I say that you could speak?' I asked, feigning casualness. Lance, predictably, had been right about me. I did get off on dominating people. Not to the same extent as him, thank God, but the sight of Imo helpless and desperate sent a nice warm tingle through my thighs that would help me handle the night ahead. 'I bet you'd love to be in my shoes tonight,' I murmured, deliberately making it worse for her. Lance had taught me that sex is as much in the mind as the genitals, and I'd learnt my lesson well. 'Last time I fucked him I swore I never would again.'

I could still remember the shame and humiliation as the naïve innocent I'd been then had first realised what she had to do to survive, then unwillingly done it. But it would have been right up Imo's street, and telling her about it would keep her on the boil while I was out, so I sat beside her, carefully not touching her, and pretended to be talking to myself.

'He told me to strip off, and I stared at him. Couldn't believe it was happening, not here of all places.' I could laugh about it now, but back then the last thing it had been was funny. 'He said I'd have to be nice to him if I wanted to pass the course module.' I'd known that I could have stormed out and gone to the college authorities, but it'd have been his word against mine, and I wasn't exactly the best student in the place. So I'd accepted the inevitable and got undressed, trying to convince myself that it didn't matter, only to be proved wrong.

'He told me to sit on this typist's chair that he'd got in front of his computer in his rooms.' After so long avoiding thinking about it, it felt strange to be deliberately conjuring up every tiny detail, but it also reminded me why I was doing this tonight. At least I was getting paid for it this time, but that wasn't the point right now. The point was getting Imo so turned on that she'd still be hot when I got back, and she was such a submission junkie that she'd be really turned on by what had happened to me.

'He told me to put my legs over the arms. I asked him what sort of fucking pervert he was. He said the sort who could make the difference between me staying at uni or being sent down. I knew he'd do it too, so I did as I was told, knowing he could see everything. I could see his erection bulging, and I was sure he'd shove it up me there and then. But the bastard was cleverer than that.'

I stroked a finger down Imo's thigh, wiping away the pain of the memories with this reminder of how good life was now. She shivered at my touch, and I knew she was imagining being in the mess I'd been in, and getting off on it.

'He lowered the chair until I was sitting at his feet; my mouth at just the right height for his cock. Then he told me to unzip him...' Talking about it still hurt a year later. I'd felt sick and ashamed and, although I'd refused to admit it at the time, a little turned on as I'd unzipped him, then waited for his next order.

'You know what you've got to do next.' The sick feeling redoubled, because I'd known he was enjoying seeing me humbled and humiliated, but I still hadn't argued. Instead, I'd eased the boxer shorts he wore – navy ones with a fine red stripe down and his cock had sprung free as if it had a life of its own.

'If you ever say a word to anyone I'll finish you,' he'd said pleasantly.

I'd known he meant it and I'd hated him almost as much as I'd hated myself when I'd taken him into my mouth and begun to lick. Maybe that's when I made that flaming list of the things I'd never do that caused me so much hell, but it doesn't matter now.

'I hoped he'd come fast. He groaned when I slid my tongue under his glans, and grabbed my hair, pulling me towards him, but that wasn't what he'd got in mind.

His cock was wet and sticky when he slid it out of my mouth, but I was still as dry as when I'd arrived for my tutorial. Not that that put the bastard off!'

'Did he hurt you?' Imo was trembling, and I wondered what it would be like not just to abase yourself so thoroughly, but to revel in it. Maybe I'd ask Lance to show me some day, but it'd be a long, long time in the future.

'No. The bastard was too clever for that. He got a tube of KY jelly out of his desk drawer, and I realised he'd planned it all along. He covered his fingers with it until they were as sticky as his cock, then raised the chair again, making a big deal out of adjusting it until I was level with his cock.

'"All I've got to do," he muttered, pushing his cock against my opening, and I shook my head. I really think I would have run then.'

Judging by Imo's expression she'd have been begging for the mercy she knew she wasn't going to get and trying to egg him on. It was a shame that she wasn't going instead of me, but the job's the job and Liberty, as ever, was right. This one would be special and exorcise a few ghosts.

'But he pulled back,' I went on, 'and began to run a finger round and round my fanny, not pushing inside, just spreading the jelly round my lower lips. It didn't turn me on.'

I hadn't been turned on at any time during that hellish evening, which was why it had been so humiliating. But when he'd finished I'd been wet enough that he could do whatever he wanted without leaving any telltale damage. And, courtesy of the condom, no proof, even if I had been prepared to risk having my private life dragged through the mud by accusing him. But those were details Imo didn't have to know. She was quite turned on enough already, and I was running out of time.

'Lift your legs,' I ordered.

She obediently rolled back on her hips, lifting her legs straight up. I knew she'd like me to whip her. Maybe I would, later, but I wanted to make sure she'd be hot and ready for me when I got home, so I was going to leave her unsatisfied. I might have to play submissive tonight, but knowing that Imo was helpless and waiting for me would remind me of who and what I really was. I'd need that to deal with that bastard.

'Now lower them,' I ordered, gripping her ankles. As she moved I dragged her down the bed until her feet were resting on the bed rail, then cuffed her ankles so you could see between those widespread legs all the way down the dark, wet, tunnel. Then I looped a length of chain between her wrist cuffs and tied it round the top bed rail, and I was ready to begin.

My first job was something to keep her amused while I was out. I took a triple-pronged dildo that would bring back all sorts of memories for her out of the locked box beneath her bed and sucked it until it was gleaming, enjoying her little pants and breathy moans. Then I lined it up carefully and pushed the flat of my hand against it. The fine probe slid up her arse, the dildo squelched into her wet sex, and the tiny penguin nestled against her clit. I considered my handiwork, then put a couple of pillows beneath her hips to make sure that she couldn't bring herself off. Imo's eyes were widening impossibly, and I knew she'd worked out what I was up to.

'You've forgotten the power unit,' she risked saying, and I smiled.

'Oh, no I haven't.' I smiled sweetly at her as I went across to the locked cabinet that held Imo's very private selection of videos. I flicked through them until I found the one that had been made the night that I'd seen her trussed up like a chrysalis, and begun to realise what I was. That slotted into the player, and I hit the start button as I borrowed her comb to tidy my hair.

'See you later,' I said cheerfully. 'And I shall be very, very angry if I find that you've come before I get back.'

She shivered, biting her lip, and I knew that she remembered what I could do to her. 'Just one orgasm?' she pleaded, starting to cry. I almost relented and gave it to her, then I remembered that she'd enjoy the wait almost as much as what I'd do to her when I got home. Such simple things please a submissive, and make a dominatrix's life a constant challenge.

'Think about me,' I murmured, rubbing salt into the wound, then locked first her bedroom door, then the flat.

She'd be alone and helpless now, her only companion that three-hour tape. She didn't know how long I'd be, but I did, and so, more importantly, did Liberty. I was out on a job, so I was taking precautions. I'd been a bit dubious about this one at first, and a damn sight more angry. Then I got the point that the clients always miss. They think they've got the power because they're paying you, but they are so, so wrong. They might have the cash, but we've got the memories.

And those memories meant that after tonight my first-class degree was guaranteed just as a regular supply of freelance work on a good paper was assured for me once I'd graduated. Courtesy of Liberty's contacts, Trickie Dickie had become an editor on one of the posher papers, and he didn't seem half as keen on uncovering the sexual peccadillos of the great and the good as he'd once been. What's more, he'd booked in at the Hall for a long weekend next month, so whatever he'd learnt about himself couldn't have been that awful.

But I wasn't going to waste time thinking about him when I'd got Dirk the lecturer to handle. What he wanted was a particularly nasty little game even by my newly liberated standards, but I'm not a nice girl, so I was looking forward to it. I straightened the knee-length kilt that was so unlike anything I'd ever wear from choice and smiled at the doorkeeper as I went out. My coat hung open over my twin set, and I knew I looked like one of the posh students I'd once been stupid enough to envy. Just as I'd expected, Dirk's car was waiting outside, and he reached across to open the door.

'Thanks for the lift,' I said, and tossed my coat on the back seat.

'No trouble,' he smiled, hit the central locking, turned up Tony Bennett on the car stereo, and the big black car purred down the road.

'We're not going back to your rooms?' I feigned surprise a few minutes later as we headed out into the countryside. 'I thought I was having an extra tutorial.'

'You are. A very special tutorial.' When he smiled I didn't have to act the shiver I gave, because his expression reminded me of a piranha, or Lance. Both of them without an ounce of humanity between them, and with only one plan in mind; to take what they wanted and to hell with the rest of the world.

'What about the books?' I kept to the script, struggling not to smile.

'Sod the books! I've had enough of you and your goody-two-shoes image. You all talk about life as if you know it all; you and your cash and your glittering careers ahead of you.'

Oh my, I thought as he ranted on. Someone really

hates his students, doesn't he? Mind you, I could see why. Fame and fortune had eluded him, but I was going to be different. 'What are you going to do with me?' I asked when he turned off the main road, then down a dark country lane, and parked the car in a driveway of a dark, unlit house behind high gates.

'I'm going to fuck you like you've never been fucked before,' he snarled.

'You can't,' I whispered, and reached for my seat belt.

He got there first, and he had a knife in his hand. He held it against my throat and I began to feel scared. Liberty had said that this was his favourite scenario, and having a real student to play it out with would make it better still for him. But what if she hadn't realised how caught up this fantasy was with real life? He moved the blade away when I flinched, and I knew it would be all right. I might be about to be 'raped', but he'd make sure that I'd enjoy it. He'd assert his wonderful male power over me, never guessing that I'd get off on his fantasy, then go home to my bound and helpless flat mate and do stuff to her that would have blown his brains out.

'Don't hurt me,' I whimpered, right on cue.

'Don't make me have to,' he retorted, and slid the knife gently along the knitted jumper. It fell apart, and he smiled as he folded the cut edges back from my breasts. 'You're so beautiful. I've wanted you ever since I saw you, but you didn't notice me, did you?' Of course, I hadn't. It's only in fairy tales that the princess kisses the toad, and I've never believed in them. 'You'd spread your legs for any spotty student, but you wouldn't even look at me. Well, tonight you're going to do a damn sight more than spread them for me!'

He sliced through my bra, leaving me glad it was one of my old ones rather than one of the new silk and lace confections that I'd bought with Dickie's money. Dirk pulled my cardigan off, jerking the remains of my jumper away simultaneously. He left the bra hanging, presumably to increase my feelings of helplessness, then began to unfasten the kilt, and I knew it was time to up the stakes. In his fantasies, the girl was always reluctant to begin with, but was won over by his manly prowess, to use the purple prose he had; the same prose that he'd have torn apart if any of his students had submitted it to him. But I wasn't going to submit to him – yet. Before he could react I was out of the car, running into the night, kicking off my shoes so I could move faster, but not too fast.

I didn't actually want to get away, but the thrill of the chase and all that, and I was finding it pretty thrilling. My breasts bounced as I ran, and the kilt had dropped away. All I was wearing were the remains of my bra, tights and a pair of sensible cotton knickers of the sort that Bridget Jones made famous. I knew my tights were laddering, and he was hard on my heels so that was the least of my problems. I'd let him catch me soon, and thinking that left me wondering where we were. Chances were that he'd have picked somewhere private, because he wouldn't want to be caught. But I wanted to get caught, so I slowed down. Seconds later he brought me down with a clumsy rugby tackle that left me face down in the leaf mould, with him kneeling astride me. I could feel his erection pressing into my back, and he was panting.

'Thought you'd run, did you?' He'd been excited before, but now he was elated. 'Thought you'd get away from me? Now I'll have to teach you a lesson.'

Thanks to Lance, there was nothing he could teach me, and a lot I could enjoy so that didn't worry me the way it would once have done. I lay quietly while he tugged my tights down, his knee in my back stopping me moving. The knife flashed again as he cut them in half.

'And you thought you could get away,' he repeated smugly as he tied my ankles together, then used the other half of the tights to tie my hands.

I whimpered, just as he'd expect me to, grinding my thighs together and enjoying the stimulation that reminded me how different this was from last time. I'd hated it then and hated him even more, had been swearing revenge while he'd used me. Tonight would be very different. Tonight I'd be his dirtiest, kinkiest fantasy, and in the morning I'd remind him of every detail and never have trouble with him again!

I whimpered as if I was too scared to manage coherent words, and he laughed. The knife slashed through the sides of those sensible cotton panties, and then I was naked except for the bra, slit open at the front, its sides now lying forlornly against the grass.

'Please, don't hurt me.'

He stopped and I wondered if I'd overdone it and he'd come to his senses. The knee came out of my back, and he knelt beside my head, staring down at me, his eyes wide, his face flushed in the dying light.

'Please?' As my mouth opened he stuffed the panties inside, using the cut sides as cords to fasten them behind my head. I could taste myself on my knickers, smell myself too.

'I'll only be a minute,' he said over his shoulder as he headed back to the car, and I knew it would be all right. The tights were tied tightly enough to keep me secure, but not tightly enough to hurt. Besides, I'd spent hours in bondage while Lance trained me and kept others in bondage for longer. This was still a neat trick, and his next refinement wasn't bad either. He was carrying two large torches, the sort you keep for breakdowns and power cuts. He arranged one by my head, the other by my feet, so I was spotlit.

'You wanted it rough,' he said, as if he were criticising my homework, and I knew this was going to be good.

I'm still not into pain or humiliation, but I wasn't feeling humiliated. I was enjoying myself. Hasn't everyone fantasised about being bound and helpless, held prisoner by a mysterious stranger who was planning to fuck your brains out? Now I was going to live it, and he struck me as the sort who'd put a lot of effort into it. For his scenario to work I'd have to come again and again, which suited me just fine. He rolled me onto my back, then shoved his head between my thighs and got to work.

'You're wet,' he whispered, as he lifted his face to stare at me. His chin was wet with my juices, so I didn't know why he was bothering to state the bloody obvious. But he was paying, so I turned my head from side to side, whimpering to make it clear that the last thing I wanted was to come beneath his pitiless torment, and all the rest of that crap and he laughed exultantly.

'You want this. Admit it, little whore. You want this.'

Lance had used the same B-movie script, and I found myself wondering if there was a book – sort of the dummy's guide to domination – and if not, if I should write one. Then I stopped thinking. Dirk's head was between my thighs again, his mouth slurping across my clit, then sliding down further, each long stroke of his tongue slithering along my channel and into my sex. I moaned, this time not in protest, and tried to wriggle. Not away, but closer, and he knew it. His hands fastened on my hips, and I knew he'd decided to make me come and to hell with what I wanted. That suited me fine, but I still made him work for it, jerking my body from side to side as if I was still trying to get away.

Up and down and in and out his tongue slid. I got wetter, and my breasts harder, and my belly began to tighten. I squealed as he slid two fingers up inside me, pressing hard against my G-spot, and came, my hips tightening round his neck to hold him in place. Then, before I'd enjoyed it properly, he was kneeling over me, unfastening the gag.

'Go on, admit it. You want me!'

I did, but he'd nowhere near got started, and it seemed a shame not to sample his entire repertoire. From what Liberty had told me, he was a pretty impressive lover. If his personality hadn't been the human equivalent of an oil slick, he'd have had girls queuing up for him. As it was, he'd got one bound helpless one he'd had to pay for, even if he didn't yet realise how much I'd cost him.

'No.' I gave a little shuddering sob, making sure my breasts heaved, and he smiled.

'You wanted that, didn't you?'

'You made me,' I whimpered, closing my eyes as if I couldn't bear to look at him.

'And I'm going to make you come again and again, you little bitch!' He stripped his clothes off with more speed than finesse, dropping them in a heap beside me, then knelt astride me, moulding my breasts round his cock. I knew he really had played this game before, because he was going for a quick orgasm now, then a slower second one. 'I'm going to come over your breasts.' He grunted, twiddling my nipples as if they were knobs on his car stereo.

'No, don't, please don't.'

Those of us who are into domination are funny

people. Me asking him not to was just the trigger he needed. When I let my mouth fall open to catch his come, I thought he'd either come again on the spot or have a heart attack. But he caught on fast, swinging his body so that he shot spunk all over my face. I moaned as if that was one humiliation too many, and he laughed.

'You're going to love it,' he swore, then turned me back onto my belly and began to rub my back in long, lazy strokes.

I always like being massaged, but I remembered to moan protestingly when he began to rub the scented cream he was using round my anus.

'Ssh,' he whispered. 'You'll love it really.' I clamped my arse muscles down, making sure it wasn't too easy for him, and he began to pant again. 'Don't tell me you've never had it up the arse?'

I didn't tell him, because Liberty doesn't like us lying to the clients. I just sobbed and struggled and gloated because I knew I'd got him right where I wanted him.

'You haven't, have you?' His cock was coming back to life, and his breathing speeding up, so I shook my head. 'No one's ever had you there.' He sounded as eager as Lance at his worst, but I wasn't scared.

'Don't,' I whispered. 'I'll do anything you like, but not that.'

He wasn't the only one buying into this fantasy now. I was a naïve student who'd probably had a crush on him. I'd hoped he'd make sweet, tender love to me tonight. The last thing I'd expected was the drive into the countryside or for him to turn savage. I'd struggled to get free, not knowing where I was running to, just that I had to get away, but he'd still caught me. Now he was about to do something unspeakable to me, and there was nothing that I could do to stop him. I was so caught up in the fantasy that I even managed a real sob when he finally managed to ease a finger past my tightly clenched anus.

'Don't,' I whispered again, but he didn't withdraw. Instead, he waited with his finger tantalisingly inside me, and I felt the familiar dark, dirty pleasure begin. Not that I gave any sign of it. 'Please don't. I can't take it. You're too big.' I protested instead.

'Yes you can. Just relax and let me teach you.'

'Please.' The nice thing about enacting domination scenes as the submissive is that there's never much dialogue to learn, but I made my whimper a good one. Part dying hope, part horror, laced with a tiny bit of shamed excitement to encourage him.

'I'll make it good for you,' he promised, and I knew he'd fallen for it hook, line and sinker. He really believed that no one had ever had me there before, and I wondered what he'd think if I told him about my initiation. He'd be creaming himself, but he wasn't going to know. He'd think he'd tied me up and forced me, and I'd reap the benefits.

'I don't want to have to gag you again,' he said, but it didn't stop him doing it when I began to struggle. Then he was kneeling on top of me, holding me down with his weight, and I embraced the fantasy again.

I didn't want this. All I wanted was to escape, but the warm male weight on top of me was making it impossible. All I could do was lie there while he slid that finger up inside me, then lifted me so he could slide his free hand beneath me. One finger rubbed against my clit, another two slid inside me, and I moaned against the gag. I didn't want to come like this, but I was so helpless, and he was so strong. A second finger joined the first in my arse, and I turned my head to one side, keeping my eyes tightly closed. He laughed.

'You're starting to like it.'

I moaned, because he was right. He straightened up and, much to my relief, pulled a condom out of his pocket. He was so high on his sick little game that I'd begun to wonder if he would, and what I'd do if he didn't. There were some risks I'm not prepared to take, and I knew I could get free if I wanted to, even if I wasn't sure how I'd get back to college when my clothes lay beside me in shreds. But I didn't want to, so I lay quiet and still, as if all the fight had gone out of me.

'I won't hurt you,' he repeated, and I knew he'd forgotten that this wasn't real, which suited me perfectly. This had been specifically ruled out of the original deal, but I guess I'd always known that it would happen. He pushed his thighs between my knees, forcing them apart so he could lie between my legs with my bound ankles pressing against his calves. I could feel his hairy legs, and his cock pressing up against my anus and I knew he'd do it to me and to hell with my pleas and protests.

I moaned, fighting my own body as well as him, because I knew I mustn't make it too easy for him. But God, there was something about this that really turned me on. He was so sure that he was in control, never realising that he was losing it with every breath. He slid his fingers in front of me again and began to rub my clit with long, slow strokes that had my juices soaking into the grass. Then, when I was moaning incoherently against the soiled knickers that gagged me as I edged towards another climax, he set the head of his short stubby cock against my tight rear entrance, and began to push. I screamed, but it was more for effect than because it actually hurt, and it got me my reward. He stopped with his cock about an inch inside me, and began to work my clit. His breath came hard and I knew he was struggling to control himself; the urge to rut like an animal fighting with his image of himself as a great lover. He took a deep, harsh breath, then stuffed three fingers in to me, fucking me until my moans and sobs weren't faked. He'd splayed his fingers until I was stretched, his finger on my clit working its magic until my stomach was knotting with the need to come, but he wasn't going to let me get there yet. I whimpered, this time pleading with him.

'Soon,' he whispered, stilling his fingers. 'Relax and I'll make it good for you.'

I gave a sobbing sigh, as if I'd come to the end of my reserves, and did as I'd been ordered. He grunted as he pushed home, and I whimpered, not quite able to hide my surprise. The bastard was good at this. I liked the feeling of fullness, the knowledge that he was getting off on me getting off, even the helplessness. For a while he lay motionless with just his fingers working on my clit, letting my body adjust. Then, when I wriggled against him, he began to move. Slowly at first, then, when I no longer fought him, with increasing confidence, sliding up and down my slick rear channel as his fingers pounded into me. I raised my arse to meet him and gave myself over to the sensations.

Fullness, dirty, rich, dark pleasure. I could feel his cock through the thin inner membrane and I was plugged and helpless. I began to moan constantly, wordlessly urging him on. He gave a guttural grunt of delight, and the fingers inside me slid upwards. As he hit my G-spot, I didn't give a damn that he was a bastard who'd once reduced me to shamed tears. I howled with delight, my arse clamped down on his cock and that tightening brought him off as I came, and came, and came. One orgasm blended into another and another, all of them laced with triumph and a sick dark anticipation of what lay ahead that even Lance would have been proud of. By the time I was aware of the outside world again he'd untied me and draped my coat over me.

'Are you all right?' His voice had changed. The exultation was gone, and I knew that he'd realised what he'd done. He'd sodomised a student, and now he was in deep shit.

'That wasn't in the deal.' I remembered those shamed tears he'd forced from me before, but this time the tears were fake. 'I agreed to your game, but not this,' I gulped as if I couldn't say the word, and his gulp was far louder.

'I didn't hurt you.' He protested.

'That's easy for you to say, isn't it?' Actually he hadn't, but why spoil a good game with the truth? Who knew, if I put enough of the fear of God into him maybe he wouldn't play this game with any other student. I'd be their great benefactor, even if they never knew.

'I said I hadn't, that I didn't want to.' I was really into this scene now, crying so hard that I could hardly manage coherent words. 'And you just . . .'

'You enjoyed it,' he said guiltily, and I cried harder still, just as I'd done when Liberty thrust that butt plug up me and left me alone to realise what I was really like. But these were crocodile tears, because life was looking good.

My body ached with the after-effects of a good fucking, and I'd got plenty of cash in the bank. Soon, when I'd made him feel guilty enough, I'd let him console me with an easy ride through my last year at university and a guaranteed first-class degree. He'd spend the rest of his career looking over his shoulder and waiting for the rape accusation, so I'd got my revenge at last. Actually, I'd got a hell of a lot more than that.

At home, waiting for me, probably desperate by now,

was Imo. When I got back I'd tell her all about what I'd done, letting her envy me every tiny humiliating detail. Maybe, if she was good, I'd re-enact it on her. Ahead of me lay the holidays and Liberty Hall. Fuck being the good girl I'd once claimed to be, I thought, glad that my face was still resting against the ground so Dirk couldn't see my triumphant expression. The bad girl I'd become had everything I'd ever wanted, and I was loving every second of it!

Visit the Black Lace website at
www.blacklace-books.co.uk

FIND OUT THE LATEST INFORMATION AND TAKE ADVANTAGE OF OUR FANTASTIC FREE BOOK OFFER! ALSO VISIT THE SITE FOR . . .

- All Black Lace titles currently available and how to order online
- Great new offers
- Writers' guidelines
- Author interviews
- An erotica newsletter
- Features
- Cool links

BLACK LACE — THE LEADING IMPRINT OF WOMEN'S SEXY FICTION

TAKING YOUR EROTIC READING PLEASURE TO NEW HORIZONS

BLACK LACE

LOOK OUT FOR THE ALL-NEW BLACK LACE BOOKS – AVAILABLE NOW!

All books priced £6.99 in the UK. Please note publication dates apply to the UK only. For other territories, please contact your retailer.

STICKY FINGERS
Alison Tyler
ISBN 0 352 33756 7

Jodie Silver doesn't have to steal. As the main buyer for a reputable import and export business in the heart of San Francisco, she has plenty of money and prestige. But she gets a rush from pocketing things that don't belong to her. It's a potent feeling, almost as gratifying as the excitement she receives from engaging in kinky, exhibitionist sex – but not quite. Skilled at concealing her double life, Jodie thinks she's unstoppable, but with detective Nick Hudson on her tail, it's only a matter of time before the pussycat burglar meets her comeuppance. **A thrilling piece of West Coast noir erotica from Ms Tyler.**

SILKEN CHAINS
Jodi Nicol
ISBN 0 352 33143 7

Fleeing from her scheming guardians at the prospect of an arranged marriage, the beautiful young Abbie is thrown from her horse. On regaining consciousness she finds herself in a lavish house modelled on the palaces of Indian princes – and the virtual prisoner of the extremely wealthy and attractive Leon Villiers, the Master. Eastern philosophy and eroticism form the basis of the Master's opulent lifestyle and he introduces Abbie to sensual pleasures beyond the bounds of her imagination. **By popular demand, another of the list's bestselling historical novels is reprinted.**

THE WICKED STEPDAUGHTER
Wendy Harris
ISBN O 352 33777 X

Selina is in lust with Matt, who unfortunately is the boyfriend of the really irritating Miranda, who was Selina's stepmother for several years until her poor old dad keeled over years before his time. When Miranda has to go to the US for three weeks, Selina hatches a plan to seduce the floppy-haired Matt – and get her revenge on the money-grabbing Miranda, whom Selina blames for her dad's early demise. With several suitors in tow, the highly sexed Selina causes mayhem, both at work – at the strippergram service she co-runs – and in her personal life. **Another hilarious black comedy of sexual manners from Ms Harris.**

DRAWN TOGETHER
Robyn Russell
ISBN O 352 33269 7

When Tanya, a graphic artist, creates Katrina Cortez – a sexy, comic-strip detective – she begins to wish her own life were more like that of Katrina's. Stephen Sinclair, who works with Tanya, is her kind of man. Unfortunately Tanya's just moved in with her bank manager boyfriend, who expects her to play the part of the executive girlfriend. In Tanya's quest to gain the affection of Mr Sinclair, she must become more like Katrina Cortez – a voluptuous wild woman! **Unusual and engaging story of seduction and delight.**

Coming in March

EVIL'S NIECE
Melissa MacNeal
ISBN 0 352 33781 8

The setting is 1890s New Orleans. When Eve spies her husband with a sultry blonde, she is determined to win back his affection. When her brother-in-law sends a maid to train her in the ways of seduction, things spin rapidly out of control. Their first lesson reveals a surprise that Miss Eve isn't prepared for, and when her husband discovers these liaisons, it seems she will lose her prestigious place in society. However, his own covert life is about to unravel and reveal the biggest secret of all. **More historical high jinks from Ms MacNeal, the undisputed queen of kinky erotica set in the world of corsets and chaperones.**

LEARNING THE HARD WAY
Jasmine Archer
ISBN 0 352 33782 6

Tamsin has won a photographic assignment to collaborate on a book of nudes with the sex-obsessed Leandra. Thing is, the job is in Los Angeles and she doesn't want her new friend to know how sexually inexperienced she is. Tamsin sets out to learn all she can before flying out to meet her photographic mentor, but nothing can prepare her for Leandra's outrageous lifestyle. Along with husband Nigel, and an assortment of kinky friends, Leandra is about to initiate Tamsin into some very different ways to have fun. **Fun and upbeat story of a young woman's transition from sexual ingénue to fully fledged dominatrix.**

ACE OF HEARTS
Lisette Allen
ISBN O 352 33059 7

England, 1816. The wealthy elite is enjoying an unprecedented era of hedonistic adventure. Their lives are filled with parties, sexual dalliances and scandal. Marisa Brooke is a young lady who lives by her wits, fencing and cheating the wealthy at cards. She also likes seducing young men and indulging her fancy for fleshly pleasures. However, love and fortune are lost as easily as they are won, and she has to use all her skill and cunning if she wants to hold on to her winnings and her lovers. **Highly enjoyable historical erotica set in the period of Regency excess.**

Black Lace Booklist

Information is correct at time of printing. To avoid disappointment check availability before ordering. Go to www.blacklace-books.co.uk. All books are priced £6.99 unless another price is given.

BLACK LACE BOOKS WITH A CONTEMPORARY SETTING

☐ THE TOP OF HER GAME Emma Holly	ISBN O 352 33337 5	£5.99
☐ IN THE FLESH Emma Holly	ISBN O 352 34498 3	£5.99
☐ A PRIVATE VIEW Crystalle Valentino	ISBN O 352 33308 1	£5.99
☐ SHAMELESS Stella Black	ISBN O 352 33485 1	£5.99
☐ INTENSE BLUE Lyn Wood	ISBN O 352 33496 7	£5.99
☐ THE NAKED TRUTH Natasha Rostova	ISBN O 352 33497 5	£5.99
☐ ANIMAL PASSIONS Martine Marquand	ISBN O 352 33499 1	£5.99
☐ A SPORTING CHANCE Susie Raymond	ISBN O 352 33501 7	£5.99
☐ TAKING LIBERTIES Susie Raymond	ISBN O 352 33357 X	£5.99
☐ A SCANDALOUS AFFAIR Holly Graham	ISBN O 352 33523 8	£5.99
☐ THE NAKED FLAME Crystalle Valentino	ISBN O 352 33528 9	£5.99
☐ ON THE EDGE Laura Hamilton	ISBN O 352 33534 3	£5.99
☐ LURED BY LUST Tania Picarda	ISBN O 352 33533 5	£5.99
☐ THE HOTTEST PLACE Tabitha Flyte	ISBN O 352 33536 X	£5.99
☐ THE NINETY DAYS OF GENEVIEVE Lucinda Carrington	ISBN O 352 33070 8	£5.99
☐ EARTHY DELIGHTS Tesni Morgan	ISBN O 352 33548 3	£5.99
☐ MAN HUNT Cathleen Ross	ISBN O 352 33583 1	
☐ MÉNAGE Emma Holly	ISBN O 352 33231 X	
☐ DREAMING SPIRES Juliet Hastings	ISBN O 352 33584 X	
☐ THE TRANSFORMATION Natasha Rostova	ISBN O 352 33311 1	
☐ STELLA DOES HOLLYWOOD Stella Black	ISBN O 352 33588 2	
☐ SIN.NET Helena Ravenscroft	ISBN O 352 33598 X	
☐ HOTBED Portia Da Costa	ISBN O 352 33614 5	
☐ TWO WEEKS IN TANGIER Annabel Lee	ISBN O 352 33599 8	
☐ HIGHLAND FLING Jane Justine	ISBN O 352 33616 1	
☐ PLAYING HARD Tina Troy	ISBN O 352 33617 X	
☐ SYMPHONY X Jasmine Stone	ISBN O 352 33629 3	

□ THE HOUSE IN NEW ORLEANS Fleur Reynolds   ISBN 0 352 32951 3

□ NOBLE VICES Monica Belle   ISBN 0 352 33738 9

□ STICKY FINGERS Alison Tyler   ISBN 0 352 33756 7

□ STORMY HAVEN Savannah Smythe   ISBN 0 352 33757 5

□ THE WICKED STEPDAUGHTER Wendy Harris   ISBN 0 352 33777 X

□ DRAWN TOGETHER Robyn Russell   ISBN 0 352 33269 7

BLACK LACE BOOKS WITH AN HISTORICAL SETTING

□ PRIMAL SKIN Leona Benkt Rhys   ISBN 0 352 33500 9 £5.99

□ DEVIL'S FIRE Melissa MacNeal   ISBN 0 352 33527 0 £5.99

□ WILD KINGDOM Deanna Ashford   ISBN 0 352 33549 1 £5.99

□ DARKER THAN LOVE Kristina Lloyd   ISBN 0 352 33279 4

□ STAND AND DELIVER Helena Ravenscroft   ISBN 0 352 33340 5 £5.99

□ THE CAPTIVATION Natasha Rostova   ISBN 0 352 33234 4

□ CIRCO EROTICA Mercedes Kelley   ISBN 0 352 33257 3

□ MINX Megan Blythe   ISBN 0 352 33638 2

□ PLEASURE'S DAUGHTER Sedalia Johnson   ISBN 0 352 33237 9

□ JULIET RISING Cleo Cordell   ISBN 0 352 32938 6

□ DEMON'S DARE Melissa MacNeal   ISBN 0 352 33683 8

□ ELENA'S CONQUEST Lisette Allen   ISBN 0 352 32950 5

□ DIVINE TORMENT Janine Ashbless   ISBN 0 352 33719 2

□ THE CAPTIVE FLESH Cleo Cordell   ISBN 0 352 32872 X

□ SATAN'S ANGEL Melissa MacNeal   ISBN 0 352 33726 5

□ THE INTIMATE EYE Georgia Angelis   ISBN 0 352 33004 X

□ HANDMAIDEN OF PALMYRA Fleur Reynolds   ISBN 0 352 32951 3

□ SILKEN CHAINS Jodi Nicol   ISBN 0 352 33143 7

BLACK LACE ANTHOLOGIES

□ CRUEL ENCHANTMENT Erotic Fairy Stories   ISBN 0 352 33483 5 £5.99
    Janine Ashbless

□ MORE WICKED WORDS Various   ISBN 0 352 33487 8 £5.99

□ WICKED WORDS 4 Various   ISBN 0 352 33603 X

□ WICKED WORDS 5 Various   ISBN 0 352 33642 0

□ WICKED WORDS 6 Various   ISBN 0 352 33590 0

□ THE BEST OF BLACK LACE 2 Various   ISBN 0 352 33718 4

□ A MULTITUDE OF SINS Kit Mason   ISBN 0 352 33737 0

BLACK LACE NON-FICTION

❏ THE BLACK LACE BOOK OF WOMEN'S SEXUAL   ISBN 0 352 33346 4   £5.99
     FANTASIES Ed. Kerri Sharp

To find out the latest information about Black Lace titles, check out the
website: www.blacklace-books.co.uk or send for a booklist with
complete synopses by writing to:

   Black Lace Booklist, Virgin Books Ltd
   Thames Wharf Studios
   Rainville Road
   London W6 9HA

Please include an SAE of decent size. Please note only British stamps
are valid.

Our privacy policy
We will not disclose information you supply us to any other parties.
We will not disclose any information which identifies you personally to
any person without your express consent.

From time to time we may send out information about Black Lace
books and special offers. Please tick here if you do <u>not</u> wish to
receive Black Lace information.   ❏

Please send me the books I have ticked above.

Name ....

Address ....

....

....

....

Post Code ....

Send to: Cash Sales, Black Lace Books, Thames Wharf Studios, Rainville Road, London W6 9HA.

US customers: for prices and details of how to order books for delivery by mail, call 1-800-343-4499.

Please enclose a cheque or postal order, made payable to Virgin Books Ltd, to the value of the books you have ordered plus postage and packing costs as follows:

UK and BFPO – £1.00 for the first book, 50p for each subsequent book.

Overseas (including Republic of Ireland) – £2.00 for the first book, £1.00 for each subsequent book.

If you would prefer to pay by VISA, ACCESS/MASTERCARD, DINERS CLUB, AMEX or SWITCH, please write your card number and expiry date here:

....

Signature ....

Please allow up to 28 days for delivery.